Crazy About Cressida

A Romantic Comedy

Abby Matisse

ISBN: 97809859612-3-7

To the fabulous Mills girls.

Prologue

Cressida Ann Wentworth spotted the open suitcase and screeched to a halt as her worried gaze drifted over the neat stacks of shirts, underwear and socks piled high in the oversized valise.

She frowned and suppressed the first stirrings of alarm as she tried to remember whether Cal had mentioned a medical convention or speaking engagement. He seemed to have more and more of those lately. Of course, that pile consisted of far more clothing than he'd need for a short business trip.

Her frown deepened as that little tidbit sank in.

For the life of her, she couldn't recall him mentioning a trip of any kind, but she'd been more than a little preoccupied for the past few weeks, so she might've missed it.

"Cal?" she asked, voice laced with uncertainty.

Her husband emerged from the closet with a selection of neckties draped over his arm. He briefly met her gaze and then quickly looked away, steadfastly avoiding her as he laid the ties on the bed. Though brief, the look in his eyes had spoken volumes as to his intent.

Her chest tightened. Was this the moment he'd make good on his threats? Was he actually going to leave her?

It took several moments before she mustered the courage to speak. She swallowed, her throat suddenly dry.

"What are you doing?" she asked, trying to sound calm.

Cal Wentworth lifted a blue and white striped tie, folded it with meticulous precision and then placed it in the suitcase, arranging it just so. He paused and then moved it next to a stack of blue shirts.

Color-coded. Of course. Her husband approached everything with a deliberate and unforgiving exactness, a quality that served his plastic surgery practice well but which made everyday life infinitely more challenging than was necessary. Especially for her.

Cal turned and his gray eyes swept over her with cool clinical detachment.

Suddenly, she wished she'd worn something other than her favorite gardening outfit. An outfit Cal despised.

She cringed and resisted the urge to look down. To be fair, she'd dressed for a morning of tending to her flower beds and technically, Cal should've been at the office by now, not here playing fashion critic. Still, she could've chosen something that at least approached cute or even better; something that veered towards sporty chic, like his partners' wives would wear. Of course, his partners' wives didn't work in their gardens. Their hired help did that sort of thing. But Cressida didn't have hired help. Her gardening time was sacred.

Cal's eyes grew hard as they drifted over her slightly frizzy flame red waves and then down to her tattered black t-shirt, where his gaze lingered just long enough to convey his disapproval. He could make her feel completely inadequate without saying a word.

Cressida raked shaky fingers through her shoulder length tresses, carefully styled just an hour before to achieve the smooth look Cal preferred. Unfortunately, her blow-drying prowess proved no match for the relentless South Florida humidity and her stubborn waves had already reappeared.

She straightened her spine and tugged self-consciously at the hem of her comfy t-shirt, once again trying to resist the overwhelming urge to check her reflection in the mirror. She didn't need to. Cal's expression told her everything she needed to know.

He shook his head and shrugged as he turned back to his packing. "I'm tired, Cress." His icy tone matched the hard resolve in his eyes.

A slow shiver slithered up her spine and Cressida wrapped her arms protectively around her waist. "Tired of what?"

She knew but pretended not to, preferring denial to the sobering reality she'd seen taking shape for months. So despite the packed suitcase and half-empty closet, she clung to the illogical belief he'd change his mind. In a few minutes he'd slip his arm around her waist, draw her close and blame all this drama on another tough week at the office. Like he'd done every other time he'd threatened to leave.

She held her breath and waited; certain he could hear the pounding of her heart as alarm turned to panic.

Cal yanked the suitcase zipper closed and heaved the oversized bag onto the floor. It landed on the thick Persian rug with a decisive thud as he eyed her with a steely resolve.

"You know," he said, his tone laced with accusation. "We both do. I...*we*...need a break."

Her heart pounded so hard she feared it might burst through her chest as a childlike voice inside whispered her greatest fear. *Don't let him leave. He'll never come back.*

She'd lived this scene before except then she'd been five—too young to prevent her father from walking out but definitely old enough to understand what it meant. Thirty-one years had passed but the stab of panic felt sickeningly familiar.

Cressida drew in a long, shaky breath. For the first time, she actually felt grateful they didn't have an innocent child who'd be wounded by this drama. She knew that pain all too well. The relentless ache. The never-ending guilt. And a debilitating soul wound that could haunt well into adulthood and in some cases, a lifetime. Of course, her inability to bear a child seemed the likeliest reason for Cal's packed suitcase. Their endless quest to get pregnant had exacted a deep emotional toll and now it appeared the price of infertility might very well be her marriage.

The childlike voice verged on hysteria as it cranked up the volume. *Don't just stand there and do nothing. Say something, you idiot!*

Something that'll convince him to stay.

Her throat convulsed. "But…" She smoothed sweaty, trembling palms down the front of her jeans and tried again, forcing herself to sound calm as she said, "But we can't work on things if we're not together." She tried to smile but her trembling lips wouldn't cooperate.

Cal blinked.

Interpreting his hesitation as an opening, she stepped closer. "Please." Her fingers wrapped around his forearm and squeezed; her voice husky as she said, "Stay." Much as she prayed he'd reconsider, pride kept her from saying more.

Cal opened his mouth as if to speak but then closed it again. His features hardened as he picked up the suitcase, turned on his heel and strode from the room.

A moment later, his footsteps sounded on the stairs.

The air burst from her lungs as if she'd been punched in the stomach by some invisible force. Her hands balled into little fists and she squeezed her eyes shut, willing him to stop. To reconsider the dreams they shared and the family they longed for.

Please don't leave.

The front door opened.

Her stomach dropped but something inside propelled her to action.

"Cal!" She raced after him, prepared to drop all pretenses and beg; plead with him to stay. But she arrived at the top of the stairs just as the front door slammed, rattling the glass.

A lump formed in her throat as Cal—the blurry outline of his body still visible through the wavy glass and wrought iron door— jogged down the steps, clearly in a hurry to leave.

Cal had left her. For real this time.

Her knees buckled. She grabbed the stair rail and collapsed onto the top step. Her head dropped into her hands but for some reason, the tears she'd fought for the last thirty minutes didn't come. Instead, she found herself treading water in a swirling sea of emotions too raw, too terrifying to acknowledge.

Cressida sat there for the longest time, vacillating between panic and despair until a wave of numbness washed over her. Its soothing emptiness felt so much better than the searing pain and she surrendered to it, letting the quiet calm surround her wounded spirit and carry her away.

Chapter One

Two hours passed and Cal still hadn't returned. As each moment crawled by at an agonizing snail's pace; uncertainty morphed into full blown panic and breathed life into her deepest, darkest fears.

What if Cal didn't come back? What would she do without him?

They'd been together ten years. Basically her entire adult life. If she wasn't Cal's wife, she didn't know who she was and that realization terrified her. Still, she refused to lie to herself. They did need a break. She wouldn't even try to deny it. By anyone's standards, the past five years had been tough and a chance to reset their relationship could be just what the doctor ordered but she would've preferred to have arrived at the decision together. At least then, she could've viewed the separation as temporary and positive instead of the way it seemed, which was terrifying and sad.

She'd had her fill of sadness. They both had. Especially after her third failed IVF attempt just three weeks before. Granted, she hadn't allowed herself even the faintest glimmer of hope this time. She'd just gone through the motions or so she'd told herself. But when the doctor had called to relay the bad news, she'd still spent the afternoon in bed, blinds drawn and crying her eyes out. For his part, Cal hadn't said a word and in retrospect, his stoic response had been a huge red flag and if she'd been paying even the slightest bit of attention, she would've noticed it. Maybe then she could've said or done something to prevent his leaving, but she hadn't noticed. Instead, she'd been too caught up in her own pain to see the signs and now it was too late.

Cressida glanced at her watch, a gift from Cal on their fifth anniversary. The sharp stab of sorrow almost brought her to her knees as memories of the romantic trip to Bermuda rushed back. The uncharacteristic sentimentality of the stainless Cartier watch inscribed simply 'Forever' below a monogram of their interlocked initials.

She pushed the bittersweet memory aside and focused on the dial.

Ten-thirty. She really should cancel lunch with Shay before it got any later or she'd never hear the end of it. Her best friend's work schedule was beyond crazy these days and she hated last minute cancellations.

Cressida reached in her purse and pulled out her cell phone, punching in a hurried excuse about unexpected errands. She hated to lie to Shay but she just wasn't up to pretending to enjoy their typical gossip and cocktail-infused lunch when her life had just fallen apart. And she definitely didn't feel like confessing that Cal had just walked out. Then again, she didn't need to. Shay would learn all about his leaving soon enough, if she hadn't already. In their close knit community, everyone seemed to know everything the instant it happened.

The doorbell chimed.

Cressida's head jerked up and despite the voice of reason that warned her not to get her hopes up, her heart soared.

Cal was back!

She shoved the cell phone in her pocket and raced down the stairs planning to fling the door open and shower her husband with kisses. But halfway down, her footsteps slowed as realization dawned.

Cal wouldn't ring the doorbell, he'd use his key.

She paused on the bottom step and squinted at the door but all she could see was a blur of brightly colored fabric.

Hopefully Shay hadn't dropped by early. She did that

sometimes. Or even worse, it could be a nosy neighbor. Cressida had more than her fair share of those and they seemed to have a sixth sense, always stopping by at the most inopportune moments. And right now, she wasn't in the mood for chatting, sympathy or pretty much anything else.

She needed to hide until they went away.

Cressida slipped around the corner, out of sight of the front door and counted to ten. Then she inched forward and peered around the wall, craning her neck to get a good look at her visitor.

A flash of red hair caught her eye.

Cressida gasped and yanked herself back, pressing herself flat against the wall. She squeezed her eyes shut and made the sign of the cross, even though she wasn't Catholic.

Please, please, pleaaassseee let it be anyone but her.

Her visitor pressed and held the doorbell about ten beats longer than could be considered polite. Another sign.

Cressida drew in a long, dread-infused breath and peeked again. Her heart fell through the floor at the sight of the face pressed against the cloudy glass.

Dear God, no. Not my mother. Not today.

She heaved a long-suffering sigh and pushed off from the wall, feet dragging as if tethered to a ball and chain as she tried to determine what she'd done to deserve this unexpected little gift and today, of all days.

Cressida painted on as big a smile as she could muster as she grasped the doorknob and pulled it open.

Her mother, former showgirl and current star of the hit Vegas act *Roxie Reynolds' Real Rock Revue,* threw her arms in the air as if posing at the end of one of her onstage numbers and flashed a mega-watt smile. "Surprise!"

Cressida's mouth dropped open as she eyed the waist-high heap of Louis Vuitton luggage. From the looks of that pile, her mother planned to stay awhile. Maybe even permanently. Heaven forbid.

She gazed up at the sky. *Why me?* When it came to her mother, she'd posed the question more times than could be counted but the universe had yet to deliver an answer.

"Hello darling." Slanted green eyes twinkled knowingly as if she'd read Cressida's thoughts and found them ever so amusing.

Cressida scanned her mother's voluptuous size four figure, showcased in a form-fitting pair of True Religion jeans, a cheetah print cleavage baring halter top and sky high Jimmy Choo's—a look best described as Las Vegas Fabulous. Her mother was something else.

Costa, Roxie's over-the-top stylist slash make-up artist slash partner-in-crime, peered over her shoulder, lifted mirrored aviator shades and winked as he blew an exaggerated kiss. "Hey girl." He waggled his fingers. "Looking fabulous," he said, but his gaze lingered disapprovingly on her tattered t-shirt.

Thanks to Cal's departure, she hadn't gotten around to pulling those weeds or changing clothes. Too bad. Costa could get over it.

Cressida managed a half-hearted wave and forced her frozen smile to remain intact.

Roxie threw her head back and gave a throaty laugh. Then she flung her arms wide and wrapped Cressida in a huge bear hug, squeezing tight as she rocked back and forth.

After several long moments, Roxie pulled away and pinched her cheek, eyes dancing. "Try to contain your excitement, dear. I'm not moving in."

Cressida's shoulders sagged with relief.

"Mothe…" She caught herself, stopping short and expelling a long sigh before she tried again. "I mean…Roxie, what are you doing here?"

Last visit, Roxie had declared herself far too young to have a daughter her age and had forbidden Cressida to call her mother. While Cressida didn't love the edict she sort of understood. Her mother had given birth when barely seventeen and now, thanks to two-hour-a-day workouts and the help of the best plastic surgeons Nevada could offer, the fifty-three-year-old vixen didn't look a day over thirty-eight. Roxie's carefully crafted professional persona had been built to support the over-the-top, ever-youthful, life-of-the-party vibe she presented onstage and a thirty-six-year-old daughter did nothing to reinforce that image.

"I'm in town for a two-month gig at the Hard Rock casino down in Seminole. We reserved the penthouse at the W South Beach but on the plane, I"—Roxie shot a conspiratorial wink at Costa—"*we* decided it would be much more fun to stay with you."

Costa nodded in vigorous agreement.

Cressida pasted on what she hoped looked like a sincere smile. "Great!" she said, through gritted teeth.

God help me.

She didn't get it. Didn't understand how they could look so alike, yet be so different. Where her mother oozed fun and could be considered as flamboyant a personality as had ever emerged from Vegas—which was saying something—everything about her own Cal-approved image screamed conservative and uptight.

She worked endlessly to tame her thick red waves and dressed to minimize her voluptuous curves. And unlike her mother, Cressida did everything possible to avoid center stage. While she shared Roxie's passion for singing, thanks to a rather traumatic middle school experience during which she'd frozen up onstage in front of the entire school, she'd sprint down Las Olas Boulevard in her birthday suit before she'd sing in front of a live audience. If the resemblance weren't so uncanny, it would be impossible to believe them related.

Cressida managed to stifle yet another sigh and tried to manufacture an enthusiasm she didn't feel as she stepped aside and held the door open wide, gesturing for the two to enter. "Wonderful. Come on in."

Roxie squealed and did her trademark hip shimmy—the sexy kitten move that had helped elevate her to cult-like status among her largely gay fan base. Then she waved a hand above her head and waggled her fingers. "Yoo-hoo! Carlton!"

A pudgy middle-aged uniformed driver sprang forward and began pulling bags from the massive pile as Roxie and Costa sashayed inside, arm-in-arm.

Cressida eyed the growing pile of bags in her foyer with concern. She cleared her throat and searched for a way to convince her mother to stay elsewhere without revealing what had just gone down with Cal.

"Uh…Roxie, I'm not sure it's a great idea for you to stay here right now. Things are a little…um…crazy." She arched a brow. "I could stay with you down in South Beach. That might be more fun."

Roxie tilted her head and studied Cressida intently. "Is something wrong?"

While Roxie liked to think of herself as big sister, her Momdar could detect the most subtle of her daughter's distress signals without fail.

"No, of course not," Cressida said, a little too quickly. "I'm kind of stressed right now, that's all. Cal's practice has really taken off and he's just so busy. Actually, he's at a medical conference right now"—she crossed her fingers behind her back at the little white lie—"and…well…you know how it is."

"So how is Cal these days?"

Despite her neutral tone, Roxie's pinched expression made her feelings clear. Her mother despised Cal and as Cressida knew all too well, he felt the same about her. And Cal's feelings about Costa defied description. This little break might actually be a gift from God because it would certainly save her from a world of unpleasantness over the next few weeks.

She supposed it wouldn't hurt anything if her mother stayed a few days, but she'd definitely need to figure out a way to get Roxie and Costa settled into a South Beach hotel before Cal came to his senses and returned or he might actually leave her for good. Her conservative right-wing husband considered Roxie's style of dress inappropriate for her age and her boy toy-loving, freewheeling lifestyle a complete embarrassment. Cal could be a tad judgmental when it came to anything outside the mainstream and her mother could easily reign as queen of the outside-the-mainstream kingdom.

"Would you like a cup of coff...?" An enormous racket drowned out her words. Cressida waited for the noise to die down and tried again. "I just made a pot of co...." It happened again; the screeching sound of industrial brakes and metal rubbing against metal. "What in the world?" Cressida frowned and headed for the kitchen.

Roxie and Costa bopped along behind.

"It sounds like World War III erupted in your backyard," Roxie said, leaning close. "We saw a bunch of construction guys out front."

"Yeah, some real hotties too. Are you having work done on the house?" Costa sounded hopeful. "It would be fun to have that crew around for a while."

"No." Cressida rounded the corner and stopped in her tracks, eyes rounded in disbelief at the scene unfolding out the back window.

Two dump trucks full of dirt sat on her lawn as a sea of construction workers buzzed around—a few with sledge hammers slung over muscular shoulders seemingly intent upon destroying something.

Costa dove for the window and pried the blinds apart, nose pressed against the glass. Roxie wasn't far behind and neither moved, eyes glued to the brawny workers.

Cressida's frown deepened as she marched stiffly toward the back window, anger rising inside like a volcano about to erupt. In the past few hours, she'd endured about all she could handle.

She grabbed the cord and yanked up the wood blinds to get a clear view. Her eyes bugged out as she spied the crane and wrecking ball situated at the back of the yard.

Pulse racing, she flew to the door, flung it open and charged onto the deck.

"What's going on out here?" she shouted at no one in particular.

Everyone ignored her.

She held a hand to her brow to shield the hot morning sun as she scanned the backyard, looking for someone in charge.

The dump trucks had gouged enormous craters that crisscrossed the lawn, destroying the carefully tended sod.

Cressida wrung her hands as she paced the deck, surveying the destruction. Cal was going to have a fit when he got a load of the damage to his precious landscaping. But grass and shrubs could be replanted. She needed to get these guys out of here before they damaged something more expensive to replace.

Cal tended to be on the cheap side so he wouldn't take kindly to laying out unnecessary cash to fix something that never should've been destroyed in the first place. And he'd blame her for not stopping them.

She spotted a tall, dark-haired man with several rolls of paper tucked in the crook of his arm. He stood just off the back deck surrounded by a cluster of men clad in orange vests and hard hats. He kept pointing to the crane and wrecking ball.

Cressida had just started towards him when Roxie and Costa sidled up.

Costa grabbed her arm and squeezed as he pointed to one of the sledge hammer guys.

"That one, right there," he breathed reverently, eyeing a beefy hunk with shoulder length sun-bleached hair and bulging biceps. "He looks just like Chris Hemsworth!"

"Ooooo," Roxie cooed. "He does…"

As if on cue, Thor looked up and zeroed in on Roxie, his lust-filled gaze drifting over her curvy figure. He straightened, puffed his chest out and slung his sledge hammer over a muscular, bronzed shoulder while shooting her a lascivious wink.

Roxie and Costa collapsed together, giggling.

"Do you mind?" Cressida glared at them, hating that she had to be the adult in the room whenever the two were around. By the time she turned back, the boss guy had vanished.

"Where did he go?" she muttered.

"Where did who go?" Roxie asked, still preening and giving Thor the hot eye.

"The guy with all the paper under his arm. He seemed like the one in charge. I want these guys out of my backyard before they do something that can't be undone."

She'd barely finished her sentence when Thor and his two steel-wielding buddies swung in unison. Their sledge hammers smashed into her newish wood deck. A large section of custom wrought iron railing bent and fell to the ground.

"Hey!" she yelled, blood pressure rising.

She might as well have been invisible because the workmen ignored her and reared their hammers back to strike another blow.

Refusing to be discounted a millisecond longer; Cressida balled her fists and stomped over. Just as the men started to swing, she stepped directly in their path, flung her arms wide and hollered, "Stop!"

The men halted mid swing but the momentum of their hammers threw them off balance. One guy ended up twisted like a pretzel. Another lost his balance and fell onto his side. The third barely missed Cressida's foot.

"What the hell!" Thor thundered as he picked himself off the ground.

Costa recoiled and partially hid behind Cressida, peering over her shoulder as he whispered, "He looks pissed. And he's sweaty. That's hot."

Cressida's lips compressed into a thin, hard line as she reared her head back and glared at Costa. Then turned to Thor, determined to stand her ground.

She pointed an accusing finger, her tone meant to sound menacing as she said through gritted teeth, "Listen—"

"No, *you* listen," drawled a deep sexy voice drenched in east Texas twang. "Steppin' in front of a sledge hammer is a real good way to lose a limb. Or worse. Just what do you think you're doin'?"

Finally! Someone in charge.

Cressida spun around, hands on hips. "I'd like to ask you the same thing…" Her voice trailed off as a pair of velvety brown eyes captured hers. The effect momentarily rendered her speechless. She cleared her throat and tried again. "I…uh…"

"Well, helloooo." Roxie stepped forward, batting her lashes. "Roxie Reynolds." She flashed her Hollywood perfect smile. "And this"—she wrapped an arm around Cressida's shoulders and squeezed— "is Cressie Ann."

Cressida cringed at the hated nickname and elbowed her mother in the side.

The man's face split into a broad grin, made all the more dazzling by his sun-bronzed skin and square-jawed, rough-hewn good looks.

Cressida blinked.

"Hey Roxie." He adjusted the papers under his arm and shook hands with her mother. His gaze shifted back to her and his smile broadened, crinkling the skin around his eyes. "Cressie Ann."

Cressida's cheeks grew warm as she caught herself gawking. She forced herself to look away. "Cressida," she corrected weakly. Then she stood a little straighter, trying to sound stern as she said, "And you are?"

"Ben Carrington," he said. "I'm the architect overseeing this renovation. And we're on a tight schedule."

"No." She folded her arms and lifted her chin, preferring to think of the architect hottie as the enemy. "You're at the wrong house."

Chapter Two

Ben smirked and Cressida tried hard not to focus on the way his full lips tugged up at the corners.

He pulled one of the rolls from under his arm and thrust it at her. "Here's the contract. I also have the blueprints and construction permit. I'm at the right house. And I have to get started. *Now*."

Mesmerized by the gold flecks in his eyes, it took a few moments to break free of his spell. She shook her head and cleared her throat, forcing her attention to the contract.

Before she could respond, Ben started rattling off the high points. He gestured toward the house. "We have to take down this entire back wall, gut most of the kitchen and enlarge the upstairs master suite," he said. "And I don't have a second to spare. If I don't finish this job in six weeks, I don't get my on time bonus."

His rugged gorgeousness fueled her angst and she nearly told him to stick his on time bonus where the sun doesn't shine. She stopped herself just in time. Instead, she forced a smile and with all the faux sweetness she could muster, said, "I'm sorry, if my husband planned to renovate our—"

"Your husband," he scoffed.

Her brows knit together and she found impossible to keep the defensiveness from her tone as she responded. "Yes."

He rubbed his jaw and eyed her with disbelief. "You expect me to believe *you're* Mrs. Wentworth."

Cressida bristled. Something about the way he said it. Like it was the most outlandish thing he'd ever heard.

She straightened her spine. "I *am* Mrs. Wentworth. Cressida Wentworth." She decided to put a stop to the nonsense once and for all. "You know what? I'm calling Cal so we can sort this out."

Cal might've just walked out on her but he'd come back. And when he did, he wouldn't be happy to learn that a wayward construction crew had damaged his lawn and demolished part of his deck. And that she'd just stood around and watched.

"Mom"—Cressida stopped, rolled her eyes and heaved a long sigh of resignation, wishing for what had to be the millionth time that she had a normal mother—"I mean, Roxie…can you bring me my cell? It's on the kitchen table."

Roxie shot a flirtatious glance at Thor as she spun on her heel and pranced toward the back door.

Ben held up a hand which stopped Roxie in her tracks. With the other, he reached in his pocket, pulled out his cell phone and with an air of superiority said, "Please. Allow me."

He punched a series of buttons, held the phone to his ear and waited.

Roxie eyed the architect with calculated appreciation, leaned close and squeezed Cressida's elbow. "He's cuuuute." Her exaggerated stage whisper could undoubtedly be heard two houses down, even with all the construction noise.

Cressida's cheeks flamed as she poked her mother in the side. "Stop it!" she muttered out of the corner of her mouth. Luckily, Ben seemed preoccupied with his phone call and didn't appear to have heard.

"Dr. Wentworth, please." He paused. "Yes. Tell him Ben Carrington is on the line and I need to speak with him immediately."

A brief pause ensued during which he pulled the phone from his ear and punched the speakerphone button.

A moment later, Cal came on the line. "Ben,"—her husband sounded surprisingly cheerful given the fact that he'd just walked out his wife— "what can I do for you?"

Cressida narrowed her eyes. They sounded like buddies. Not a good sign.

"I'm at the house trying to get the back wall taken out so we can stay on schedule. Some woman here is claiming to be your *wife*," Ben looked her up and down, as if he considered the notion ridiculous. "And she's refusing to let me and my guys proceed."

Cressida self-consciously tugged on her t-shirt and wished again that she'd changed clothes.

The silence seemed to last an eternity.

Finally Cal sighed and sounded decidedly less upbeat as he said, "Let me talk to her."

Ben handed her the phone, a triumphant gleam in his eyes.

She bit her lip as she accepted the device, her thoughts so jumbled and confused, it didn't occur to her to take the phone off speaker as she said, "Cal? What's going on?"

He sounded matter-of-fact. "I hired Ben to gut the kitchen, add onto the master suite and a few other things."

Her mind raced as she struggled to make sense of his words. "But why wouldn't you have involved me? Do you really think we need this right now given the fact that"—suddenly aware she had an audience of at least two dozen workmen, the cute boss guy and Roxie and Costa, she turned her back to the group and slunk to the opposite side of the deck, lowering her voice to a whisper before continuing—"you know...since we're taking a break and all?"

"We're putting the house up for sale in two months."

"What?" Cressida cried, forgetting the audience. "Sell the house? No! We're trying for a baby!"

"No. We're taking a break," Cal shot back. His words sounded harsh and brittle in their finality. After an uncomfortable pause, during which Roxie and Costa exchanged a worried glance, he

18

assumed a more persuasive tone. "Think about it, Cress. Wouldn't it be nice to have a fresh start in a new place? One without all the memories of failed pregnancies and disappointments and depressing doctor visits?"

"A fresh start," she repeated, chewing her lower lip. A fresh start actually did sound nice.

"Yes." Cal spoke faster as his charm offensive picked up steam. "We could move to South Beach since my practice is so busy these days. I need to be closer to the office. South Beach sounds nice, doesn't it? We could use a change of pace."

"I guess." Cressida nibbled a fingernail and tried not to think about his possible motives for not involving her in the renovation or the idea of selling the house and moving to South Beach or why the hot architect seemed so convinced she wasn't Cal's wife.

"Let Ben and the guys get started. If you don't want to stay there while the work is underway, I'll get you a hotel suite," said Cal.

She arched a brow, her trouble meter now on full alert.

The day her frugal husband voluntarily forked over cash for a hotel suite was the day she could no longer deny that something was up. Something she didn't feel ready to acknowledge but couldn't completely ignore, which left her feeling confused.

"Now, be a love and hand the phone back to Ben," he said.

Cressida wanted to push back, wanted to ask more questions but she couldn't form a coherent thought, so she plodded over to the architect and handed him the phone.

As Ben rejoined the men in hard hats, Roxie looped an arm through Cressida's, her tone overly bright as she said, "Let's grab a bite to eat. I'm famished. That flight lasted an eternity."

"And the food in first class was inedible," said Costa. "Thank God for the mimosas."

"We might need some more of those," Roxie said, nodding her head toward Cressida while shooting Costa a meaningful glance.

Numb and more than a little confused, Cressida let them guide her through the kitchen and into the living room where Roxie grabbed their purses and Cressida's car keys from the foyer table as the ear-splitting construction din grew louder.

Costa opened the front door and the trio stepped onto the porch.

A burly man clad in an orange vest and hard hat spotted them and barked into a walkie-talkie. "Clear!"

As Costa locked the front door, the wrecking ball crashed through the back wall, demolishing part of the kitchen and what remained of Cressida's peaceful, perfect little world.

Cressida slid into the booth and tossed her Marc Jacobs bag onto the purple vinyl seat. "Sorry I'm late. It's all Roxie's fault."

She heaved an exaggerated sigh and reached across the table for Shay's margarita.

"Roxie's in town?" Shay's face lit up and she leaned forward, eyes dancing.

Cressida rolled her eyes and nodded, taking a generous sip. The tequila flamed a path down her throat, melting some of the numbness of the past twenty-four hours. She took another healthy sip.

"Fabulous!" Shay rubbed her palms together, blue eyes gleaming with devilish anticipation. "Ooo, I hope she brought her sidekick. I need to have some *fuuunnn!*" She drew out the last word in a way that made her intentions clear.

Cressida pursed her lips. "Yeah, almost as fabulous as the wrecking ball that smashed through my back wall during the surprise renovation yesterday." She arched a brow. "By the way, don't bother plotting any crazy adventures with Costa this trip. The last time did Roxie in and she told me she plans to keep you two apart this time, which is the most sensible thing she's said in a decade."

"Spoil sport." Shay made a face and snatched her glass back. "So what's all this about a wrecking ball?"

"Oh, *that*." Cressida waved a hand dismissively, not bothering to hide the sarcasm in her tone. "That arrived yesterday. No biggie. Just your average two-ton destruction device. To Costa's delight, it came complete with a hot architect and a sea of sweaty construction workers."

Shay chuckled and shook her head, causing her shiny blond bob to swing back and forth. "You're ridiculous. Stop kidding around." She took a sip of margarita.

"Oh, I'm dead serious. Unfortunately." Cressida raised a hand to flag the waiter. "The construction crew showed up a few hours after Cal moved out." When she failed to get the server's attention, she stretched taller and waved more frantically. "I wish he'd hurry. I need a cocktail."

Shay's mouth gaped open and her eyes grew round. After a brief pause, she leaned forward and placed her palms on the table, searching Cressida's face.

"Wait. Let me get this straight. Cal moved out?" Shay's brows shot to her hairline. "We'll get to the hot architect later."

"He packed his stuff and walked out yesterday morning. A few hours later, the construction crew arrived to complete a six-week renovation he'd apparently been planning for ages but never bothered to mention. Oh, and in between, my mother and her evil twin of a stylist arrived for a two-month surprise visit, though judging by the volume of luggage, they might've just moved in permanently." Cressida waved her hands and made a goofy face. "Surprise!"

Shay giggled. "Oy vey." She pushed her half-finished margarita toward Cressida. "You need this more than I do."

"You can say that again." Cressida accepted the drink and sipped a generous amount.

"So how hot is the architect?" Shay lifted a calculated brow and without waiting for the answer, fired another question. "Single?"

Two years post-divorce, Shay rarely missed a beat when it came to attractive, potentially eligible men, a habit that usually amused Cressida but which today, she found irritating in the extreme. She opened her mouth to say as much but the waiter arrived to take their order.

Both ladies ordered a margarita and he left two menus behind.

After the harried waiter scurried away, Cressida drew in a long breath and decided to humor her friend. "Scale of one to ten?" she asked, playing their usual rating game.

Shay nodded, eyes dancing with anticipation.

Cressida gazed up at the ceiling and sipped her friend's margarita as she considered her answer. "I'd say about a seventeen point five."

A pretty fair assessment in Cressida's mind, though perhaps a little on the conservative side since she'd graded him down due to the fact that he'd destroyed her house.

"Really. Usually no one gets more than a 9 with you." Shay leaned forward, elbows on the table. "Do tell."

"Six foot gorgeous and a Texas accent to boot. You'd love him." Cressida spread her napkin in her lap and then reached for a chip. "But believe it or not, I had a few other things on my mind yesterday so I failed to catch his marital status."

She shot her friend a look intended to chastise as she dipped her chip into the salsa and took a bite.

"Fair enough," Shay had the grace to look slightly embarrassed. "So what's Cal's deal?"

Cressida shrugged. "He informed me we're taking a break. Whatever that means."

Shay pushed back in the booth and her mouth twisted into a know-it-all smirk. "Ah, the ole taking a break ploy. I swear." She shook her head and pursed her lips. "Amazon must sell a manual on how to ditch your wife. All these guys use the same excuse and frankly, it's getting a little tired." She paused and her eyes narrowed. "Is Princess Graciella still in residence?"

Shay's sour expression made her feelings about Cressida's cousin clear.

Cressida plucked at her linen napkin, too preoccupied with her own thoughts to rise to Shay's bait. Her cousin had stayed five long months while trying to land a modeling gig down in Miami that had never materialized. Her presence hadn't exactly helped a marriage already limping along. And during the length of her visit she'd defended Gracie endlessly against Shay's constant nitpicking.

"She moved out two days ago," Cressida said. "Thank God. Having her around when he left would've been too humiliating."

Shay's brow furrowed. "Where did she go?"

"South Beach. Cal helped her put a down payment on a condo or something. I don't know." Cressida tossed her napkin on the table and leaned back in the booth, eyeing her friend with determination. "Right now, I couldn't care less where Gracie moved. Help me think this Cal thing through. It doesn't make any sense."

Shay's eyes grew into two huge round pools of concern. "El Cheapo shelled out cash on a condo for your *cousin*?" Her voice cracked as she added, "*Seriously?*"

The waiter returned, set a frozen margarita in front of each girl and rushed off.

Cressida frowned. Put that way, it did seem weird that her financially conservative husband had volunteered to help Graciella. Enticing Cal to part with his precious cash normally took a lot of persistence and a compelling reason. Considering she hadn't even broached the subject but instead Cal had volunteered did seem suspicious now that she thought about it, but she'd worry about that later. Right now, she had more pressing problems to contend with.

Cressida pushed the troubling thoughts away and continued. "Anyway, it took me a few hours but after he left, I convinced myself the separation made sense. That taking a little break might actually be a good thing. It could help stoke the fire a little. You know, absence makes the heart grow fonder and all that." She frowned and slowly shook her head. "But then the construction crew showed up. I mean…who hires an architect to renovate a house without even consulting their spouse?"

Shay nibbled on a chip, her brow furrowed.

Cressida gazed up for a long moment, eyes focused on the rotating ceiling fans as she mulled over the troubling thoughts that proved impossible to push aside. Then she sucked a generous amount of margarita through her straw before continuing. "And when I called to confront him, all he would say is that we're selling the house. No discussion. No emotion." Her expression darkened into a scowl. "He just informed me in that autocratic way of his that we're selling it."

"Why does he want to sell the house?"

Her frown remained steadfastly in place as she plucked distractedly at her napkin. "Apparently, he wants to move to Miami."

"Miami." Shay pursed her lips.

"I don't know," Cressida continued. "Maybe Cal's having a midlife crisis. He's been acting weird for two months. Now that I think about it, a few weeks ago I was cleaning out his pockets before a run to the dry cleaners and I found a business card from Hair Club for Men. And I think he might actually be going." She leaned forward and whispered, "He's looking a little fuller on top, don't you think?"

"Miami," Shay repeated, more insistently this time. She arched a brow and paused three beats before she added with pointed emphasis, "Where Graciella just moved."

Cressida sat up straight and stirred her drink with her straw before taking another long sip. "Anyway, I've done nothing but obsess for twenty-four hours and I think it's best if I just take this whole Cal leaving thing at face value. It's important not to overreact in situations like this." She lifted her chin. "We're going through a down cycle, that's all. I mean, every marriage goes through down cycles, right? And we're entitled given all the baby drama of the past few years." She squared her shoulders. "You have to stick through the tough times. That's the key to a successful marriage."

Shay pushed out her lower lip and eyed Cressida intently. "This doesn't sound like a down cycle to me."

Cressida glared at her friend, tired of the innuendos and endless jabs. She loved Shay but the bitter aftermath of her friend's marriage had planted seeds of suspicion which had blossomed into full blown paranoia of all husbands. According to Shay, all men cheated and while Cressida knew many did, she refused to hop on the don't-trust-any-of-the-scumbags bandwagon. Life was too short.

"Cal isn't Jerry. He wouldn't cheat. It's not his style."

Cal worried too much about appearances to cheat. He obsessed about putting forth the right image to the right people. The image of the perfect life. The perfect couple. The perfect wife. Then again, nothing and no one had ever really been perfect enough for Cal. Certainly not her, though God knows she'd tried. But she'd fallen woefully short in his eyes. And in her own.

"Yeah," Shay said. "I thought the same thing. I thought Jerry was a nice, loyal, semi-nerdy Jewish guy who'd stick with me till the end. And I continued to think that right up until the day *after* the divorce when he married the twenty-one-year-old hoochie he'd secretly shacked up with." She shook her head, her voice dripping bitterness. "I'll tell ya. These South Florida plastic surgeons are something else. A hot young thing struts in one day looking for a boob job or some Botox she doesn't need and two seconds later, the faithful wife gets shoved to the curb."

"Cal is different," Cressida said, jumping to his defense though she had no idea why given the way he'd treated her yesterday. Still, the idea of Cal and Gracie running off together seemed too ridiculous to even consider.

Cal didn't approve of sexy clothes and shunned over the top

lifestyles—hence his disapproval of Roxie—and Gracie fell squarely into both categories. Graciella exuded a larger than life persona—a bombshell in every sense of the word. Cal, on the other hand, protected his ultra-conservative image at all costs lest he risk becoming an outcast among the country club set he considered so important, a group that pontificated about family values—even though more than a few kept a mistress on the side—and sat in judgment of those they considered beneath them.

Shay shifted around in her chair, tucked a few honey blond strands behind her ear and cleared her throat. "Listen," she began, eyeing Cressida cautiously. "I've..." She cleared her throat and tried again. "Well, I've heard rumors about Cal and Gracie. I didn't...you know...*believe* them at first, but since she just moved to Miami and Cal followed the day after, I wonder if—"

A portly man barged up to their table. He wore a wrinkled suit that strained to fit over his enlarged mid section and reeked of stale cigarettes.

The man glanced at a crumpled piece of paper in the palm of his hand. "Crez..."—he squinted and tried again—"Cree...zeeda Wentworth?"

"Cressida. Like the car." She issued the correction automatically. Nobody ever got her name right, no doubt finding it hard to believe she'd been named after the dilapidated red Toyota her mother had driven for a decade before landing her first recording contract.

She held up an index finger. "Hang on a sec." She narrowed her eyes, her voice determined. "I'm sorry, what about Cal and Gracie?"

Undeterred, the man pulled an envelope from his jacket pocket and thrust it into Cressida's hands.

She gazed at the crumpled envelope with wide-eyed surprise. "What—?"

"Divorce action, sweet cheeks. Served and witnessed. Have a nice day." He gave a mock salute and waddled away.

Chapter Three

The envelope, emblazoned with the logo of Cagney, Anderson and Doyle, slid from Cressida's grip and onto the table.

The girls stared at it for several long moments and then locked eyes.

In her friend's worried expression, Cressida detected sympathy mixed with a healthy dose of fear.

Cressida narrowed her eyes. Shay knew more than she'd volunteered that wasn't okay. She wanted the truth and wanted it now.

Her hands balled into fists and her voice took on a sharp edge as she said, "What about Cal and Graciella? And why am I just hearing about this *now*?"

Shay held her gaze for a moment longer and then looked away, shifting in her chair uncomfortably. "There's been talk," she said softly.

Fear and disbelief intermingled with something else Cressida couldn't quite identify. Or didn't want to. A lump formed in her throat as she slumped back in her seat, shoulders sagging.

She swallowed hard, her voice a hoarse whisper as she said, "Oh. *Talk*." She knew what that meant and she grew quiet as the realization sank in.

No wonder the dinner invitations had dried up. And now she knew why the Ladies Guild had *accidentally* forgotten to invite her to last week's planning luncheon for the White Ball. The pieces of the puzzle had started to fit together and she didn't like the picture coming into view. She knew all too well what happened to the discarded wife in their crowd.

Shay squeezed her hand. "I know I should've said something. I just...I didn't want to mention it until I knew for sure." She leaned forward, eyes pleading with Cressida to understand as she whispered, "You know how people around here like to gossip. Sometimes it's hard to know what's true versus the crazy talk of the week."

"You should've told me," Cressida said softly. But she sort of understood why Shay hadn't wanted to. Being the person who delivered the bad news about a cheating man could doom a friendship, whether true or not.

Tears welled as reality sank in. She blinked fiercely and took another long sip of margarita.

The idea of Cal and Gracie sneaking around behind her back and in her own home sounded so embarrassingly cliché and so unlike anything she'd imagined Cal capable of, it didn't seem possible. She wondered what his hoity-toity friends would say.

She gulped down a healthy portion of frozen margarita and then pinched the bridge of her nose against the onslaught of brain freeze.

The friends with the secret mistresses would probably congratulate him—especially since her gorgeous cousin had just celebrated her twenty-fifth birthday. Meanwhile, at the ripe old age of thirty-six, almost thirty-seven, she suddenly felt as if an expiration date had been tattooed on her forehead.

Shay flagged down the waiter. "It's time for serious carbs and some real cocktails," she announced. "Enough with these girly drinks."

When he arrived, Shay handed him the menus and began rattling off their order. "We'd like guacamole, chips and salsa, the largest bowl of chili con queso you can get your hands on and two extra dry, *extra grande* martinis." She winked and leaned closer. "And keep 'em comin."

After he left, Shay opened her purse and fished around, pulling out a dog-eared business card. She slid the card across the table and gazed at Cressida expectantly.

Cressida picked up the card. "Gray Portell."

"The best girl power attorney south of the Mason-Dixon Line," Shay said with a devious smile. "They don't call him Scoretell for nothin'. I wish I'd discovered him while going through my divorce. The outcome would've been completely different."

Cressida shook her head and pushed the card away.

"I'm not ready to hire an attorney."

Just an hour earlier, she'd planned to enlist Shay's help in devising a strategy to put the spark back in her relationship. She'd been thinking lacy black lingerie and a long weekend in Key West which made it all the more difficult to wrap her head around the possibility that her ailing marriage might actually be over.

"I need to think. Too much has happened in the past few days." She chewed the inside of her lip and then announced, "I need to talk to Cal."

She straightened her spine. Yes. If she could just talk to Cal, she could make sense of all this craziness. His leaving and serving her with papers might just be another ploy for attention. It had to be. And if so, his tactics had succeeded. Cal now had her full attention and Cressida would literally do anything to piece her marriage back together. To get her life back to normal.

"You don't *have* time. Trust me. You need to get in front of this situation. Take control. Before things go too far." Shay pointed at the envelope. "If Cal wanted to talk, *that* wouldn't have arrived."

Cressida sat up straighter and found it impossible to keep the defensiveness from her tone as she said, "Look, I know your divorce got ugly but Cal is different. He wouldn't hurt me."

Or would he? Suddenly, she didn't feel as confident as she had an hour ago.

"Seems to me he already has." The gentleness in Shay's tone softened her harsh candor. "Cal's done, honey. Even if you don't want to believe he's cheating with Gracie, here's your proof." She tapped the envelope with a French-tipped fingernail. "And I can tell you from personal experience, if this situation wasn't going to get ugly he wouldn't have hired the CADs."

Cressida frowned. "The CADs?"

Shay pointed to the logo of Cagney, Anderson and Doyle. "Believe me, that acronym is no coincidence because every two-timing midlife crisis-experiencing man scum in South Florida uses them. That's why Gray's practice is booming. Gray Portell fights back and he loves nothing better than ripping the CADs to shreds. Apparently there's some bad blood from law school or whatever."

She leaned forward and locked eyes with Cressida. "But Gray isn't a miracle worker. Don't give Cal too big a head start. As you know all too well, by the time I got served Jerry had already hidden most of the money."

Cressida's jaw went slack. "You think Cal could be hiding money?"

Shay arched a brow. "His Royal Cheapness? You tell me..." She tilted her head to the side. "Did you know there's a law firm up in Palm Beach that actually offers a class on how to hide your assets? I saw an advertisement at the Cinemark up in Boca last weekend, just before the movie previews. Apparently, there's a whole infrastructure down here built around how to screw your wife. Or husband, I guess, as the case may be." She sipped her martini.

Cressida's mind raced to process through this sudden and troubling turn of events.

What had happened to her perfect, orderly little life?

Okay, maybe perfect stretched the truth a bit but orderly sure fit. Or it had, anyway. But in the past two days her life had been ripped up and tossed into the gutter where it now lay in tattered, filthy little bits.

Cheating, secret house renovation, attorneys, hiding money, divorce. Overnight, her world had morphed into a Lifetime Movie of the Week with an exceptionally trite plot and somehow she'd been cast in the role of clueless wife like some D-list movie actress. Nothing could be farther from her dreams of babies and romance and happily-ever-after.

The waiter returned with their appetizers and martinis. He placed a glass in front of each girl and then left.

"Chin up," Shay said, lifting her glass. "My divorce was the best thing that ever happened to me. You've said so yourself millions of times. It set me free. If I hadn't experienced such a financial catastrophe, thanks to my loving ex-husband, I might never have discovered I'm such a genius entrepreneur."

"You already had the boutique on Las Olas when Jerry left," Cressida pointed out.

"But it really took off after that. You know that. It had just been a hobby before. And I never would've expanded to Boca if I'd stayed with Jerry."

"I don't have any hobbies." Cressida's voice sounded dangerously close to a whine. She knew she sounded pitiful but couldn't help it.

"We'll find you one. Now let's drink to brighter days ahead. Come on," Shay coaxed and raised her glass. "You'll feel better."

Cressida picked up her glass and took a long fortifying sip. Her head was spinning. She definitely needed to talk to Cal.

She set down her drink, pulled her cell phone from her purse and punched in the number for Cal's office.

His receptionist picked up after three rings. "Hi Monica, its Cressida. Can I speak with my husband please?"

Shay shook her head violently, shot out of her chair and strained across the table, trying to swipe the phone from Cressida's hands. "No!"

Cressida pushed Shay's hand away and leaned back in the booth as she waited for the receptionist to connect her with Cal. If she could just hear his voice, she'd know everything would be okay. He'd tell her to stop worrying. That the break was temporary. That in the weeks to come, they'd be picking out a new house down in South Beach.

"I'm sorry Mrs. Wentworth…" After a long uncomfortable pause, the woman continued. "Dr. Wentworth is in surgery at the moment. May I give him a message?"

Cressida bit her lip and frowned. "Yes. Could you have him call me please?"

"Of course."

Cressida disconnected the call and set the phone gently on the table. She lifted her drink, her voice raw as she said, "Cal doesn't do surgeries on Thursday. This is his day for consultations." She sipped her cocktail. "He's always available on Thursday."

She blinked back the sudden rush of tears, determined not to cry in the middle of lunch hour at Rocco's Tacos. "It's true, isn't it?" Her voice trembled. "My marriage is over."

Shay reached for her hand and nodded. "I think so." Her eyes held a gentle sadness. "I'm so sorry, Cress."

She tossed back a healthy gulp of martini and blinked away the fresh tears that sprang to her eyes, uncertain whether they'd come from the stiff cocktail or the sudden realization that yesterday's departure wasn't just another dramatic gesture on Cal's part. This time, Cal seemed serious and she had the divorce papers to prove it.

She was two seconds from being flung into the unforgiving South Florida world of divorce attorneys and bed-hopping bachelors looking for a good time and she didn't feel ready. She wasn't prepared. She wanted to be a mother, not a single woman. She didn't want to date, she wanted her husband. She didn't even want a career, she wanted to stay home and take care of her family. While she knew many would think those aspirations old fashioned, she didn't care. It's what she wanted. Was that so wrong?

She took another drink. It didn't matter what she wanted. She appeared to be headed down a path of Cal's choosing and she'd been left with no choice but to suck it up and deal with it.

Cressida sipped her martini as her depressing new reality sank in.

"Good girl." Shay bit the olive off the plastic spear and chewed. "Have one more sip."

Cressida dutifully sipped and set the drink down. She felt numb. Whether from the alcohol or the sudden turn of events in her marriage, she had no idea.

She reached for the chips and salsa and then thought better of it. If she wasn't careful, she'd pack on a heap of unwanted pounds which would only make matters worse. She'd always been an emotional eater and with all the baby drama, she already carried fifteen unwanted pounds—all of it on her hips—and Cal never let her hear the end of it. She hadn't eaten so much as a morsel of a carb in front of her husband in nearly two months.

With great effort, she pushed the chips away and made a mental note to head to the gym first thing in the morning.

"There you go." Shay nodded approvingly as she set her glass on the table and picked up her cell phone. "I'm calling Gray." She punched in his number. "We need to get you an appointment. Before it's too late."

Cressida gulped down half her martini and then slumped back in the booth as Shay scheduled a meeting with Miami's most ruthless divorce attorney.

❧

The cab rolled to a stop in front of Cressida's house. Her car would be delivered later that evening by the Rocco's Taco's valet crew. Her twenty-five dollar tip had seen to that.

Cressida thrust a wad of crumpled bills at the driver, climbed out of the cab and stumbled up the sidewalk, clutching the envelope that had destroyed all her hopes and dreams.

After several failed attempts, she managed to insert the key into the lock and stepped inside, letting the comforting warmth of home embrace her.

Cressida closed the door quietly and collapsed against it, grateful for the silence as she pressed the envelope to her chest. She hadn't summoned the courage to open it. She couldn't. That would just make this whole nightmare seem too real.

Roxie's throaty laugh drifted down the hall and Cressida groaned inwardly. So much for hoping she'd be at rehearsal.

Despite the abundance of vodka coursing through her veins, she didn't feel up to dealing with Roxie, her ever-present sidekick or the unholy mess the construction crew had made of her kitchen. She just wanted to be alone so she could sink into a giant tub of lavender-scented bubbles and throw the pity party to end all pity parties.

She slipped off her heels and tiptoed toward the staircase. On the second step, the wood creaked in protest.

Cressida froze, uttering a quick silent prayer that Roxie hadn't heard her.

"Is that you, Cressie?" Roxie called, her timing perfect, as always. "Come join us!"

Cressida threw her head back and groaned, silently cursing her mother's supernatural hearing.

She briefly considered ignoring her mother's call and heading upstairs as the siren's cry of the bubble bath was strong. But she knew better. Roxie wouldn't hesitate to come looking for her and she might bring her sidekick with her and Cressida wasn't up for a bathroom chat fest.

Besides, she'd have to confess the truth about her marriage eventually and now seemed as good a time as any. At least the two martinis would take the edge off the humiliation of getting served with divorce papers in the middle of a busy restaurant.

Envelope in hand, she headed to the kitchen, dropping her purse on the foyer table as she passed.

As she entered, she immediately spotted Roxie perched on a bar stool at the kitchen island, chin resting on laced fingers as she gazed up at Ben with adoration.

Costa stood nearby, checking out the buff carpenter busily taking measurements of the kitchen appliances.

Ben sat between them looking so ruggedly gorgeous that she briefly considered turning around and heading upstairs. Something about the sexy architect unnerved her.

"Hiya Honey!" Roxie pulled out the stool next to her and patted the seat. "You're just in time. Ben is about to update us on all the progress." Her grand sweeping gesture encompassed the boarded back wall and stripped floors. "Isn't it wonderful?"

Cressida gazed about, eyes narrowed and lip curled as she weaved toward the island, a little unsteady on her feet. She traced a fingertip over the temporary plywood counter where just yesterday, a newish and perfectly nice granite countertop had been.

She eyed the black residue with disgust and snarled, "What progress?"

Roxie's brows knit together as she searched Cressida's face. "What's wrong, dear?"

"Oh, I don't know." Cressida swept her arm broadly. "Maybe I'm just a little cranky because Mr. Hot Stuff architect here"—she glared at Ben—"destroyed my kitchen."

For some reason, it felt good to vent her frustrations on the builder, especially since he seemed so chummy with her two-timing husband. And her mother, the traitor.

Roxie's lips twitched and she appeared to be fighting back a smile which pissed Cressida off to no end.

Cressida glared at her mother. "If you think that's funny, you'll love this." She smacked the envelope down on the plywood counter.

A puff of sawdust wafted up.

Roxie and Costa sneezed in unison.

"Gesundheit," Ben said.

Cressida gestured dramatically toward the envelope. "That arrived during lunch, compliments of a paunchy little hobbit in a badly fitting suit."

Three sets of eyes locked onto the offending packet.

"Cal filed for divorce." Her eyes welled and voice shook as she added, "And he ran off with Graciella."

Roxie gasped and shot to her feet, outrage written all over her face. But the outrage quickly changed to uncertainty as she studied Cressida's face, looking as if she was trying to gauge whether her sympathy would be welcomed.

She tentatively touched Cressida's arm and then pulled it away, clasping her hands in front of her. "Oh baby, I'm so sorry…" She turned to Costa, fire shooting from her eyes. "I can't say I'm surprised. That girl's mother is a husband-stealing tramp. She's pulled that same stunt more times than I could count."

Costa sniffed. "Apparently the hoochie doesn't fall far from the tramp."

Roxie reached for her arm but Cressida yanked it away.

Sorry? Fat chance. More like her mother had been praying for this moment for a decade. That realization stuck in Cressida's craw where it festered like an infected wound right along with the rest of her unresolved Roxie baggage.

"Please," Cressida spat. "Like *you* care. You *hate* Cal."

"He's not my favorite, no, but I know *you* love him." Roxie turned to Costa and rolled her eyes.

Costa shook his head sadly as if to say he considered Cressida a lost cause.

"And I love *you*," Roxie said. "So I *do* care. I care a lot."

Cressida stumbled over to the cabinets, opened one and pulled out a wine glass. Then she popped the cork from an Argentinian Malbec. A healthy portion chugged into the crystal stemware.

"No, you care about *you*." She turned and jabbed a finger at Roxie, causing wine to splash out of her overfilled glass and onto the floor where it mixed with little sawdust particles and turned into a congealed burgundy-colored mess.

The trio gaped at her, eyes wide.

"And you care about your precious singing career and your *fans*." More wine sloshed out as Cressida waved the glass toward Costa. "And you care about your little sidekick over there."

Costa froze, looking as if he wanted to bolt.

Ben jabbed a thumb toward the door. "I, uh…I need to go check on the guys. Make sure they're wrapping up for today." He backed away slowly, eyeing her cautiously in the way one would a rabid dog.

"I'll go with you." Costa tiptoed after him.

"Stay!" Roxie barked.

Both men halted on command and froze in place.

Roxie didn't take her eyes off Cressida and the steely gleam in those green depths indicated she'd broach no arguments.

"My daughter needs to apologize for being so rude."

Ben looked from one woman to the other, shifting his weight from one foot to the other.

Costa peered over his shoulder, eyeing Cressida with concern.

Cressida lifted her chin. "I'm not apologizing to *him*." She jabbed a thumb at Ben. "He wrecked my kitchen!"

"Don't you think you've had enough?" Roxie said, zeroing in on the wine glass.

"Not even close," Cressida said. "I've spent *years* trying to be perfect—first for dad, then for Nana and now for Cal. And where has it gotten me? Dumped, that's where. I deserve a little wine." Cressida tossed back a large quantity, swallowed and proclaimed, "From here on out, I'm going to live exactly as I please."

Chapter Four

Roxie sighed. "That would sound a whole lot better if you weren't slurring your words." Roxie gazed into Cressida's eyes. "Honey, Cal wasn't right for you. It's that simple."

Cressida scoffed. "Oh, and you're the expert on relationships." She drank a long swig of wine. "Daddy left the day after I turned five and you didn't do a thing to stop him. Not one damned thing! You just let him gradually disappear from our lives."

Roxie lifted her chin as Cressida continued. "And your last guy"—Cressida's mirthless laugh sounded as hollow and as raw as she felt— "well, he put the *boy* in boy toy. He couldn't have been a day over thirty."

Roxie's narrowed eyes didn't waver as she studied Cressida for a long moment.

Costa and Ben glanced at each other and then down at the floor, looking as if they'd like to disappear.

"Actually, Corey turned twenty-nine last week, not that I owe you any explanations," said Roxie.

"Corey." Cressida snorted and swallowed more wine.

Roxie stepped closer and pried the wine glass stem from Cressida's clenched fingers. She set it on the counter.

"Now enough with the tantrum." Roxie lifted a perfectly arched brow. "What's next? Are you going to hold your breath and start stamping your feet?" She put her hands on Cressida's shoulders. "I need you to pull yourself together."

"I don't care what you need." Cressida jerked out of her

mother's grasp. "Why should I listen to you?"

"Hey…" Costa stepped forward, obviously trying to come to Roxie's defense. "Easy now."

"No…seriously." Cressida turned to Costa. "What does she know about having a successful marriage?"

She turned back to Roxie. "You and your endless string of boyfriends and the way you carry on and the ridiculous way you dress."

Her eyes swept over Roxie's too-tight-for-polite-company black skinny jeans, open-toed stiletto booties and zebra print top displaying what Cressida considered to be an indecent amount of cleavage for a fifty-three-year-old.

"I mean…do you own anything that's *not* animal print? Honestly. It's embarrassing."

Costa stepped forward. As Roxie's stylist, he clearly felt the need to defend his fashion choices.

"Excuse me, but everyone knows animal print is a classic and…" His voice trailed off as Roxie shook her head. But he couldn't let it go. Costa turned to Ben and said, "Well it *is*." He cupped a hand around his mouth and leaned closer to Ben as he whispered loudly enough for everyone to hear. "And from what I've seen of her frumpola wardrobe, she could use a little animal print in her life."

Ben stared at Costa for several moments as if he didn't quite know what to make of him and then directed his attention back to the women.

Even through her drunken haze, Cressida registered the hurt that flashed across her mother's face but ignored it, refusing to see things from Roxie's point of view.

Roxie hid her emotions quickly, fixing her features into an unreadable mask as she said, "I'm sorry you feel that way. Perhaps one day you'll realize the only person you need to please is yourself." She turned to Costa. "We need to go or we'll be late."

"No, wait." Cressida folded her arms in front of her chest, not ready to give up the fight. "What are you trying to say?"

Roxie sighed and turned to face her. "Haven't you done enough to please Cal? To fit his image of the woman he *thought* you should be?" Roxie spread her arms wide. "Look at you! You've turned yourself inside out for ten long years and where has it gotten you?"

She let the words hang in the air for several moments before she continued. "And while you seem so disapproving of my life choices, it might do you good to spend a little time trying to figure out what you actually want from life instead of constantly obsessing over what that pompous ass of a husband might want you to do."

Cressida lifted a brow. "Did you ever stop to consider that this might be exactly the life I want to live?"

"Heavens, no! What a travesty *that* would be." Roxie's eyes seemed to bore into her soul for several moments. Then she shrugged. "I don't think you've allowed yourself to consider what you want from life in a very *very* long time."

Filled with indignation, Cressida jammed balled fists onto her hips.

"You think my life choices are wrong because I didn't want to grow up to be like you," Cressida said. "You never could accept that I didn't want to be a singer; that I wanted to do something else with my life."

"No baby," Roxie said softly. "My only problem is that you tried to *be* someone else. Just to please your husband. Big difference. You have so much to give. Just as you are."

She cupped her daughter's cheeks and kissed her gently on the forehead. "I just hope you realize that one day." She glanced at Costa and pointed toward the front door. "We need to go or we'll be late."

Cressida slumped against the counter as they left, riding the emotional roller coaster between euphoria and despair. She'd been dying to say some of those things to her mother for years and she'd meant every single word, hence the euphoria. So how come she felt like such a low down jerk and why was Roxie's hurt expression etched onto her brain?

Ben headed for the back door as Cressida yanked a string of paper towels off the roll. Then she knelt down and began wiping up the spilled wine sawdust goop.

Cressida paused and looked up as Ben grasped the doorknob. Unable to stop herself, she said, "I guess you think I'm a big jerk."

She didn't know why she cared. Hot or not, she'd placed the architect in the friendly-with-my-soon-to-be-ex file which technically classified him as the enemy, so she shouldn't care what he thought. But she did. She cared much more than she'd ever admit.

"No," he said. "But for what it's worth, Roxie's right. You shouldn't give two hoots what other people think."

She squared her shoulders in protest. "I don't."

"That's good. Because most people don't know their ass from a hole in the head."

Despite her foul mood and his enemy status, a slow smile spread across her face.

He grinned, revealing the tiniest little dimple in his right cheek and her eyes fixated on it.

"If you do what makes you happy, you can be pretty sure you're headed down the right path. At least that's what Uncle Rex always says."

Happy. She bit her lip and chewed on that little tidbit. In truth, she didn't have a clue as to what would make her happy. Roxie had nailed that one, though Cressida would never give her mother the satisfaction of admitting it. But she wouldn't even try to deny the truth to herself.

She'd traveled a long lonely road the past ten years which had led to a destination about as far from happy as one could get. Somehow, in attending to her husband's never-ending needs, her own desires had gotten lost in a barren wasteland of neglect, denial and eventually self-loathing. Aside from her determination to have a child, she hadn't bothered to think about what would make her happy in longer than she cared to remember.

"I'll see you tomorrow," he said and closed the door behind him.

Cressida stood and wadded the wine-soaked paper towel into a ball eyes locked on Ben as he joined a group of men in orange vests and hard hats.

Everything about him drew her in. She couldn't seem to get him out of her head. The night before she'd even awakened in the middle of night thinking about his sexy grin and hadn't gotten another wink of sleep after that.

This was not a good thing. In the past few days, her life and any semblance of security or normalcy had dissolved like a puff of smoke. She didn't need any distractions right now.

Cressida turned away from the window and tossed the dirty paper towel into the trash.

She'd just have to avoid Ben Carrington from here on out. That shouldn't be too hard. After all, Cal had hired him so Cal could deal with him. Plus, the renovation would be complete in six weeks and after that; she'd never see him again. So until then, she'd just steer clear of the sexy architect and focus on getting her life back on track.

Now, if she could just figure out how to do that...

༻·❀·༺

Cressida yawned widely as she plodded into the kitchen. She'd lain awake until the wee hours staring at the divorce papers spread out on Cal's pillow, her thoughts shifting wildly between devising an elaborate scheme to win him back and plotting his murder. She'd finally fallen into a restless sleep just before dawn.

But she was awake now and the rich aroma of Columbian coffee enveloped her and drew her in with its promise of the morning caffeine jolt she needed so badly.

She sniffed appreciatively as she opened the cupboard, pulled out a mug and filled it to the brim with steaming brew. She didn't even bother to add her usual cream and stevia. Straight black and piping hot. The morning after a three martini overdose demanded no less.

Cressida trudged into the living room as she blew on the hot beverage. She took a sip, pulled the curtains aside and frowned.

Where was her car?

She craned her neck and looked up and down the street but it was nowhere in sight. And it wasn't in the driveway which meant it was probably still in the parking lot of Rocco's Tacos.

Great. Just what she needed when she was in a hurry. Now she'd have to hit up Roxie for a ride.

She strolled to the base of the stairs and cupped a hand to her mouth as she shouted, "Mom? Costa?" She peered intently up the staircase and waited a full minute before she tried again. "Roxie?"

No answer.

She headed back to the kitchen.

Maybe Roxie and Costa were in the backyard. Given the swarm of scantily-clad construction workers, it seemed a good bet. She should've thought of that first.

As she approached, the back door opened and Ben stepped inside.

Cressida's cheeks flamed as embarrassing scenes of her drunken fit the night before drifted back. Between their first meeting on the back deck and her behavior last night, she hadn't exactly made a good first impression. Not that she cared, but still…

She cleared her throat and attempted to sound dignified as she said, "Have you seen Roxie?"

"They left an hour ago." Ben appeared distracted as he strode past. He laid the papers on the makeshift plywood countertop, spread them out and studied them intently. "Something about morning rehearsal."

He removed a pencil from behind his ear and made a notation in the margin.

Her gaze drifted over his broad chest and muscled arms, displayed to full advantage in a tight white t-shirt, half tucked in to his well-worn and very nicely fitting jeans. His skin glistened with a thin veil of sweat and his t-shirt clung to his flat abdomen.

She swallowed and tried to stop her mind from conjuring up images of chiseled, rock hard abs and muscled pecs. Cal never looked that good sweaty and he wasn't that…firm. Her husband's style veered more toward metro sexual and while he spent endless hours obsessing about his appearance, he hadn't stepped foot in a gym in years.

Sweaty suddenly seemed so much more appealing.

Ben glanced up from his papers and wiped a hand across his brow. "Damn, it's hot out there."

Her cheeks burned and she quickly averted her eyes, embarrassed to have been caught checking him out.

"Uh-huh," she mumbled, suddenly wishing Cal had hired a pudgy senior citizen architect for the surprise renovation. She turned away and began fiddling with the mail as she sipped her coffee.

"Cressie Ann, I—"

She heaved a great sigh and her voice sounded harsher than intended as glanced over her shoulder and said, "Please don't call me that."

His brow creased as he scratched his chin. "What should I call you?"

"Cressida," she said, thinking how nice he looked with the beginnings of a five o'clock shadow.

She fantasized briefly about running her hand along the rough stubble of his angular jaw.

"Cressida, like the car?" His face broke into a grin which lit his eyes from within, making him look rather mischievous.

She cleared her throat and nodded as she went back to the bill flipping—anything to distract herself.

"What can I say?" She shrugged, feigning nonchalance. "My mother had an odd attachment to her old Toyota. She only calls me Cressie Ann to irritate me."

"Oh." He shifted his weight from one foot to the other, sounding decidedly uneasy as he said, "Listen, I hate to ask, but your husband…err…Dr. Wentworth called this morning and asked me to direct all questions about this renovation to you."

"To me?" She arched a brow, dropped the mail and turned, gaping in disbelief. "You've got to be kidding." Her face twisted into a scowl.

"That's what he said." He shrugged and shoved his hands into the pockets of his jeans. "I wanted to see if you could head up to Boca with me tomorrow. You need to make some design choices. Things like cabinets, tile and carpet can take up to six weeks to arrive and I don't have anywhere near that long."

Her jaw set. "Forget it. No way." She shook her head fiercely from side to side. "Have a designer do it."

Cressida didn't give a flying fig about carpet or tile colors and hadn't since Cal had imperiously informed her she wouldn't be living here in a few months. So she had zero intention of spending one second of her life selecting the perfect décor for this house she had once loved but which in the past week had become a monument to her failed marriage. Doing so would be the equivalent of rubbing her own nose in the dirt of her failed marriage. Cal wanted out. He'd made that crystal clear with the divorce papers. He'd decided the house would be sold. Fine. She wanted nothing to do with the renovation. After all, the overhaul was part of his grand plan, not hers. So she considered the décor Cal's problem and she'd gladly tell him as much if need be.

"Sorry," he said, ruffling his hands through his thick dark hair. "The contract is clear that this reno must be done to your specifications. If it's not, I don't get my—"

"Let me guess." Cressida held up a hand and lifted a brow.

"Your on-time bonus?"

He nodded with a sheepish grin.

Cressida sighed inwardly. She'd heard enough about the godforsaken bonus.

"Let Cal and his girlfriend do it." She glanced at the clock on the stove. She needed to get a move on or she'd be late. "I don't have time to discuss this right now. I have to call a cab."

She reached for the phone.

"I'll give you a lift. Where are you going?"

She stopped dialing and turned. "Seriously? I left my car down on Las Olas yesterday. The valet crew promised to deliver it last night but for some reason, they didn't. I have to be down in Miami in about an hour." She arched a brow. "You sure you don't mind?"

"If you'll meet me up in Boca tomorrow to pick out the décor, I'll take you to your car." He grinned, looking quite pleased with himself. "Deal?"

Her mouth twisted as she considered his proposal. She checked the clock again. This was her only chance of getting to Miami on time. A cab would most certainly take too long.

She sighed. "Deal."

She dumped her coffee in the sink and then dashed for the stairs. "Be back in a flash," she called over her shoulder.

While she dreaded the prospect of Boca with Ben the next day, she was grateful for the ride. The best attorney in Miami had squeezed her in this morning and he might very well be her only hope of leaving with the assets she deserved after a decade of marriage. There was no way she was going to show up late.

Chapter Five

Ben's gaze drifted lower, drawn to the subtle sway of her hips where it lingered far longer than could be considered appropriate. But while he knew he should, Ben just couldn't look away.

A bolt of desire electrified every cell in his body, sending parts of him that had laid dormant for years into high alert.

The black sleeveless dress hugged her curves in all the right places and her legs seemed to go on for miles. Her flame red hair cascaded over creamy shoulders in a smooth shiny curtain.

He swallowed and tamped down the urge to move closer. He'd been obsessed from the moment he'd first laid eyes on her. Obsessed in a way he'd never experienced before. He couldn't stop himself from imagining what it would feel like to bury his hands in those thick silken strands. He could almost feel the tantalizing brush of her locks caressing his chest as she leaned forward to—.

Ben caught his reflection in the microwave and tore his gaze away.

For God's sake. He was gaping at her like a lust-filled thirteen-year-old. He cleared his throat and gathered up his papers, trying to seem interested in anything but her. But in truth, Cressida Wentworth was hot. Smoking hot. And he needed to get over it. *Now*. She was someone else's wife regardless of her marital situation. And even if she weren't, she was a client and clients were off limits—especially for just north of broke, self-employed architects trying desperately to get their businesses off the ground.

He didn't need distractions and couldn't risk letting his hormones lead him around like some horny teenager. He had work to do. Work that had nothing to do with a hot, curvy redhead who'd enjoyed the starring role in the most outrageously sexy dream last night.

He rolled the papers more vigorously than was necessary and shoved them under his arm. "Ready?"

She squared her shoulders, appearing to steel herself for some great challenge ahead. "Ready as I'll ever be, I guess."

He didn't bother to ask what she meant. Better to not get too involved. Especially since his nonstop fantasies of her seemed headed toward ever more X-rated territory.

Get a grip, Carrington. Don't blow this job. You need that damned bonus.

Clearly, he needed to find some female companionship. Or more accurately, he needed to find a woman who could punch all the right buttons. Someone like Cressida. But not Cressida. Someone else. Someone available. And someone not related to his livelihood.

She followed him out the door, pausing to lock it before she trailed him down the sidewalk.

He tried not to think about the sexy little swish of her hips and instead forced his thoughts back to the job. As of this moment, they were on schedule. But a six week timeline bordered on the undoable. If he wanted to finish on time, he'd have to micromanage every minute little detail of this job and…

When the steady tip tap of her heels went silent, Ben glanced over his shoulder.

Cressida stood gazing up at his truck, her eyes big and round, like two huge green pools of disapproval.

"Is everything okay?" he asked.

"Please tell me we're not riding in *that.*" Her brows knit together as she pointed at his new pride and joy—his Chevy Silverado—and looked as if she'd just spent half an hour sucking on a lime without the benefit of the tequila shot.

He stiffened. "What?" His couldn't keep the defensiveness out of his tone as he looked from her to the truck.

What was her problem? By anyone's standards his truck looked positively pristine. His kids were under a strict 'no French fries in the car' rule and he still washed the exterior twice a week.

He shifted his gaze back to her and felt compelled to explain. "It's clean," he said. "I just took it through the car wash."

"It's not that," she said, waving a hand dismissively. "How am I supposed to climb into that thing? The first step is almost three feet in the air!" She gestured to her linen dress. "As you can see, I didn't dress to scale the truck equivalent of Mount Everest."

Despite himself, he smiled and motioned her forward. "It's not that bad. You'll see."

Maybe he shouldn't have gotten the lift package. But it had been impossible to resist. After all, you could take the guy out of Texas but wild horses couldn't drag the Texas out of the guy.

Besides, he hadn't had any complaints thus far. Of course, his last date had been a boat ride in the Everglades and they'd both worn tennis shoes and shorts. While his date hadn't complained about the truck, everything else about that afternoon had been an unmitigated disaster. Just an hour into it, with her constant complaining about mosquitos and the heat, he'd contemplated jumping overboard and letting the alligators feast on him for dinner. He hadn't. Instead, he'd made a bad excuse about a forgotten business appointment and cut the day short.

A date with Cressida would never end that way. His suddenly Technicolor imagination conjured up an image of her lying in his bed, hair fanned out on the pillow and gazing up at him with a lazy smile.

He shook his head and forced his thoughts to neutral territory. He really did need to find some female companionship. And quick. Maybe he should take his uncle's advice and join one of those online dating sites.

He opened the passenger side door and tried to sound encouraging as he said, "It'll be fine."

Cressida looked irritated as she shuffled towards him, her quick short steps reminding him of a geisha.

His gaze drifted downward. Now that was a tight skirt. Not that he was complaining. But she definitely wouldn't be able to climb into the passenger seat wearing that getup, though it could be fun to watch her try.

He bit back a grin as she came up beside him. "Here, I'll give you a hand."

She looked about to protest but he didn't give her a chance. He grasped her firmly around the waist, suddenly enveloped by her intoxicating scent of wild flowers and vanilla.

He inhaled deeply. Man she smelled good. It was all he could do not to pull her closer but he resisted the urge and instead, hoisted her up.

Her legs dangled awkwardly. One of her shoes fell off and clattered onto the concrete driveway.

She reached out with her toes, straining to get a foothold on the running board and once she did, she propelled herself forward and then grasped the back of the seat for dear life.

"You got it?" He kept his arms up just in case she tipped back.

"I'm good." She started to slide into the passenger seat but stopped, glancing down as she tugged at the leg that still donned a shoe.

"What's wrong?"

"My heel is wedged. I don't want to ruin these pumps, they're my"—she rocked back and forth and then yanked her foot hard—"Oh!"

She lost her balance, clawing desperately at the seat. Her arms waved frantically and she let loose a prolonged blood-curdling scream as she fell backwards.

Ben rushed forward, arms up. Before he had time to react, she plopped down on his outstretched hands.

He grunted from the sudden and unexpected weight as he locked his arms and tried to figure out what to do.

Her scream died off as her bottom—her nicely curved bottom—molded around his fingers. But she wasn't steady and she teetered dangerously from side to side, crying out in alarm.

So Ben exercised the only option available to him. He shoved her up and forward as hard as he could.

Cressida sprawled headfirst into the front seat, legs spread and offering a nice view of her shapely thighs. And her cheetah print thong.

Ben bit back a grin as he bent down to retrieve her nude-colored pump and then placed it on the floor in front of her as she struggled to sit upright.

He shut her door and then strode around the back of the truck, unable to contain the shout of laughter that escaped. But when he got to the driver's side, he paused and focused on wiping the silly grin from his face before he opened the door. He sensed she wouldn't share his perspective on the situation.

As he climbed behind the wheel, he stole a quick sideways glance at Cressida who gazed out the side window, trying to appear unfazed. But he didn't miss the subtle tinge of pink in her cheeks.

Ben cranked the ignition and couldn't resist teasing her. "Costa would be happy to learn that you *do* own some animal print."

She lifted her chin ever so slightly and cleared her throat, staring straight through the windshield. But her complexion turned a charming shade of crimson which highlighted the delicate sprinkling of freckles across her cheeks.

It was all he could do to resist the urge to lean over and kiss the pert little tip of her nose.

"Where are we headed again?" he asked, his brow creased.

For the life of him, he couldn't recall a single thing they'd discussed in the past hour. Cressida Wentworth—with her shapely thighs, cute little freckles and cheetah print thong—had proven far too distracting for his own good.

"Rocco's Taco's on Las Olas," she sniffed, a haughty edge to her tone.

Ben shook his head. "Right. Sorry. Too many things on my mind."

He backed down the driveway and headed for the restaurant, trying to resist the urge to whistle. For some inexplicable reason and for the first time in longer than he cared to admit, he felt happy.

As they cruised along the residential streets that led to Las Olas Boulevard, he snuck another sideways glance and amended his earlier conclusion. Hot didn't really describe her. She could best be described as exotic meets apple pie. With that mass of red hair and Cupid's bow lips mixed with the slanted green eyes and cute little freckles, she was the kind of woman mothers loved and men lusted after. Classy with an effortless sex appeal and a fire simmering just below the surface that hinted at a passion that couldn't be contained. He'd bet there was a lot more to Cressida Wentworth than met the eye and he definitely couldn't fathom a world in which a man walked out on a woman like her.

His thoughts drifted to her temper tantrum from the night before. Of course, she did seem like a handful and appeared to have the temper to match the hair. Maybe that's why her husband had run off. Or maybe her crazy family had scared him away. Now *that* he could understand. They all appeared to be looney tunes— especially that Costa character.

Ben switched on the radio to try to force his thoughts onto something besides the woman seated beside him and as he did, he caught her studying him. He tapped a thumb on the steering wheel and pretended not to notice.

She cleared her throat. "Can I ask you something?"

"Sure." He turned down the radio.

She shifted her body around so she faced him. "That day in the backyard. When we first met. You didn't think I was Cal's wife." She tilted her head and gazed at him more intently. "Why?"

Ben shot a quick sideways glance and then forced his attention back to the road. He didn't want to get involved but she'd thrown him right into the middle of their sticky divorce situation with *that* question.

His jaw tightened.

The light turned red and he brought the truck to a gentle stop.

The silence lengthened until it became downright uncomfortable. He wracked his brain, searching for the right words but drew a blank. He barely knew her but you'd have to be blind to have missed her shock at the sudden downward turn of her marriage. She'd had a tough couple of days and he definitely didn't want to be the one to break it to her that her husband had a girlfriend. Plus, he couldn't afford to piss her off. He needed that on time bonus so badly, he almost couldn't see straight.

Ben tapped his thumb harder. "Uh…."

The click clack of the blinker sounded abnormally loud.

She pressed him further, her soft tone laced with steel. "He brought her with him when you met regarding the house renovations, didn't he?"

He cast a sideways look. The set of her jaw, the determined glint in her eye told him what to do. She deserved the truth. If actions accounted for anything, and in his mind they did, her husband appeared to be a cheating low life. Ben had initially thought him okay if not a little too slick, with his GQ style of dress and fussy comb over. But now that he knew the truth, he liked Cal a lot less.

"I guess so," he muttered. "Tall, curvy, Sofia Vergara type?" He shot her a quizzical look and when she nodded, he continued. "He called her Gracie."

Cressida squeezed her eyes shut and a single wayward tear trickled a path down her cheek.

He fought the temptation to brush the moisture away.

"When?" she whispered, her voice low and raw.

"Two months ago."

She nodded and dragged in a long, ragged breath.

"I'm sorry," he said, aching for her. He knew how it felt to get blind-sided by a cheating spouse.

She gazed out the windshield.

"I knew," she said softly. "I saw the divorce coming but I didn't want to face it." She shot a quick sideways glance at Ben. "I mean, I didn't know about the Gracie thing. She's my cousin by the way."

He winced.

"We weren't close or anything. She's my father's sister's kid. The father who walked out on us when I was five so there wasn't exactly a lot of family time. Plus, she's twelve years younger than me. I was just trying to help her out while she was in between work." She smiled through watery tears. "I guess I should've known better than to let her stay with us."

"You couldn't have known," he said. He knew all about the guilt number, too. He'd spent a few years on that one himself.

"I knew something wasn't right between us." She studied her fingernails and then clasped her hands tightly. "You see, we've been trying to get pregnant for five years and for the last three, we've tried in vitro." She gazed down at her hands. "I thought our problems were related to all the baby stress. I assumed everything would be okay if I could just get pregnant. I never thought he'd cheat." Her lips trembled as she blinked back the tears fighting for release. "I guess I saw what I wanted to see."

Anger welled inside as painful memories rushed back and Ben was consumed by the overwhelming urge to belt the idiot who'd broken her heart. He gripped the steering wheel so hard his fingers hurt.

The light turned green and a few moments later, he pulled into the parking lot of Rocco's Tacos. It was empty, still too early for the lunch crowd.

Their eyes met and held for several beats longer than was probably wise.

Despite his better judgment, Ben lifted a hand and he'd barely touched her cheek when she shifted away from him, blushing scarlet.

"I'm sorry," she said. "I shouldn't have told you all of that."

He cleared his throat and dropped his hand to the gear shift. "That's okay. I'm sorry you're going through this."

She opened the door.

He moved to open his own door. "Need help getting down?"

"No. I can manage." She placed a foot on the running board, turned to face him and then wriggled down to the pavement in as dignified a manner as the form-fitting dress would allow. Then she gazed up at him with a slight smile. "Thanks for the ride."

She reached up to shut the door.

"Hey Cressida," he said quickly, leaning over the center console.

Those big green eyes locked with his, telling him far more than she would ever say about the depth of her pain. He wished he could do or say something to make the hurt and anguish go away.

"Yeah?"

"It gets better. Easier." He gazed at her intently, hoping she believed him. "I promise."

Cressida nodded and softly shut the door.

Ben sat there, staring into the rearview mirror as she made her way to the valet stand. With effort, he dragged his eyes away from her and yanked the gearshift into drive.

His jaw clenched and he resisted the urge to look into the rearview mirror again, though every fiber of his being cried out to do so. Everything about her invited him in; beckoned to him in the same dangerous way that a flame entices a moth. But getting involved with a client's soon to be ex-wife in the middle of a complicated renovation while they were in the midst of what seemed likely to be an incredibly messy divorce, spelled trouble. Like the moth that ventures too close to the blaze, allowing himself to feel anything for Cressida Wentworth seemed like a real good way to get burned.

Chapter Six

"Followed!" Cressida didn't even attempt to hide her outrage as she eyed the attorney with disbelief. "Why would he have *me* followed? *He's* the one who cheated!"

An insincere smile touched Gray Portell's lips and he twisted a platinum cufflink as he leaned back in his overstuffed burgundy leather chair. "That, my dear, is precisely why."

Cressida narrowed her eyes.

She'd taken an instant dislike to the slick operator and didn't appreciate the endearment but she bit back the retort that sprang to her lips. Instead, she studied his every move, trying to figure out if, despite her feelings, she could trust the attorney to protect her interests. Everything about Gray Portell screamed ruthless—from the meticulously maintained highlights, fake tan and custom tailored suit to the ultra-swanky downtown Miami office—an image likely cultivated to instill confidence. But his slick-willy veneer left her feeling uneasy.

"Sorry," she said, not bothering to hide the frostiness in her tone. Hopefully he'd get the message and stop with the condescending endearments. "I'm not sure I understand."

Gray swaggered around his desk, leaning against the edge as he gazed down at her.

"Your husband did the cheating. He's the bread winner. *He's* got the most to lose because you could take everything he has." He smiled, but the glint in his eyes hinted at a ruthlessness that increased her discomfort. "And we'll certainly try." His smile broadened.

His pointy teeth reminded her of a shark.

"He's almost certainly having you followed and has probably done so for quite some time." Gray gestured to the sofas near the window. "Please. We'll be more comfortable over there."

Cressida let his words percolate as she moved to the sumptuous cream suede couch. Gray did this for a living so he clearly knew what to expect, but no matter how hard she tried she couldn't make sense of his viewpoint.

"Why would he do that?" She sat and crossed her legs.

His predatory gaze drifted downward and lingered.

She tugged at the hem of her dress and primly clasped her hands in her lap.

"So he can catch you doing something wrong." He joined her on the sofa, sitting far closer than he should have. "He's probably already planted someone in your life. Someone who can feed him information they can use."

Cressida frowned at his invasion of her space and inched away. "Something they can use?"

She felt like an idiot for parroting his words but she wasn't following. How could her husband's attorneys discover her doing something wrong if she wasn't doing anything wrong?

"The most frequent approach used in cases like this—especially cases handled by the CADs—is to catch you with someone and then claim you cheated first. They'll turn it into a he said she said. Or try to, anyway."

She reared her head back. "But that's ridiculous! Just a few months ago, I underwent my third in vitro procedure. Who in their right mind would believe *I'm* the one who cheated?"

"It happens. You'd be surprised."

He leaned close, completely encroaching her space as he stretched an arm along the back of the sofa, brushing against Cressida's shoulders.

She stiffened and it took every ounce of self-restraint not to reach around and remove it. Instead she leaned away, hoping the back-off body language would be received.

"One recent client was having an affair with her fertility specialist. And another—a lesbian trying to hide the fact from her husband—was sleeping with their fertility specialist's nurse."

She shook her head. This sounded like the stuff prime time soap operas were made of.

Gray shrugged and his lust-filled gaze slid over her. "You know, you're a very attractive woman, Cressida." His hand brushed against her thigh. "They'll try to bill your husband as an extremely busy doctor. Long days. Night shifts. A beautiful young wife who got lonely and…strayed."

She moved closer to the edge of the sofa. She'd never even considered the possibility that Cal might try to paint her as the villain and the thought caused her blood to boil. On top of the humiliation of his cheating, attempting to portray her as the wrong doer would just be too much.

Gray slid closer. Too close.

She shifted further away, suddenly wishing she'd stayed in the chair.

"The divorce could drag out for months." He trailed a finger down her arm. It drifted dangerously close to her breast.

Her eyes locked on his fingertips and it took everything she had to stop herself from slapping him. She needed a good attorney and supposedly he was the best in South Florida but if he tried that move again, the smooth operator might lose an appendage.

"It's natural that at some point, you'll want…"—the look in his eyes turned positively pornographic—"companionship."

She had to fight to keep from rolling her eyes. Now she knew how he'd earned the nickname Scoretell and unfortunately, it seemed to have little to do with his courtroom prowess and everything to do with his sofa. She intended to give Shay an earful as soon as she left his office.

His smile morphed into a lecherous grin. "You'll change your mind. I can assure you of that. The months will drag on and you'll want some fun. If you expect me to represent you, you'll have to be careful. I don't like surprises and I don't like to lose. You'll need to find someone to play with who knows how to be…discreet."

He abandoned any subtlety and pressed his thigh against hers, his spicy cologne overpowering.

Cressida glanced over her shoulder. She'd run out of couch. Another inch and she'd be on the floor.

She stood and straightened her skirt.

"I appreciate the advice but I'm not looking for a playmate." She frowned as an image of Ben formed in her mind. Where had that come from? She deleted the mental picture and got back to business. "Do we need to discuss anything else?"

Gray inclined his head and appeared to accept that his overtures would not be reciprocated that day.

He probably encountered few divorcees who resisted his charms. She supposed he could be considered good-looking if you could get past the über-slick appearance and lounge lizard approach to the law. She wondered if he gave retainer discounts in exchange for a little couch action. Not that she was tempted.

Gray strode to the door, suddenly all business.

"My receptionist has all the necessary documents. Fill them out as soon as possible. We need to freeze the finances before your husband has time to move them." He smiled. "Let's meet again early next week. Perhaps dinner?"

She slipped her handbag over a shoulder. "We'll see."

Dinner with the slick operator would be about the last thing she needed right now. She'd struggled to sidestep his moves in the cold light of day. It wasn't hard to imagine what might happen at a secluded table in a dark restaurant.

He assumed a more serious expression. "Remember, be wary of anyone who's just appeared in your life and seems more interested than they should be. Most likely that person was planted there by your husband's attorneys."

She nodded, though the idea seemed very far-fetched. She struggled to envision Cal in the role of lady-killer let alone believing him so calculated that he'd attempt to manufacture outright lies about her. Then again, her entire life had been turned inside out in the past few days, so who knew? At this point, anything seemed possible.

"You can leave your retainer deposit with my receptionist."

Gray ushered her out the door and immediately shifted his attention to a glamorous and designer-clad woman seated on a white leather wing chair. "Francesca, please come in."

The tall, voluptuous brunette grasped her red Hermes bag and breezed by in a cloud of expensive French perfume—all overly plumped lips, amply displayed bosom and artfully tousled hair. She headed straight for the sofa.

Gray smiled as he shut the office door.

Cressida's lips twisted. He'd undoubtedly find the fabulous Francesca a much easier mark.

She gave herself points for recognizing him for the shark he was and not falling prey to his charms. Maybe she was finally getting wise when it came to men with less than honorable intentions. She certainly hoped so. She'd spent enough years being deceived.

Cressida paused in the kitchen doorway, frowning at Roxie and Ben. Her brows shot clear to her forehead as Ben leaned close and murmured something in Roxie's ear. She narrowed her eyes. Since when had those two become so chummy?

Roxie threw her head back and roared with laughter as she smacked Ben playfully on the arm. "You devil!"

Ben chuckled and teasingly rubbed his arm as if in pain.

Cressida cleared her throat and strolled into the kitchen, pretending to scroll through her text messages while trying to tamp down the disturbing stab of red hot jealousy that came out of nowhere.

Was Roxie trying to put the moves on the sexy architect?

Cressida's frown deepened. The possibility shouldn't have surprised her since Roxie rarely let an attractive man enter her orbit without engaging in a little flirtatious fun but the thought bothered her far more than it should have.

"Hiya honey." Roxie dragged her gaze from Ben and spun around on the barstool, eyes dancing. "Whatcha been up to?"

"Meeting with my lecherous divorce attorney down in Miami," Cressida grumbled as she tossed her purse and keys onto the plywood counter. She opened a cabinet, pulled out a mug and poured herself a cup of coffee. "Quite the experience let me tell you."

"I'm proud of you for being proactive, honey."

Proud. Right.

Cressida's lips twisted as she blew on the steaming beverage. She knew better. Her mother had likely spent the better part of the day doing the happy dance at the thought of her impending divorce as she'd no longer have to consider Cal family and therefore, would no longer have to pretend to be nice. Not that she'd done a very good job of it.

Ben pushed his stool back from the island and stood, gazing down at Roxie with what looked like regret. "I need to get back to work."

Try as she might, Cressida couldn't take her eyes off him as he ambled to the door.

As if sensing her scrutiny, Ben paused and glanced over his shoulder. "We still on for the design studio tomorrow?"

"Sure." She tried to sound chipper but in truth, she dreaded the trip. Spending time with Ben was about the farthest thing from a good idea right now as her infatuation only seemed to be getting worse. But a deal was a deal.

"Ten o'clock?"

"That works. Just leave the address on the counter and I'll meet you there."

Ben nodded and closed the door behind him.

Roxie expelled a wistful sigh and rested her chin on a balled fist. "He's soooo dreamy."

"I guess." Cressida tried to sound disinterested but the truth was, dreamy didn't even begin to describe him. Still, she had zero intention of letting her mother know she thought so.

She blew on her coffee and couldn't resist a lighthearted dig. "He seems a little old for you, don't ya think? I mean…he's gotta be pushing forty. I thought your age limit these days was thirty."

"Good one." Roxie giggled and waved a dismissive hand. "Don't be silly. I'm not interested in Ben."

She wasn't surprised that her mother didn't bother to correct the age comment. Roxie preferred her men young, embarrassingly so from Cressida's perspective. She pulled out a barstool and sipped at her brew. "What were you two talking about?"

Her mother grinned impishly. "You."

Radar activated, Cressida narrowed her eyes. "What about me?"

Her mother loved nothing better than to meddle and stir up drama in her life and Cressida wasn't having it. Not this visit. She had enough real life drama to contend with right now and didn't need any help from her mother.

"He's got the hots for you. I can tell." Roxie's eyes danced with mischief as she picked up her iPad and started surfing the internet.

Cressida's brows knit together as the attorney's warning drifted back. *Be cautious of anyone who's suddenly appeared in your life and seems more interested than they should be.* Ben definitely fit that criteria as he seemed to spend more time inside with them than he did outside supervising his crew.

She let that realization percolate for several minutes and then shook her head, dismissing the notion as ridiculous. The idea that

Ben had been deliberately planted in her life sounded like something straight out of a low budget detective movie.

"That's crazy. The only thing he's hot for is that on-time bonus." Cressida sipped her coffee as Roxie squinted at her tablet screen. "Why don't you wear reading glasses? You'll give yourself a headache straining your eyes like that."

Roxie scoffed. "Readers are for fogeys. Besides, if some enterprising paparazzi were to catch me wearing readers it would destroy my image." Roxie fluffed her hair and winked. "To my fans, I'm forever young."

Cressida rolled her eyes. "If Nana was here, she'd say you were ruining your forever young eyes."

"If Nana was here, she'd say a lot of things," Roxie said, not bothering to look up. "I'd say we're both lucky she decided to stay in Vegas this trip."

Cressida let that comment slide by without a response as she gazed at her mother. She really needed to apologize for her drunken fit the night before but wasn't sure where to start. She took another sip of coffee and decided on the direct approach.

"Uh…" She cleared her throat. "Listen, mom…I'm really sorry about last night." She drew in a long breath and with a sheepish smile said, "I acted like a jerk."

Roxie looked up from her tablet computer. "It's okay." The soft smile and chipper tone were undermined by the sudden rush of tears. "I know how it feels when your husband rips out your heart and tosses it aside like yesterday's trash." Her mother pulled out a tissue and dabbed at her eyes. "I'm so sorry you're going through this."

Her mother's sweet compassion caused an unexpected swell of emotion. Cressida blinked back the moisture that flooded her own eyes. She'd half expected a jab about Cal. Something to the effect of 'good riddance.' She hadn't anticipated understanding and empathy.

Her mother's outrageous persona and the way she flitted from one young lover to another made it easy to forget that at her core, Roxie was a complicated woman who'd endured more than her fair share of heartache. Those experiences had built layers of substance that, for the most part, Roxie kept hidden lest her sensitive feeling side interfere with the carefree, ever-youthful, life-of-the-party persona her fans had grown to love.

"It wasn't okay. I shouldn't have lashed out." Cressida reached over and squeezed Roxie's hand.

She couldn't bring herself to say she hadn't meant the jabs about her mother's wardrobe and lifestyle choices because she'd meant every word, but she hated that she'd hurt Roxie and had done so in front of an audience.

"I have no excuse. It's just"—her voice cracked and she drew in a long ragged breath before she continued—"well…it's been a really hard few days, you know?"

"I *do* know." Roxie's sympathetic gaze hinted at a depth of pain Cressida had only occasionally witnessed and had never before seen displayed as it related to her father. Roxie had always acted as if his leaving hadn't bothered her in the least. "I've lived it, remember?"

Roxie cleared her throat and sat a little straighter as she went back to her internet surfing.

Cressida sipped her coffee and frowned. She'd never before stopped to consider how her father's abandonment had affected Roxie. Whether she'd been hurt. Maybe even heartbroken. Cressida had simply been too busy obsessing over her own pain. A child could be forgiven that self-obsessed view, but an adult?

She bit her lip, dismayed at her own lack of sensitivity. It had taken the unexpected and jolting end of her marriage to realize what now seemed an obvious truth. It had been too easy to blame her mother—way too easy—because her father had been the one who'd walked out and never returned. Despite her faults and while her mothering instincts might be in short supply, Roxie had stayed.

Rather than risk opening painful old wounds, Cressida changed the subject. "Where's Costa?"

"He went out with a couple of my backup dancers. Apparently there's a new gay bar down in South Beach that's all the rage. Something about a foam party," Roxie said, without bothering to look up. "I would've gone but I can't afford to spend the night sliding around on foam. If I got hurt and had to cancel show dates, I'd surely get sued for breach of contract."

Cressida shook her head as she sipped her coffee. Any normal mother would turn down the foam party because sliding around on bubbles was a ridiculous way for a grown woman to spend her time, not because she wanted to avoid getting sued. Then again, no one would ever accuse Roxie of being normal.

Cressida's stomach rumbled, reminding her that she hadn't eaten since breakfast. "Wanna grab some dinner? I'm starving. There's this new restaurant on Las Olas I've been wanting to try."

"Oh honey, I can't. I have a—"

The doorbell chimed.

Cressida headed to the door, glancing over her shoulder as she said, "Who could that be?" She noted Roxie's devilish smile as she pulled a compact and lipstick from her purse. "Are you expecting someone?"

Roxie didn't respond, too intent on applying a fresh coat of lipstick.

Cressida opened the door and widened her eyes in surprise. "Micah! I thought you were away at school."

Micah Farentino lived around the corner but spent most of the year in New Haven as he was finishing his second year of law school at Yale.

His grin oozed boyish confidence mixed with a hint of anticipation. "Hi, Mrs. Wentworth. I just got back for the summer yesterday." He paused and peered over her shoulder. "Is Roxie here?"

"Uh, well…huh?" She frowned; too busy trying to figure out how Micah knew her mother to form a coherent answer.

"Well helloooo," Roxie purred as she slinked past Cressida, thrust out a hip and assumed a seductive pose.

Cressida narrowed her eyes.

Micah grinned from ear to ear. "Are you ready?"

Cressida glanced from one to the other as a sick feeling formed in the pit of her stomach.

How had her mother managed to meet and score a date with Micah Farentino in the few short hours she'd been here? Come to think of it, she didn't want to know because the truth undoubtedly involved Roxie making a spectacle of herself in front of the neighbors.

"I was born ready." Roxie winked as Micah gallantly extended an elbow.

Cressida's jaw dropped as Roxie slipped her hand through the arm of the handsome twenty-seven-year-old son of Trudy Farentino, the Ladies Guild President who'd *accidentally* forgotten to invite her to the charity event planning meeting the week before.

With a sinking heart, Cressida watched a new scandal take shape. Naturally, it involved her mother. Apparently it wasn't humiliating enough that the entire town had learned about her cheating husband hooking up with her vixen of a cousin months before she'd discovered it herself. Now she'd have to contend with her mother prancing up and down Las Olas Boulevard, seducing every red-blooded twenty something male in the vicinity. And how interesting that Micah had lived next to *her* for five years but still called her Mrs. Wentworth whereas in just one day he'd already gotten to a first name basis with Roxie. And Lord only knew how much better acquainted they'd become that evening. She didn't even want to think about it.

As the improbable couple strolled down the sidewalk—he clad in the preppiest Polo Sport had to offer and she donning the latest in Las Vegas glitz—Roxie turned and called over her shoulder, "Don't wait up, Cressie!"

The last shreds of Cressida's reputation disintegrated before her eyes. As soon as the neighbors caught on that her man-killer mother was on the prowl and had a penchant for hot young men, doors would be bolted and Cressida would undoubtedly become an even bigger social pariah than she already was.

She closed the front door and collapsed against it.

Dear God, what next? Given the events of the past few days, she could only imagine. But on the upside, maybe Roxie's age-inappropriate date was a good thing because surely it meant she'd hit rock bottom. Things couldn't possibly get any worse.

Chapter Seven

Cressida sat amidst the hammers, nails and sawdust, sipping coffee and absentmindedly playing Candy Crush on her iPad when Roxie glided in wearing the outfit she'd left in the night before.

Her brow furrowed as she eyed the artfully mussed hair and the stilettos, dangling from Roxie's fingertip. She'd assumed her mother had slept in. She hadn't even considered the possibility that Roxie might've stayed out all night.

With Micah Farentino.

Ho. Lee. Crap.

Her stomach lurched. She'd been wrong. Things *could* get worse. And they had.

Blood pressure rising, Cressida gaped in disbelief as she set the gadget on the newly-installed granite countertop with a clank. She crossed her arms and fixed Roxie with a laser hot glare intended to elicit a confession.

"And just where have *you* been?" Since her mother had clearly just sauntered down the walk of shame, Cressida had a pretty good idea but still felt compelled to ask. In her mind, Roxie had a lot of explaining to do.

Her mother looked vaguely amused. "You sound just like Nana did when I was sixteen."

Cressida arched a brow. "Considering you got pregnant with me when you were *seventeen*, I can't say I blame her for trying to keep tabs on you." Maybe Nana should've tried a little harder, though the task had probably been doomed from the outset.

Roxie sniffed. "I wasn't aware I had a curfew." She tossed her Hermes clutch onto the counter, dropped her sandals on the floor and looked decidedly pleased with herself as she added, "If you must know, I spent the night with Micah."

Cressida gulped and her voice sounded strangled as she said, "Where?"

Please don't let her say Micah's house.

Her mind conjured up a horrifying image of Roxie wandering into Trudy Farentino's kitchen and helping herself to a cup of coffee in the middle of a quiet family breakfast.

The knot in her stomach grew tighter.

That's all she needed. If Trudy learned that Roxie—a woman a good five years older than Trudy herself—had bedded her son, Cressida would have to move out of state to escape the disgrace. It went without saying that she'd be banned from the Ladies Guild for life. With her failing marriage, her membership had already entered shaky ground.

"Don't worry, dear. Micah's staying in his parent's guest house out back."

Cressida's shoulders sagged and she felt positively giddy with relief but she wasn't about to let her mother off the hook.

Roxie leaned closer and spoke in a stage whisper, eyes dancing as she said, "I snuck out before anyone woke up. I'm sure no one saw me."

Clearly, her mother considered this a game and that realization caused Cressida's blood pressure to shoot through the roof.

Her eyes shot daggers. "They better *not* have seen you."

She supposed she should be grateful her mother had even thought to try to hide her illicit activities. Discretion wasn't one of Roxie's strong suits. She put her outrageousness out there for the world to see and made no apologies.

Roxie shook her head, a disappointed expression on her face. "You're *so* uptight. I can't believe I raised such a prude."

"You didn't raise me. Nana did." Cressida sipped her coffee and tried to calm down.

She considered her prudishness a necessary counterbalance to her mother's outlandish approach to life. After all, someone had to try to retain the Reynolds' good name. She felt certain Nana would agree. She actually wished her grandmother had decided to come this visit as she was the only person who even came close to keeping Roxie on the straight and narrow.

Cressida lifted a brow, feeling like the adult in the room as she said, "Do you know who Micah is?"

While probably pointless, perhaps if her mother knew what was at stake she'd take more care to behave herself.

Roxie opened a cabinet to retrieve a mug and then glanced over her shoulder as she poured herself some coffee. "No, but I *can* tell you that he is *so*—"

"Eww." Cressida held up a hand and squeezed her eyes shut to block out the mental image of her mother and Micah doing whatever it is they had done the night before. "Please spare me."

"What?" Roxie feigned wide-eyed innocence. "I was just going to say that he's so wise."

Cressida didn't believe that for a second. Determined to set her mother straight, she drew in a long determined breath and announced, "Micah's mother is president of the Ladies Guild of Fort Lauderdale."

She also happened to be the cattiest, most mean-spirited woman Cressida had ever encountered. Probably because her husband routinely hit on every female that came within six feet. Cressida had never fully understood what a cheating spouse could do to a person's self-worth until she'd experienced the treachery herself. Now she could sort of understand how the anger and pain might eat away at your soul until you were left with nothing but a burning need to lash out at anyone and everyone you encountered.

Roxie pulled out a bar stool and shrugged. "So?"

"So *I'm* a member of the Ladies Guild of Fort Lauderdale!"

Cressida shot to her feet and jammed balled fists onto her hips. "And as it happens, I'm co-chair of this year's White Ball."

"Oh!" Roxie visibly perked up. "Has Diddy moved his annual White Party from the Hamptons to Miami?"

Cressida gritted her teeth. "No. This has nothing to do with Diddy or any of your ridiculous showbiz friends. It's our annual fundraiser and it takes place in two weeks. I've slaved away for six months to make the event a success and now, thanks to Cal and his cheating ways, I'm an outcast."

She paced the floor, unable to contain her anxiety. "They didn't even invite me to the planning luncheon last week and I'm supposed to be in charge of the silent auction!"

She paced faster. "There's another meeting this afternoon. I found out by accident when I ran into Lucinda Hearst at the grocery store yesterday." Cressida knew she'd begun to babble, but couldn't stop herself. "I've been trying to figure out if I'm brave enough to show my face there today so the very last thing I need right now"—she jabbed an accusatory finger at Roxie—"is *you* playing *Mrs. Robinson* with her *SON*!"

Her mother regarded her for several long moments and then shook her head. "I can't believe we're related."

Finally! Something they could agree on.

"My sentiments *exactly*." Cressida expelled a long yogic breath and told herself to calm down before she had a stroke. Her mother could rile her up like no one else.

Costa glided into the room looking surprisingly bright-eyed considering he'd only gotten home a few hours before. She knew the exact moment of his arrival because his drunken, stumbling entry could've awakened the dead.

He opened a cabinet, pulled out a mug and filled it with coffee. "I love South Beach," he declared. "Love. Love. Love."

Roxie beamed. "Morning sunshine."

She and Costa exchanged air kisses as he plopped down on the barstool next to hers. Then she turned back to Cressida. "If you must know, I slept with Micah but I didn't...you know...*sleep* with him."

Costa choked back a laugh as he eyed her in disbelief.

"Shush." Roxie elbowed him in the side. "We had a very nice time at dinner and went back to his place for a cocktail. We got to talking, one thing led to another and we fell asleep next to the fire. Totally harmless." She smiled. "He's very sweet and quite the gentleman."

Costa pursed his lips and blew on his coffee.

Cressida narrowed her eyes. Like Costa, Cressida wasn't buying Roxie's story but after a few moments of searching her mother's face and failing to detect a clue as to the validity of her claims, she shrugged and decided to take Roxie's explanation at face value. In this instance, denial seemed wiser than a pursuit of the truth. Contrived though it may be, Roxie's version of events sounded far more appealing than the outlandish scenarios she'd envisioned that were probably closer to what had actually happened. And the sanitized version seemed less likely to result in a public lynching at the Ladies Guild meeting this afternoon should she muster the courage to attend.

Her mother sighed. "You know dear, you can't continue to live your life obsessing over what others think of you. All that matters is what *you* think. I mean seriously...who cares?"

"*I* care," Cressida said. And she'd spent a lifetime wishing her mother cared as well but clearly, she didn't.

Roxie turned to Cressida. "Listen. I know you think I don't get it." She waved her hands next to her face. "You think I'm *reeaaally* out there, I know. But the truth is, you only go around once in this life." She held up a finger. "We get one shot. Are you really going to let the Trudy Farentino's or Cal Wentworth's of the world determine how you feel about yourself?"

"Yeah girl," Costa said. "You gotta grab life by the jewel-encrusted lapels and show it whose boss." He doubled up his fist and pumped it twice.

"That's right!" Roxie cried and fist-bumped Costa. Then the pair launched into what appeared to be a synchronized victory jig on their bar stools.

As Cressida eyed the gyrating pair, she couldn't help but wish they'd stayed down in South Beach as originally planned. Life would be so much easier right now.

"I don't let others determine my worth," she mumbled, all the while knowing very good and well that she did. Aside from a few close friends—a circle which had grown even narrower since her marriage to Cal—she obsessed over everything she said and did, constantly worrying what others might think. Always had. Her entire life had felt like one enormous prolonged struggle to fit in; to find acceptance, to strive to be good enough. Though good enough for whom and for what purpose had remained a constantly shifting target. Even more depressing, she couldn't recall a single instance in which she'd actually measured up. But she'd rather die than admit Roxie might be right.

"Fine. Prove it." Roxie crossed her arms and her fiery emerald gaze issued a challenge. "Prove you're not the co-dependent people pleaser I think you've become."

Cressida crossed her arms as well and jutted out her chin. She could be just as stubborn as her mother when the situation called for it. "How?"

"By marching into that ladies luncheon this afternoon with your head held high," Roxie sniffed. "So they didn't invite you. So they're trying to make you feel like an outcast because your marriage fell apart. So what? You're a Reynolds. And Reynolds' women do their own thing. We don't let the Trudy's of the world—or anyone else for that matter—dictate what we do or how we feel about ourselves. We're fabulous and we own that very simple but very profound truth."

"You know it." Costa nodded vigorously. "You need to strut in to that meeting rockin' that beige linen Versace number hanging in your closet. Let those uptight country club snobs drool over your fabulousness."

Cressida scowled. "Why do you always feel compelled to inspect my closet? And without an invitation, I might add."

He shrugged. "I'm a stylist. That's what I do." Costa leaned forward and stage whispered, "By the way, we need to take an afternoon next week to hit the boutiques." He lifted a brow. "We need to dial up the vixen if you're gonna be single again."

Roxie nodded in energetic agreement.

He sniffed and scrunched up his face as if he'd just smelled something foul. "Oh, and that black *thing* you were wearing when we arrived has been discarded."

"Hey! You can't just rifle through my closet and start tossing my clothes without asking!" Cressida glared at him. "I'll have you know that was my favorite gardening t-shirt."

Costa pursed his lips. "I wouldn't use that rag to bathe a stray dog." He glanced sideways at Roxie. "Her closet positively *screams* last year."

Roxie shook her head sadly and shrugged. In the past, she'd made it all too clear that she considered Cressida's style sense beyond repair, which Cressida actually found somewhat validating. Living up to her mother's questionable taste in fashion had never been a focus. And never would be.

Cressida strode to the door with renewed purpose. She needed to hurry if she wanted to be on time to meet Ben up in Boca. Much as she dreaded the task of picking out décor for a house she wouldn't even be living in, she didn't mind leaving. She wasn't sure she could stomach any more life or fashion wisdom from the two most outrageous people she'd ever known.

"Make sure you pair that Versace with those stunning turquoise teardrops—the ones with the little pave crystals," said Costa.

So he'd gone through her jewelry box as well. Cressida couldn't resist a little dig as she breezed out of the room. "They're diamonds not crystals," she called over her shoulder.

"Even better." Costa cupped a hand next to his mouth and shouted at her retreating back. "Oh and pair it with those cheetah print Louboutin peep toes. You need to stop playing it *so safe!*"

Cressida trudged up the stairs and once again, tried to figure out what she'd done to deserve this surprise visit from Roxie and her meddling sidekick. Despite reassurances, Cressida wasn't buying Roxie's story about her evening of canoodling with Micah and uttered a silent prayer that Trudy Farentino had slept in that morning.

꺼◦ᲠᎧ

Cressida headed downstairs wearing the beige Versace sheath and teardrop earrings. But she'd chosen nude pumps instead of the animal print peep toes. She might be a Reynolds but she still cared what people thought and with their preference for pearls, cardigans and sundresses, the Ladies Guild could only take so much glitz on a Wednesday afternoon.

She breezed out the door totally focused on responding to a text message from Shay when she ran headlong into a solid wall of unmoving male flesh.

"OH!"

The sudden stop threw her off balance and she teetered backwards.

Ben grabbed her shoulders to prevent her from falling. "Whoa…!"

A sizzle of energy rippled through her body and she took a quick step back, out of reach of his strong grasp.

"Hey there." His warm brown eyes smiled down at her and caused her stomach to do one of those little flip flops it seemed to do whenever he was near.

"Sorry," she murmured, rubbing a shoulder that still tingled from his touch. Why was it that every time he came within ten feet, every nerve in her body went into over drive?

His face broke into a broad, slow grin. "Textin' and walkin' is a hazard, you know. Didn't you see that YouTube video where the lady fell into the fountain?"

She shook her head and dragged her gaze away from his twinkling brown eyes with effort, pretending to check her texts.

"I thought we were meeting up at the design place."

"Something came up and I needed to swing by. Give me a second to get things under control with my crew and then we'll ride up there together," he said. "Deal?"

"Uh, okay." She bit her lip. She definitely didn't think it would be a good idea to be confined in a small car for two hours round trip. After all, she was supposed to be avoiding him.

She glanced at her watch and made one last ditch effort. "Listen, I have to be back here by two for a meeting. Maybe we should take separate cars." She arched a brow.

"Nah. I need to get back here anyway." He held up a finger. "Be right back."

As he disappeared into the house, Cressida sighed.

Good job Cress. Really workin' that big plan to avoid him.

Irritated, she pressed the key fob and the doors of her silver BMW unlocked. She slid in, fastened her seat belt and started the engine.

Ben joined her a few minutes later. "Nice ride." He ran his hands admiringly over the dashboard. "Now I understand your aversion to my truck."

He reached down to the side of the seat and adjusted the electronic controls to allow for more leg room.

"I don't have anything against your truck. I just don't have much in my wardrobe that could be considered even remotely truck-friendly."

She studiously avoided looking at him as she backed down the driveway but his masculine scent proved impossible to ignore. He smelled of fresh laundry and vanilla, mixed with a hint of spice. Heaven.

Cressida turned on the radio to focus on Oprah—anything to divert her attention away from the man seated next to her.

She tapped her finger on the steering wheel. After another few miles, she switched to a music station and turned up the volume.

None of the distractions worked. All she could think about was Ben.

She sneaked a sideways peek as he gazed out the window.

He had the kind of face that inspired fantasies and broke hearts. A chiseled nose and square jaw softened by warm brown eyes and lips that could morph into the sexiest smile she'd ever seen. Lips she longed to kiss and—.

"Uh…Cressida…," he began.

The sharp blare of a horn shattered her fantasy.

Her eyes darted back to the road.

Crap!

She slammed on the brakes, missing the car ahead by mere inches.

"Sorry," she muttered.

Her cheeks flamed, embarrassed to have been so caught up in Ben that she'd nearly rammed the car in front of her.

What was wrong with her anyway? She considered herself sensible and level-headed—at least most of the time. So how could she be so drawn to Ben when she wasn't yet divorced? When just a month before she'd been plotting ways to reinvigorate her marriage? It didn't make any sense.

Unlike her mother, Cressida didn't flit from one man to another. Never had. To her, vows were sacred and marriages worth making the effort to save. And she'd been focused on just that—saving her marriage—for years. Still, just because the marriage had been hard and now appeared to be over, it didn't excuse her sudden obsession with a new man—no matter how outrageously sexy—just to escape the disastrous turn of events in her marriage. That wasn't who she was. That was something her mother would do.

Determined anew to ignore him, she tightened her grip on the steering wheel as they merged onto I-95 North.

Ben's cell phone buzzed.

He glanced at the display and then at Cressida as he connected the call. "Hello, Dr. Wentworth."

Cressida pressed her lips together but kept her attention focused straight ahead. She hadn't talked to Cal since the day this whole mess had started when he'd announced—in front of Roxie, Ben and the entire construction crew—they were taking a break. She hadn't heard a peep from him since, despite the fifteen messages left with his receptionist and the countless voicemails on his cell phone. Not even the day he'd served her with divorce papers—the weenie. After ten years of marriage, he could've at least had the decency to break the news himself. Instead, Cal had hidden behind the 'we're taking a break' ploy and then paid someone else to do it while he'd casually waltzed off with her sex-on-a-stick cousin.

Anger stirred at the injustice of Cal's approach.

"Everything is right on track," Ben said. "We're headed up to Boca to make the design choices right now." Ben paused to listen to Cal's response. "Yes." He stopped again and glanced at her uncertainly as he listened. "Uh…sure."

Ben handed her the phone with an apologetic look. "He wants to speak with you."

Cal wanted to speak with her? A little late in her estimation.

Already riled by the direction of her thoughts, she snatched the phone from Ben, pressed the device to her ear and snapped, "What do you want?"

Chapter Eight

After a lengthy pause, Cal said, "I…uh…I had such a busy schedule I didn't have a chance to get back to you before now."

Cressida lips pressed together at that bit of news. She felt confident he'd had all the time in the world for Graciella. Her fingers tightened around the steering wheel.

"I just…well, I wanted to check in to see how things are going."

His tentative tone surprised her. Cal usually sounded so autocratic, so in control.

Her lips twisted. The harshness of her tone had probably caught him by surprise. In all their years together, she'd rarely uttered a cross word and she'd *never* called him out on his bad behavior. It had always been about protecting his ego, building him up, trying to be the perfect wife. Well, those days were over.

"Things? If you're referring to the renovation, ask Ben." She spat the words, not caring how nasty she sounded. He deserved every ounce of her ire. "He'd know better than I would."

It took several moments before he spoke and when he did, he sounded hesitant and gruff. "When Ben mentioned you were with him, I wanted to see how you were doing. To make sure you're holding up okay."

She frowned, pulled the phone away from her ear and held the device in front of her, staring at it in disbelief.

Blood boiling, she put the phone back to her ear and said, "You served me with divorce papers in the middle of lunch hour at

Rocco's Tacos. You ran off with my twenty-five-year-old cousin—the one you no doubt slept with in my home and in *my bed*! How the hell do you think I'm doing?"

The raw anguish in her voice came from the depths of her soul.

Ben turned and gazed out the passenger window, looking as if he'd like to disappear.

"You know about Gracie?" Cal sounded shocked.

"*Everyone* knows about Gracie!" she hollered in a voice loud enough to rattle the windows. "Certainly all of our friends know—and apparently have known for months!" She dragged in a few deep breaths in an attempt to calm herself but her voice still shook as she said, "Seriously, Cal. How *could* you?"

He didn't speak for several moments. Finally he sighed, sounding weary as he said, "I was going to tell you. I mean…I meant to tell you sooner."

"Sooner? As in *before* you slept with my cousin? *Before* the *whole town* knew? That might've been nice."

He sounded defensive as he continued. "Everything just got too hard with us. You know it, too. We weren't working. Every time we turned around there was another failure to contend with, another piece of bad news. It started to feel like we were cursed," he said. "I saw a chance to change my life and I grabbed it. One day you'll realize this was all for the best."

She fantasized briefly about pounding the phone on the dashboard until it shattered into a million little pieces, but she didn't. Primarily because it wasn't her phone.

Instead, she said, "You know what? I'm beginning to believe that myself. Don't bother checking up on me again. Just focus on that *new life* you grabbed for yourself and leave me the *hell* alone!"

She disconnected the call and tossed the phone onto Ben's lap. "Sorry," she muttered. "That wasn't like me."

But it sure had felt good to finally say what was exactly on her mind. During their marriage she'd turned herself inside out trying to please Cal. She hadn't let herself question him about much of anything. If something hadn't felt right, she'd simply ignored it or come up with a million excuses to explain it away. Not because he'd demanded it, but because she'd wanted to believe the best of him. Doing so had made her feel more secure. Safe.

Her needs in the marriage had been simple. She'd wanted Cal's approval; his love. And she'd sensed—had *known* deep down inside—she wouldn't receive it if she'd actually let herself *be* herself, though she'd never before acknowledged that little tidbit to herself. So she'd transformed into someone else; the person Cal wanted her to be.

Cressida gazed broodingly out the window as a dark cloud of doom descended.

Her life had melted down into what could only be described as a spectacularly hot mess. Fat lot of good all that effort to please Cal and save her marriage had done her. While she'd been busy molding herself into Cal's dream woman, she'd lost herself. After a decade of marriage, she no longer knew who she was or what she wanted. While her friends had been experimenting, dating, building careers and discovering more about themselves and the gifts they were meant to contribute to the world, she'd been trying to please an unpleasable man and denying her own dreams and aspirations in the process. And at the end of that long lonely journey, she'd ended up with nothing. Her dreams were nonexistent and her confidence almost completely shot. After ten long years she felt nothing but a disturbing numbness that apparently—judging by her reaction to him now—hid a deep seething pool of anger and resentment.

Ben's voice held a quiet sympathy as he said, "I'm sorry. I shouldn't have mentioned you were with me."

She shrugged. "It doesn't matter."

Nothing mattered anymore. Nothing except dealing with this mess. Getting past the house sale and just moving on with her life. Whatever that meant.

They rode in gloomy silence for several miles. She could feel

Ben's scrutiny but did her best to ignore him.

"Do you want to talk about it?" he asked quietly.

She shook her head. "There's nothing to talk about. My marriage is over."

She knew that for sure now. Granted, the divorce papers and his shacking up with Graciella had been huge red flags but Cal had just helped her realize the degree to which she'd blinded herself to the truth. She'd seen the signs for years. She hadn't been happy, not really. And clearly, neither had he. But the thought of losing Cal had been too terrifying a prospect for her nonexistent self-esteem, so she'd cloaked her fear in denial and busied herself with trying to get pregnant and be the perfect wife and hostess, which had only succeeded in delaying the inevitable.

"Nothing hurts quite as badly as having your spouse cheat," he said.

Cressida lifted a brow as she cast a sideways glance at Ben. "You were married?"

He nodded. "Twelve years. Married my college sweetheart. That's why I'm in Florida now and not Texas."

"Wow. Twelve years. What happened, if you don't mind my asking?"

"No, its fine," he said. "We met senior year of college, fell in love and married two years after we graduated. We were happy, or so I thought. Then I found out about her affair with my business partner."

She frowned. "Your partner?"

He sighed. "Ex-partner. For the first eight years after college, I worked at a big architectural firm down in Miami. Hated everything about it—the politics, the mediocre design. Everything." He shook his head. "I dreamed of opening my own place. A boutique firm where I could do great work; the kind of work that means something. The kind of work I love. Phil and I shared the same dream. He's incredibly talented and great at all the things I'm not. We decided to strike out on our own four years ago so we scraped the money together and put up a shingle."

"That's wonderful," she said.

"It was," he said. "Until a year later when I discovered their affair."

She grimaced. "How did you find out?"

He expelled a long sigh. "I came back a little early from an offsite meeting with a client and found them in Phil's office. Total cliché." He glanced over and a faint smile touched his lips. "Amazing how badly a cliché can hurt, huh?"

She shot him a sideways glance and their eyes met for a brief electrifying moment. She knew exactly what he meant.

"I'm sorry," she whispered. "That must've been awful."

He nodded. "Especially for the kids."

Cressida arched a brow. "You have kids?" For some reason, she hadn't pictured that.

"Two. Ten and eight. Just old enough to—"

She finished for him. "I know this one. Just old enough to understand what was happening but too young to do anything about it."

"You got it. Pretty harsh thing for a kid to go through," he said. "And for me, it meant I had to start all over again—personally and professionally. For a year, I dragged around feeling sorry for myself, certain she'd come back. And since I couldn't work with Phil anymore, I didn't have an income and with the recession it was tough to find a job so I burned through my savings."

He shook his head. "It was a tough time. It damn near ruined me financially but six months ago Uncle Rex stepped in—he's my dad's brother—and loaned me enough to start over again. He grabbed me by the scruff of the neck and told me to buck up and get my ass in gear." He grinned at the memory. "So…I signed a lease, bought some advertising and hung out a shingle. It's been hand to mouth ever since. This is actually my first big job."

"Ah." Her lips spread into an ear to ear smile. "Now I get the obsession with the on-time bonus."

"That bonus equates to twenty percent of my fee for this project and that'll allow me to pay back Uncle Rex plus have a little in the bank." He glanced at her. "So anyway, I'm living proof that as bad as your life seems today, it gets better. The hurt and sense of betrayal will fade. You just have to keep going even when you think you can't and when there's enough distance between you and the relationship, you'll realize it was all for the best."

"Do you really believe that?"

As angry as she was and as much as she'd begun to realize how unhealthy the relationship had been for her, Cressida couldn't imagine life without Cal.

"I do. I believe life unfolds the way it's supposed to and our job is to pay attention to the lessons we learn along the way and then do something with them."

She chewed the inside of her lip. "Sounds a little too easy to me. Doesn't that prevent you from holding people...or yourself...accountable?"

He shrugged. "The philosophy probably makes it easier to forgive and forget but I actually believe it's true. It's not about the speed bumps and detours we encounter in life. We all get our own special version of those. The important thing is the lesson each speed bump delivers. How the journey shapes who we become."

"How can you be so sure your divorce was for the best? I mean...you're still single, right?"

"Yeah but I'm so much happier. So are the kids." He studied her profile. "We weren't working for a long time but I only saw that after I got a little distance. My ex picked up on it before I did, that's all. And while I would've preferred she not cheat, I think it was her way of getting out, of forcing an end to the relationship."

She nodded slowly as his words sank in. She could relate. She'd known for ages that her marriage had issues but she still couldn't twist her perspective enough to view her impending divorce as a blessing. Not yet anyway. She'd much rather be struggling through endless counseling sessions and difficult conversations in an effort to patch things up. Even now, after knowing Cal had cheated with Graciella. Reconciling—as difficult as it would be—seemed far preferable to building a new life alone. That way, at least she wouldn't have to view the past ten years as a complete and total waste of time.

"I'll share a big learning with you," he said. "When someone walks out on you like that, you have to get right back on the horse."

She frowned. "What horse?"

"You should start dating."

Her brows shot up and her voice cracked as she said, "Already? It just happened!" Cal's side of the bed still had a little indentation. His pillow still smelled vaguely of his cologne and up until a few days ago, she'd still snuggled up to it, drinking in his scent and remembering the way things used to be. That was before he'd served her with papers. Now his pillow was in the guest room closet so she wouldn't have to be reminded of him.

Still, while she suddenly wasn't sure if her happy memories of the relationship were even based in reality, it was still much too soon for dating or even thinking about dating. Or fantasizing about a certain sexy architect, for that matter.

"Maybe not next week. But don't wait too long. I know it's the last thing you're interested in but trust me; you need to force yourself to get out there again." He eyed her intently. "It's so easy to put the dating thing off. To wait until you feel better; until things settle down and you're ready." He shook his head. "But if you do that, you'll discover that life starts to happen and all of a sudden months roll by, and before you know it the months turn to years and then one day, you wake up and find yourself all alone much farther down the line than you ever intended."

Her fingers gripped the steering wheel so tightly her knuckles turned white. The mere thought of the nightmare of dating again made her want to lock herself in a dark room and never come out again. But spending a lifetime alone didn't sound any better.

"I'll need more than a few months before I'm ready for that. I thought the typical advice was to wait awhile before diving in again. Isn't the general rule to wait two months for every year?" She smiled ruefully. "Shay brought over a bunch of self-help books last weekend and I read that in one of them."

"I'm sure that's true if your spouse dies or it's a sudden thing and you're mourning the loss of your love. But this is completely different. You just discovered your husband has been messing around for months. He left you. Emotionally he probably left a long time ago which means the true intimacy in your marriage has been over for quite some time, whether you realized it or not." His voice became gentler. "And that means you either weren't paying attention or you were in denial." Ben shrugged. "Either way, you need to face the music and force yourself to move on too. Even if you don't feel like it at first."

She chewed the inside of her lip and considered his advice.

"I waited three years to feel better, to understand what had happened," he said. "Finally, I...or rather my therapist..."—his lips twisted—"helped me realize the truth. By putting that part of my life on hold, I hadn't allowed myself to emotionally move on. I stayed stuck right where we'd been, wishing it hadn't happened, blaming myself and hoping she'd come back. Finally, when I learned of her engagement, I realized my therapist was right. I needed to put myself out there again or I'd spend the rest of my life sitting on the couch watching Ice Road Truckers."

She grinned despite herself. "That show is ridiculous."

But in truth her viewing habits weren't much better. In the past few weeks, her reality show of choice had become the Real Housewives of New Jersey. She found the show reassuring since the screwed-up cast made her life feel positively sane by comparison.

"It was actually good company for a few years," he said. "Anyway, I finally forced myself to start dating two months ago. Hated every minute of it at first and don't much like it now but gradually, you get used to it." He glanced at her. "It's not healthy to isolate yourself and while we're just getting to know one other, it's easy to imagine you going down that path."

"How can you tell?" She couldn't believe he had her pegged so accurately.

"You seem a little reserved."

She lifted a brow. "With a mother like mine, do I have a choice? One family can only take so much extroversion."

He grinned. "She is something else. I'll give you that."

Cressida contemplated his advice as she exited the highway at Glades Road and turned left to head toward Boca Design Studio. She couldn't imagine dating again, let alone diving in so quickly after the end of her marriage but Ben definitely had her number. She could so easily retreat into her own little world, licking her wounded pride and letting the months pass her by until they turned to years and eventually, decades. A big part of her wanted to do exactly that—to hide from reality rather than muster the courage to face it. But an even bigger part of her knew she'd regret it down the line if she did.

Still, if forced to prioritize her get-a-life to-do list, she'd definitely slot dating in last place.

Chapter Nine

Cressida loitered outside the Tuscan Grill pretending to send a text message while trying to summon the courage to enter.

She checked her watch. The meeting would start in a few minutes.

She glanced over at the door and then gazed longingly down the street in the direction of her car. One and a half blocks from freedom. That's all. One and a half blocks and she could just hop in her beamer, floor it and get the hell out of dodge.

Glancing back at the door to the restaurant, she tried to imagine the torture the next few hours might bring. She didn't feel ready to face the inevitable gossip. The whispers. The furtive glances and knowing smirks. Under the best of circumstances, a Ladies Guild meeting could be a mixed bag—the satisfaction of doing good mixed with the knowledge that you'd never fit in, no matter how hard you tried. If you weren't in the inner circle you were an outsider and that was that. And given Cal's rampant display of infidelity, she had not doubt she'd be treated as even more of an outcast than usual. Granted, she couldn't predict how many of the women knew of Cal's cheating but given the gossip-loving nature of the group, she could be pretty sure nearly everyone had known before she did and she didn't feel prepared to face that possibility. Not yet.

As she turned to leave, Lucinda Hearst rushed by.

"Come on, Cress!" Cinda said, pointing at her watch. "We don't want to be late." She rolled her eyes. "You know how Trudy gets when someone is *tardy*." Her emphasis on the last word mimicked Trudy's syrupy, hoity-toity manner of speech.

Cressida gave a half-hearted smile. Cinda had a good heart and Cressida liked the other woman immensely. "I'll be in shortly."

"Hurry!"

Cressida nodded.

That settled it. The decision had been taken out of her hands. Pride wouldn't allow her to slink away now that she'd been seen. So she squared her shoulders and summoned every scrap of courage she could find as she pulled the doors open and stepped inside.

The Ladies Guild had rented the entire restaurant for the afternoon meeting. Probably because the floor plan fed Trudy Farentino's outsized ego.

Cressida glanced around, looking for a seat near the back.

Designer-clad women sat in groups of two or three across twenty tables. A curved balcony stood four feet high—just tall enough to draw a level of importance to the two women leading the meeting, both of whom appeared to be enjoying the spotlight immensely.

Naomi Gilligan, Ladies Guild secretary and Trudy's social terrorist of a wingman, called the meeting to order. Her artfully plumped lips and slightly frozen expression, carefully tended to by her plastic surgeon husband, gave her the look of a Stepford Wife. Her perfectly manicured hands rested lightly on the wrought iron rail. Trudy Farentino, just as perfect and just as artificially enhanced, stood to her left and surveyed the ladies in attendance as a queen would her subjects.

Cressida tiptoed in as quietly as possible so as not to call unnecessary attention to her late arrival. Under the best of circumstances, joining the meeting five minutes late would be frowned upon. Given the sad state of her personal life and therefore her social standing, tardiness would be considered unforgiveable. Members of the Ladies Guild followed the rules.

Appearances were everything. Like Cal's country club cronies, they prided themselves on their perfection and oozed an overinflated sense of their own importance.

Trudy's eyes bored into her as she crept up to a table near the back and slipped into a chair.

Cressida caught Trudy's eye, smiled and waved.

Trudy responded with a frosty glare and then pointedly looked away. To drive the snub home, she crinkled her nose and gave a friendly little half wave to one of her favored inner circle seated at the next table.

Cressida gritted her teeth.

I get it. You don't want me here. She jutted out her chin and sat a little straighter. *Too bad. I'm not going anywhere.*

Determined to tough it out, she greeted the ladies on either side—neither of whom she knew very well—and directed her attention back to Naomi and Trudy, trying to appear as if drinking in every word.

Once the minutes from the last session had been ratified, Naomi stepped back and relinquished the stage to Trudy, who whispered something in her ear as she glided by.

As Naomi sauntered down the stairs, she shot Cressida a disapproving sneer and then took a seat at the lead table while Trudy introduced the first topic.

An hour flew by.

While the women nibbled at salads and sipped Pinot Grigio, Trudy covered plans for the holiday bazaar, solicited volunteers for the senior citizen reading initiative and formed a new committee to help fund an effort for the local children's hospital. Then she announced a fifteen minute break.

The noise level increased a few decibels as the women started to mingle.

Cressida took a healthy swallow of wine and studied the printed agenda, trying to ignore how uncomfortable she felt. She didn't do well in large crowds and wasn't a joiner by nature. Actually join wasn't quite the right word for how she'd arrived in the club. One had to be invited into the Guild and Cal had arranged for the invitation through one of the partners in his medical practice who just happened to be Naomi Gilligan's husband. And of course, it hadn't hurt that Trudy Farentino was her neighbor.

Cal had insisted she get involved because all the other doctor's wives belonged. It had been expected and so Cressida had gone along with it to make Cal happy. She hadn't expected to enjoy it. But in truth, she'd discovered a deep satisfaction in giving back and connected with many of the Guild's causes, particularly those that involved children. And she'd grown truly fond of a few of the women, like Cinda Hearst. Of course, Trudy, Naomi and their catty inner circle weren't among them. There was nothing worse than a middle-aged mean girl and that's exactly what they were.

Cressida drained her glass and pushed away from the table, deciding to head to the ladies room to kill time while the other women socialized.

One hour down. One hour to go.

Thank goodness she didn't have to give an update on the White Ball. Not only did she have no idea of how plans were progressing since Trudy had excluded her from the last subcommittee meeting but the mere thought of standing on that stage made her nauseous.

Cressida leaned closer to the mirror to freshen her lipstick. Then she ran a fingertip around her lips to neaten the line. Satisfied, she slid the makeup bag back in her purse, snapped it shut and stood.

So far so good. The meeting had been uneventful thus far and had gone much better than she'd expected.

She smoothed her dress and felt almost lighthearted as she returned to the meeting.

Trudy had just called the meeting to order and the ladies were getting seated when Cressida entered the room. She edged along the wall, trying to appear invisible as she moved toward her seat.

Cressida had just placed her purse on the table and was about to sit when Trudy paused, looked directly at her and said, "Since we're lucky enough to have my co-chair for the White Ball in attendance, I think we'll do an impromptu update on the silent auction. Cressida, please come and share all the details."

Every eye in the room locked in on her and Cressida's heart stopped.

Since Trudy had excluded her from the last subcommittee meeting, she was well aware Cressida had no idea of how plans were progressing. But since Cressida couldn't very well say that, she stood and smoothed trembling hands down her dress as a mixture of panic and dread stirred inside.

"Come Cressida," Trudy said, not bothering to hide her impatience. "We have a full agenda. Just give us a quick update on the auction items since that's your domain."

She trudged to the stage, heart hammering as she tried to figure out what she'd say. Halfway there, she broke out in a cold sweat. Acutely aware of the deafening silence and the fact that every eye in the place had locked on her, she climbed the stairs with all the dread of a prisoner headed to the gallows.

When she reached the top of the stairs, Trudy lifted her chin and stepped back, gesturing for Cressida to take center stage.

Cressida's knees wobbled as she stepped up to the rail, grasping it for dear life as she gazed down at the women—two-thirds of whom she would've been thrilled to never see again. She morphed instantly into that humiliated thirteen-year-old girl who'd frozen up onstage when she'd forgotten the words to her song, which had only happened when she'd scanned the rows of proud parents and realized that, once again, despite all his promises, her father hadn't shown up to watch her perform. Fast forward twenty-three years and not much had changed. She still felt abandoned and alone.

Every set of eyes gazed up at her. Judged her. And no doubt, found her wanting.

The silence thundered in her ears. Her mouth felt parched. And the voice of thirteen-year-old Cressida hissed, *Say something for God's sake!*

Cressida opened her mouth but only managed a hoarse croak. She cleared her throat. Twice.

The ladies shifted in their chairs and stared. A few leaned to the woman seated next to them and whispered.

Naomi Gilligan crossed her legs and leaned back, grinning like the Cheshire Cat.

The voice came again, this time more insistent. *Make something up, you idiot!*

Her tongue felt two sizes too big for her mouth as she wiped beads of perspiration from her forehead.

She needed a drink of water. Or better yet, something stronger.

"I…uh…" She turned and shot a pleading look at Trudy, hoping to be rescued but instead, was met with a look of smug satisfaction.

"I…I have to go." Cressida raced down the stairs.

The room erupted as she darted through the sea of tables with all the grace and agility of an NFL running back.

She snatched her purse off the table and flew out the door. As she stumbled onto the sidewalk, she blinked several times until her eyes adjusted to the harsh afternoon sunshine. She paused for a moment to catch her breath and then sprinted one and a half blocks to her car, no easy feat while wearing four-inch heels.

Cressida yanked the car door open, slid into the front seat and slammed the door. As she caught her reflection in the rearview mirror, she barely recognized the wild-eyed woman staring back.

Her face dropped into her hands as junior high Cressida zeroed in on her self-doubt. *Loser! You can't even string three sentences together at a lunch meeting. What the hell is wrong with you?*

She lifted her head and drew in a ragged breath. Then she cranked the ignition, slammed the car into reverse and roared out of the parking lot, headed for home.

Just a block from her house, her cell phone rang.

She studied the display to ensure the caller wasn't anyone from the Ladies Guild. Recognizing the Miami prefix and assuming it must be her attorney, she connected the call.

"Hello?"

"Cres…" The unfamiliar female voice paused and then tried again. "Cress Ida Wentworth?"

"Cressida," she replied automatically, only half paying attention. "Like the car."

"Sorry," the woman replied. "Cressida, my name is Priscilla Davies. I'm executive director of Children's Hope adoption agency down in Miami and I'm calling with wonderful news." She paused dramatically and then cried, "Congratulations! Your referral for an infant girl just came through! An unwed teenage mother from a small town in central Florida has selected you and your husband to be the parents of her unborn child."

Cressida whipped the car to the side of the road, screeched to a halt and slammed the gearshift into park.

"What?" Her voice was a ragged whisper.

They'd completed the adoption paperwork nearly three years ago, after the first IVF procedure failed. She hadn't thought about the adoption in so long she couldn't even remember the last time she'd had contact with the agency. After they'd completed the paperwork and months had dragged by, she'd chalked up the domestic adoption process to a hopeless endeavor, akin to selecting the winning Powerball numbers. IVF had seemed a far more realistic solution. At least she'd felt like there'd been some semblance of choice and control.

"Your daughter will be born in four months," Priscilla continued. "I'd like you and your husband to come in next week, if possible. We need to discuss next steps."

"My husband," Cressida repeated her voice as flat and lifeless as her dead emotions.

"Yes," the woman said. "We have a number of details to go

over and we'll need both of you here so we can make any necessary updates to your paperwork since you completed it so long ago."

Cressida stared out the windshield. *My husband. Sure. I'll get right on that.*

"That's wonderful." Cressida found it impossible to infuse even the slightest hint of excitement into her voice and, because she didn't want to get into the fact that her marriage had just imploded, she simply thanked the woman and hung up.

Cressida slumped over the steering wheel and rested her forehead on her hands. She felt sick. After five years of trying—countless natural attempts, three in-vitro procedures, untold hormone shots and years on a waiting list for adoption—her dream of a baby had finally drifted within reach but was about to be cruelly yanked away once again, this time due to her impending divorce.

Tears welled and she didn't even try to stop them. They spilled unchecked down her cheeks, splashing onto her beige linen dress.

Her shoulders heaved.

The emotional dam had burst and the tsunami of pain felt good, reassuring somehow, and so much better than the emptiness that had held her prisoner since the morning Cal had walked out. So she let herself grieve. For Cal. For her marriage. For the baby girl she'd never be able to adopt. For her dreams of a family that might never be realized.

"You didn't sound too good when you called." Shay paused as Cressida shut the front door, tilting her head to study her more intently before she pronounced, "And you look even worse than you sound."

"Gee thanks." Cressida made a face before turning to head to the kitchen. But after two hours of nonstop crying, she knew she looked bad. "I'm okay," she said, stretching the truth more than a little. She definitely didn't feel okay. Far from it, actually. But she was trying to put on a brave front, mostly to keep from falling to pieces.

Shay tucked a few golden strands behind her ear. "Well? Did you go to the meeting? Is that what all this drama is about?"

"I did." Cressida's shoulders slumped. "Total disaster."

Shay reached over and squeezed her hand. "I swear. Those trollops can be so mean. I don't know why you still bother with that crew."

Cressida leveled a cautionary look. "You know very good and—"

Shay raised her hands in weary surrender. "I know...I know. You just want to finish your stint as co-chair of the White Ball so you can get that little kicker donation for your special causes. I get it. Sort of." She drew in a long breath. "Okay, out with it."

"Well, as usual, I made a complete idiot of myself by freezing up onstage but that's not even the worst of it. After I left, I got..." Her voice trailed off and she paused to drag in a long shaky breath before she continued. "I got the c...call."

Her voice broke on the last word as the tears she'd managed to keep at bay for the past thirty minutes threatened to spill over again like water seeping through the cracks of a dam. They burned her eyes, intent on coming but she blinked furiously in an attempt to hold them back, determined not to cry again.

Shay's brows knit together. "What call?"

"THE call," Cressida sniffed.

Shay leaned over and yanked some paper towels off the roll and thrust them into Cressida's hands.

Cressida blew her nose. "The call I've spent the past three years waiting for but thought would never come. From the adoption agency. My referral for a...a baby g...girl finally came through."

Shay leaped to her feet. "A baby!" She jumped up and down, clapping. "We're going to have so much fun shopping for the nursery and little dresses and…oh! Have you seen those little tutus they wear now?! I'm buying her a whole closetful!"

Someone coughed.

The women spun around in unison.

Ben backed slowly away. "Sorry. I didn't mean to interrupt." His hand gripped the doorknob and pulled it open. "I'll come back later."

His eyes never wavered from Cressida's and seemed to ask a question as he walked out the door.

Chapter Ten

"Well hello, Mr. Hot Stuff." Shay sauntered to the back window and gawked, craning her neck to get a good look. "Wowza. Six foot gorgeous is right. You weren't a kiddin'."

"I don't want to talk about him right now," Cressida warned.

"Did you find out if he's sing—?" Shay caught Cressida's reproachful glare and snapped her mouth shut, slunk back to the island and slid onto the barstool, looking like a child who's been caught doing something naughty.

"Sorry." Shay rested her chin on a fist, blue eyes dancing. "Now, down to business. Let's come up with some names."

Cressida shook her head adamantly. "No!" She blew her nose and sniffed. "No," she whispered brokenly. "Don't you see? Cal and I completed the adoption paperwork *together*. The birth mother chose us as a *married* couple. I can't proceed with this adoption unless I alter the paperwork to just me and if I do that, it'll probably take so long I'll miss the opportunity for this baby girl. Plus, the house is going to be sold so we wouldn't have anywhere to live and,"—she dragged in a long ragged breath—"who knows if I'll get any money from the divorce and I don't have a job so I probably can't even afford a baby. I don't even know if they'd qualify me to adopt on my own."

Every drop of strength had been wrung out of her like water from a discarded wash cloth. She rested her head on her folded arms and her swollen eyes drifted shut.

"My head hurts."

Shay padded to the bathroom and returned a few moments later with a bottle of aspirin. She filled a glass with water, shook out two pills and held them to Cressida, eyeing her sternly.

"I thought you were spunkier than this."

Cressida lifted her head and accepted the aspirin, popping the tablets into her mouth and chasing them with water.

She narrowed her eyes, irritation rising. "What do you mean?" She'd expected support and sympathy, not accusations.

Shay jammed balled fists into her waist. "All I'm saying is where's the redheaded feistiness? Just because something is a little difficult doesn't mean it's impossible."

Cressida gazed at her friend and tried to tamp down her irritation. She wasn't in the mood for lectures on how to be perky or resilient. What did Shay know about infertility or trying to live with the fact that you might never be a mother? Her friend might be loyal and supportive but maternal could not be counted among her strengths.

Shay folded her arms. "You're getting ahead of yourself. You're assuming it's impossible to adopt her on your own but have you actually talked to anyone about it?"

"You mean an attorney?"

Shay nodded.

Cressida crumpled her tissue and threw it in the trash.

"No. And please don't even think about suggesting that lounge lizard you sent me to earlier this week."

Shay lifted her chin. "Gray is the best. And don't even try to tell me you didn't find him cute." She leaned closer and whispered. "Also, he's great in bed." She sat up a little straighter and cleared her throat. "Or so I hear."

Cressida clamped her lips together in disapproval. "You hear that, huh?"

She shook her head. Shay had thrown herself into the dating world with abandon over the past year and in Cressida's view, she could stand to be a bit more discriminating.

"I didn't say it was me. Anyway, I don't kiss and tell," Shay said. She straightened her spine and cleared her throat. "Let's focus here." She tapped a fingernail on the counter, her brow creased. "We need to find someone you can talk to. Call Gray and see if he can refer a good adoption attorney. Where there's a will, there's always a way."

Cressida pursed her lips as she considered Shay's suggestion. "I guess."

"You don't have anything to lose." Shay regarded her for a long moment. "Listen, don't take this the wrong way but you're going to have to toughen up. Remember what you told me during my divorce?"

Cressida shook her head. She didn't but hoped it was something profound. She could use some words of wisdom right about now.

"You said if the marriage had been right it wouldn't have failed and that I needed to let it go and stay open so the right things could unfold in my life."

Cressida stared at her as the words soaked in. She shook her head in disbelief. "I said that?" It sounded like something straight out of a self-help book.

"You most certainly did and you were right."

Cressida shrugged. "That must've been when I was reading *The Secret*. Unfortunately, I never got past the third chapter."

"Well you need to dust the book off and finish it. You can't stay a Pessimistic Polly and expect good things to happen," Shay said. "It took some time but once I got to the other side of the pain, I realized you were right. I hadn't been happy with Jerry in a very long time. I wasn't myself. Actually I didn't even know who I was until recently."

She leaned back in her chair. That certainly sounded familiar. Cressida blew her nose.

"Granted, I haven't found my soul mate yet but my life is so much better, so much more fulfilling than I ever thought possible.

You've said so yourself a million times. My divorce was the best thing that ever happened to me."

"So you're saying this baby isn't meant for me."

She found that impossible to believe given everything she'd gone through to have a child. This little girl belonged with her and she was pissed beyond all measure that Cal and her husband-stealing hoochie-mama of a cousin might keep her from realizing her dream.

"I didn't say that," Shay said slowly. "You should absolutely do everything you can to move things in the direction you want them to go. Go see an attorney. Get the facts. Find out if there's anything you can do to nudge the adoption along. But then…" She shrugged. "Then, you need to let go so things can unfold in the way they're meant to."

Cressida pursed her lips as she considered Shay's advice.

Shay reached out and squeezed her hand. "Have faith."

"Faith." Cressida scoffed. Faith wasn't something she had in great supply at the moment.

Shay leaned forward and rubbed Cressida's arm. "I can promise that if you can just believe it'll all work out for the best, it will. And we'll be sitting here a year from now celebrating your fabulous life."

"We won't be sitting here," Cressida said. "We'll be sitting in the shabby one bedroom apartment I can't afford."

Shay glowered at her. "Positive."

"Fine." Cressida sighed.

She wasn't buying her friend's advice but it sure sounded good. She supposed she didn't have anything to lose by giving positive thinking a try. It's not like she had much choice.

She attempted a wry grin. "I never knew you were such a self-help wannabe."

Shay shot her a level look. "I'm dead serious. But even if you don't believe me, right now you really have no other choice. Sometimes life backs us into such a dark corner that we have no control over the events unfolding. When that happens, faith is all we have. Do what you can and then let it all go, hun. Just put one foot in front of the other and trust that everything will work out the way it's supposed to."

Cressida blew out a long breath. "I guess."

Shay pushed back in her chair and folded her arms. "Maybe it's time you started working on the things holding you back."

Cressida frowned. "Like what?"

"Well, given what happened at the Ladies Guild meeting, you might start with tackling your stage fright. That issue has bothered you since junior high. Why let a fear of any kind have that sort of power over you?" Shay lifted a brow. "It might be time to get over it, don't you think?"

Cressida scoffed. "I'm not sure I'd categorize my stage fright as holding me back."

"Oh, so you think it's normal that you can't utter a word in front of fifty women you're quite well acquainted with. And what about the nonstop obsession over what other people think? I'd say those two issues are linked and in my view, they're both holding you back."

Cressida grumbled. "Well, if you put it that way..."

"The way I see it, the perfect solution is right in front of you."

Cressida lifted a skeptical brow. "Oh really. Do tell."

Shay looked decidedly pleased with herself as she pronounced, "Roxie."

Cressida's brows knit together. "What about Roxie?" She struggled to imagine her mother as the solution to anything. She'd always seemed more like the problem itself.

"She's in town for a few months." Shay spread her arms wide. "She knows everything there is to know about working an audience. Who better to coach you out of your stage fright?"

Cressida sat still, quietly digesting Shay's suggestion. It might work but for some reason she couldn't imagine herself asking for

Roxie's help with anything. That would definitely require more thought.

"I don't know…I'll have to think about it."

Shay checked her watch and picked up her purse. "I have to run. I'll stop by later to see how you're doing."

Cressida closed the door behind her and trudged back to the kitchen. She poured herself a cup of coffee and headed for the kitchen island, but stopped.

The Secret. She still had a copy somewhere.

She spun around and strode into the living room with purpose, scanning the wall to wall bookshelves until she found the book.

She pulled the self-help tome from the shelf and then plopped down on the sofa, nestling into the cushions as she flipped to chapter one.

The front door burst open, banging against the wall with all the force of an explosion.

Cressida nearly jumped out of her skin.

"Hi Honey! We're home!" Costa shouted in sing song fashion as Roxie giggled, punching him playfully in the bicep.

Carlton the driver lumbered in behind them, barely able to see over the enormous heap of garment bags piled high on his outstretched arms.

Cressida lowered her book and peered over the top as the winded, red-faced chauffeur staggered to the nearest chair where he unceremoniously dumped the colorful array of bags. Tantalizing glimpses of sequins, feathers and crystal beads poked out from beneath the plastic.

Costa rifled through his wallet, pulled out a twenty-dollar bill and thrust the cash into the driver's hands.

The weary man executed a half bow and then bolted for the door as if the devil himself was in hot pursuit.

Cressida's lips twitched.

Lord only knew what the poor man had been asked to do in the past week. Serving as the pair's chauffeur couldn't be the easiest gig he'd ever had. The poor guy was probably on the phone this very moment, asking to be reassigned.

"Are you trying to give poor Carlton a heart attack?" Cressida lowered the book to her lap and eyed the mound of bags with curiosity.

Roxie waved a hand dismissively. "Oh please. Carlton insisted on carrying the bags inside."

"He loves us," Costa declared.

"It would be interesting to hear his perspective. I suspect his viewpoint might differ." Cressida lifted a brow and gestured to the bags. "What is all that stuff? It looks like you knocked over a few boutiques on your way home."

"We just came from the seamstress. Rox needs to try on everything in these bags so we can decide what to keep or change." He eyed Roxie sternly. "And I do mean *everything*."

Roxie groaned as she trudged to the sofa. "Not tonight though."

Costa straightened and squared his shoulders as if readying for a fight. "Yes, tonight. We're running out of time."

Roxie shot Costa the evil eye. "Slave driver. I need a night off. Would that really throw us so far behind?"

She shook her head and rolled her eyes at Cressida.

Costa sniffed and waved a hand dismissively. "Oh, stop complaining. I'll make us some margaritas and you can model the outfits between sips."

Cressida giggled, wondering when she'd actually started to enjoy their banter. Usually they irritated her but now she wondered if she'd just been too caught up in what Cal would think of the pair to really appreciate their antics.

"I swear…you two gripe at each other like an old married couple." She set her book on the sofa beside her and stretched her stiff muscles. "How was rehearsal?"

She rubbed her eyes with balled fists, glad to have the break. She'd skimmed through half of *The Secret* in the past two hours. For some reason, the Law of Attraction made a lot more sense than it had three years ago. Then again, desperate people tended to latch on to whatever random scrap of hope they could find.

Roxie flopped down on the sofa next to Cressida and propped her feet on the square leather ottoman in front of her. "Rehearsal was exhausting…" Roxie's voice trailed off on a sigh as her head dropped back on the sofa cushions. She closed her eyes and folded her hands in her lap. "Totally exhausting."

"Fabulous," Costa corrected as he perched on the arm of the sofa, beaming with pride. "Just wait until you see the new act." He leaned close and said dramatically, "To. Die. For. Seriously. I didn't think Rox could top the last one but this new show is killer."

Cressida turned to Roxie, arching a brow in surprise. "I didn't know you were changing the act. I thought all this rehearsal was because of the change in venue."

Roxie shook her head. "After three years, it's time to change things up. Past time, really. In this biz, you have to constantly reinvent yourself and honestly, I should've done it a year ago."

"But why?" Cressida arched a brow in surprise. "I mean, your show is sold out nine months in advance."

"That's not good enough," Roxie said. There's always a sexy new singing act nipping at your heels and fans are fickle. If you're not careful, one minute you're Queen of the Strip and the next you're headlining at the Hard Luck Casino ten miles outside of town and schlepping drinks between sets for fifty cent tips. You have to pull a Madonna and change things up every year or two whether you're hot or not."

"So what's different about this new show?" Cressida tucked a foot underneath her and stretched her arm along the back of the sofa, keenly interested.

Like Roxie, she truly loved to sing but her fear of the stage had relegated her singing to the shower or long car drives. She could belt out a mean Miranda Lambert but her favorites were old school rock chick acts like the 4 Non Blondes or even Bonnie Rait.

Roxie sat up straighter, her exhausted demeanor replaced with a passion that was contagious.

"Well, you know retro pop and country is my thing. So we've added a few numbers from the nineties. You know I love me some Shania."

"Me too." Cressida grinned.

"And for you, I sprinkled some 4 Non Blondes into the mix. I always loved your rendition of *What's Up*." Roxie clapped her hands in delight. "Oh! And I added our award-winning duet from your junior high variety show."

"*Hot Child in the City*?" Cressida tilted her head back and groaned. "Oh my Loooord. That was old twenty-three years ago."

"It's called retro," Costa said with an air of superiority. "And it's super cool. Just wait till you see it."

He jumped up, waggled his hips and spun around on his heel, Michael Jackson style.

"I even kept in our synchronized dance steps," Roxie said. "We've updated the moves to give the number a more hip hop edge but it's super tight. I've got one of the back-up singers doing your part."

Cressida smiled as memories of that seventh grade variety show victory drifted back. They'd taken first place with that duet. Of course, having a professional singer and dancer for a mother had given her an unfair advantage but she'd been so proud of the win. It had been the first and only time she'd won anything and she'd proudly displayed the ribbon on her dresser for years. She had it safely tucked away in a hand-carved wood box in the back of her lingerie drawer.

"Isn't that the number that inspired your little hip shimmy?" Cressida asked.

Costa nodded and wriggled his hips in a reasonably good

imitation of Roxie's signature move. "Her trademark."

"I've incorporated several new numbers too, which is why I'm testing the show here first. I can't afford to unveil my new act on the strip until it's absolutely perfect. So we'll refine it in Miami over the summer and then take the show back to Vegas in the fall."

"You're coming opening night, aren't you?" Costa asked. "You don't want to miss the after party." He leaned forward and beamed with pride. "She has so many fans here. She's the queen diva of South Beach."

Cressida didn't doubt that for a moment. While her mother appealed to a broad range of people, the gay community could easily be considered the most loyal component of her fan base and South Beach had a large population from which to pull.

"Of course I'll be there opening night. When is it again?"

"In a little more than two weeks. Your tickets are front row center," Roxie said.

"Bring Shay, too." Costa said.

"Costa…" Roxie leveled a meaningful stare. "Remember what we talked about…"

Costa cast his eyes downward and pushed out his lower lip, clearly displeased.

"Anyhoo," Roxie said. "I just hope we're ready." She ran her fingers through glossy red curls. "We're having issues with the set."

"The martini glass isn't working right," Costa declared. "It keeps getting stuck. Three separate companies have tried to fix it."

Cressida had no idea how a martini glass factored into the show or why it would be so significant but she knew better than to ask.

"I should've vetted my local crew a little more." Roxie shrugged. "I'm sure it'll be fine but I'm worried. It's challenging to put on a production of this magnitude without my regular guys. And to make matters worse, this is by far the most complicated show we've done from a special effects and props perspective. By this time in the preparations, all the little kinks should be ironed out but we still have substantial issues."

She glanced down and reached for the book. "What are you reading?"

Cressida flushed and pulled the paperback from Roxie's grasp, flipped it over and plopped it onto her lap, cover side down. "Nothing." She cleared her throat and her cheeks flamed. "I was just…"

Her voice trailed off and to hide her discomfiture, she picked up her mug and took a sip. The coffee tasted flat and was ice cold. She scrunched her nose in disgust. She'd always found it difficult to open up to her mother but when her ever-present sidekick was around, it was nearly impossible.

Roxie gazed at her more intently. Then she placed a hand on Costa's arm and smiled up at him.

"Sweetie, can you fetch me a bottle of water? I'm parched."

Costa popped up and headed toward the kitchen, breezing through the foyer just as Shay poked her head in the door. The pair spotted each other in the same instant and squealed in unison.

"Hello fabulous!" Costa skipped towards her, arms outstretch and air-kissed each cheek. "I'm making margaritas. Come help me."

Shay looped her arm through his and the two headed for the kitchen, heads together and whispering like co-conspirators.

Roxie's brow creased. "So much for keeping those two apart." She sighed. "Well, he'll just have to get himself out of whatever mischief they dream up. I'm not swooping in for the big dramatic rescue this time."

She shifted around to face Cressida. "Okay, what's up?"

Cressida tried to appear all wide-eyed innocence. "What do you mean?"

Roxie eyed her with a look that indicated she'd broach no arguments. "Why don't you want me to know you're reading *The Secret*?"

Cressida expelled a long sigh. "I don't know. I guess I just feel stupid. You know? Like I should know how to handle this divorce thing on my own. But the truth is, I don't."

"It's okay to admit you need help," Roxie said. "Everyone needs help occasionally."

Chapter Eleven

Cressida tucked a foot underneath her and turned to face Roxie. "Shay suggested I shift my thoughts away from what's going wrong in my life and instead concentrate on what I want." She shrugged. "It seemed like a good place to start."

"It's a great place to start." Roxie studied her intently and then tapped her temple. "It all starts in here, you know. Your thoughts are the source of your power. Not Cal. Not your precious Ladies Guild. Not me." Roxie pointed at Cressida. "It's about what you think and how you think about it."

Cressida bit her lip. "I know. I just…" She shook her head and shrugged, her thoughts too jumbled and incoherent to put into words.

"I like Louise Hay," Roxie said. "Try *You Can Heal Your Life* or *The Power is Within You* next. You'll love her."

Roxie took her hand and cradled it, lazily stroking her skin. The soothing motion took Cressida back to childhood and had a narcotic effect, easing the kinks in her shoulders. She laid her head on her mother's shoulder and closed her eyes.

"Your whole life you've been your own worst critic; harder on yourself than anyone else could ever be." She kissed the top of Cressida's head and whispered, "Except maybe that husband of yours."

"What husband?" Cressida grumbled.

"Exactly." Roxie playfully tugged her hair. "See? The book is already working its magic."

Cressida smiled. The time had come to dive into the deep end of the pool. To Shay's point, if she truly wanted to move forward with her life, she needed to start with the problem that had dogged her the longest.

She lifted her head and cleared her throat. "Can I ask a favor?"

"Anything." Roxie's eyes searched her face.

"I want to start working on some of the things that have been...you know...holding me back." She picked up the book and waved it. "This is part of getting started but my biggest issue is with stage fright."

"I know." Roxie heaved a sigh. "I should've forced you to get back onstage all those years ago. I could tell your freezing up episode might become a full-blown issue." Roxie shook her head. "But you were so petrified; I didn't have the heart to push you. Nana told me to wait, to give you some time." She clenched her fist and pounded it on the arm of the sofa. "Damn it! I knew we should've addressed your stage fright back then."

"No. I wasn't ready." Cressida smiled ruefully. "I'm still not sure I'm ready, but it's time. I'm not going to run from my fears any longer. I have to face them head on."

"That's my girl." Roxie beamed. "And I know just the thing. It works like a charm for me."

Cressida reared her head back, eyes wide. "You have stage fright?"

The idea didn't fit with Roxie's ever confident, über-fearless image. She'd always seemed in her element onstage; like she came alive under the spotlights and in front of a massive audience of cheering, adoring fans.

Roxie waved a hand dismissively. "Everyone does. It's simple biology. Just the quick build-up of adrenaline. The key is to channel the adrenaline—and your thoughts—productively. If you don't, the pent-up energy can turn to fear which causes all of these crazy voices of doubt to form inside your head. If unchecked, that derails your performance. But if you learn to use the nervous energy to serve you, the fear takes your performance to new heights." Roxie eyed her thoughtfully. "Why don't you stop by after rehearsal tomorrow and I'll show you what I mean."

"That works. I have an appointment in downtown Miami with my attorney tomorrow afternoon so I'll swing by after that," Cressida said. "I've wanted to catch your act anyway." She paused and raised her eyes to meet Roxie's. "Do you really think I can get past my fear after all these years?"

"Absolutely. You just need the tools to help you channel it." Roxie shrugged. "I'm guessing we'll need at least a few sessions." She smiled and patted Cressida's hand. "This is a great first step. It's time to stop hiding your light under a bushel."

Costa and Shay rounded the corner, carrying a glass pitcher and margarita glasses, bopping to some imaginary tune.

"Amen sister!" Costa set four margarita glasses on the table with flourish. "It's time to unleash the redheaded fabulous."

Shay poured some frozen mixture into each glass.

"Rox, the outfits are laid out on the bed upstairs," Costa said. "Why don't you try them on while we have our cocktails?"

Roxie winked at Cressida as she said. "Whatever you say, boss."

Costa handed each woman a cocktail.

Roxie turned to Cressida and raised her margarita, eyes twinkling. "Here's to unleashing the redheaded fabulous."

The group clinked glasses and then headed upstairs for the impromptu costume fashion show.

❧

"The balances in your accounts are not what we expected." Gray twisted a platinum cufflink. "I'm not surprised. It's important to move fast in matters such as this and they probably had a significant head start. Your husband likely had this divorce planned for some time."

Cressida frowned as she digested this unexpected bit of news. "How bad is it?"

"The balances are less than a quarter of what you indicated they should be." He shrugged. "As I said, this is not an unusual occurrence. We'll conduct a thorough investigation but I assume your husband has recently moved some of your assets."

She chewed the inside of her lip. "So what do we do?" She should've anticipated that given his midlife crisis—if one could categorize this situation with that label—one of the first things her tightwad of a husband would do is hide and try to horde their assets.

Cal worshipped money and no doubt expected her to be satisfied with whatever crumbs he decided to toss her way and she guessed the Cressida of even last week might've been. But Cal had a very unpleasant surprise in store because the new and improved Cressida wasn't going to stand for it. Scraps and crumbs weren't good enough. Not by a long shot.

"We'll start looking. I've already hired a private investigator and a firm that specializes in tracing money. If you know what to look for, it's relatively easy to find and follow the trail." His expression turned even more serious. "This will prolong the proceedings and of course"—a faint smile touched his lips—"my fee will increase."

Her eyes narrowed as she briefly considered whether Gray could be in cahoots with the CADs. He seemed like the type of slimy character that might do such a thing.

Gray gestured to the sofas. "We'd be more comfortable over there."

"I'm fine right here."

She wasn't falling for the sofa move again. She still didn't trust him and for the life of her, couldn't understand how Shay could find the slick operator so attractive. He definitely wasn't her speed.

She crossed her legs. "So how long will it take to trace the money?"

"Probably a few weeks. Maybe a month. You'll have to be

patient. These things take time."

Time wasn't something she possessed in great abundance at the moment. The ticking of the adoption clock grew louder by the second and if she had even a prayer of a chance at qualifying to adopt the little girl on her own, she needed resolution on finances. And fast.

Gray steepled his fingers and gazed at her intently. "I understand you've been contacted by an adoption agency."

Cressida's jaw went slack. It took her a full minute before she could form a semi-coherent response. "But...I don't understand. How did you know?"

"I received a call from the CADs this morning. They wanted to make it clear they won't entertain child support." His eyes glimmered. "We'll see about that."

How could Cal have known about the adoption? No one knew besides Shay. She hadn't even told her mother. Or Nana. She'd been listed as the contact on their adoption paperwork so it seemed unlikely the agency would've contacted Cal too, as Children's Hope still thought they were a happily married couple. After three years of waiting, the agency would have to assume she'd told her husband the joyful news.

She pursed her lips as another thought occurred.

Ben.

Her brows knit together. Could it be?

He'd overheard her discussing the adoption with Shay. Could he have informed Cal?

She bit her lip and briefly considered the possibility, and then just as swiftly, dismissed the idea. It couldn't be Ben. That would just be too...ridiculous. Granted, he'd been standing behind them as she'd shared the news with Shay but he probably hadn't even heard the details. After all, he'd been clear across the room.

Cressida pushed her wayward thoughts to the side and moved on to more practical matters.

"I actually wanted to talk to you about the adoption." She

clutched her purse for dear life. "This dream has taken three long years. I refuse to just write it off as impossible but in truth, it'll take a miracle to pull off a successful attempt given the divorce. I need a good adoption attorney."

"I don't have a list of adoption attorneys. My practice is about the end, not the beginning."

She eyed him with a steely determination.

Gray sighed, picked up a Mont Blanc pen, flipped open his leather organizer and scrawled something illegible onto a blank page.

"Very well. I'll look into it."

Cressida nodded and stood. "Thank you. And please hurry. I don't have much time."

As she headed to the door, Gray followed close behind. Too close.

His hand brushed against her bottom as he reached for the door.

It took every ounce of restraint not to spin around on her heel and slap him. She opened her mouth to say something, but stopped herself.

"I'll call you with a referral in a few days." He held the door open so she could pass.

"Thank you," she said through gritted teeth.

He wasn't going to get away with groping her again but she didn't want to upset him. She needed that referral and his help in getting through this nasty divorce.

Gray eyed a voluptuous blonde seated in the waiting area. "Jessica, please come in," he said, his gaze sweeping over the other woman with a predatory air.

As Jessica strutted by, her gray eyes swept Cressida head to toe as if sizing up her competition.

Cressida ignored her and strode to the elevator bank and punched the button. She stepped inside and turned just in time to see the woman kiss Gray's cheek.

As the elevator doors closed, Jessica headed straight for the sofa.

If that sofa could talk…

❦

"Thank you for seeing me on such short notice."

Cressida grasped Priscilla Davies' hand and gave what she hoped would be interpreted as a confident handshake. In truth, she felt anything but confident at the moment.

"Not at all. Happy to squeeze you in." Priscilla Davies smiled and gestured to the uncomfortable looking wood chair across from her desk.

Everything in the woman's office appeared practical to the point of looking austere. No one could ever accuse Children's Hope Adoption Agency of misappropriating funds in the pursuit of creature comforts.

"What can I do for you?" Priscilla asked as Cressida took a seat.

Her mind raced, suddenly gripped by indecision. She didn't want to do anything that could even remotely jeopardize her chance at adoption but she'd come here for a reason, so with effort, she pushed away the niggling self-doubts and forged ahead.

"Well, as you might imagine, I…"—Cressida smiled nervously and swallowed hard, hoping Priscilla hadn't caught the slip—"I mean *we*…well, we're very excited."

"I'm sure you two have a million questions and I'll do my very best to answer them." Priscilla laced her fingers, her smile genuine and encouraging. "Shoot."

Cressida swallowed. What she really wanted to know was whether she could reasonably qualify for adoption on her own. She'd been feeling so anxious, so riddled with fear that this hard won chance might pass her by that she'd felt like she'd die if forced to wait the few days it would likely take for Gray to call with a referral. That's what had driven her here. Unadulterated fear, pure and simple. But now that the moment of truth had arrived, she was too afraid to ask the question; too fearful of what the answer might be.

Her palms started to sweat.

She cleared her throat. "May I have a glass of water?" she asked, mostly as a way of giving herself more time.

As Priscilla left to fetch a bottle of water, Cressida continued her internal warfare with indecision.

Was it wise to confide in Priscilla or would it backfire? On the one hand, having the woman as her ally could certainly help the adoption proceedings. On the other, given the mess going on in her life right now, this conversation could literally blow up in her face.

As Priscilla walked back into the room, Cressida searched the woman's face as if she'd find her answer written there.

Priscilla handed Cressida the water. As she took her seat she glanced pointedly at her watch.

"I do have another appointment in fifteen minutes."

Cressida took a generous swig of water. "Of course." She smiled weakly.

She had two choices. Suck it up, confess the truth about her situation and let the chips fall where they may or stand up, walk out and risk having Priscilla think her crazy. She chose door number one.

Cressida gripped the arm of the chair. "I wanted to ask if you ever…I mean,"—she shifted around and tugged at the hem of her skirt—"well, I wanted to ask if adoptions ever change…you know…midstream."

Priscilla's brow furrowed. "Change?" She leaned forward, suddenly all business. "Change how?"

Cressida sighed and gave up all attempts at pretense. Best to just lay her cards on the table. She straightened her spine but found it impossible to maintain eye contact. While completely illogical, she felt more than a little ashamed to have been dumped.

As if Cal's cheating somehow marked her as less of a woman. As if, once again, she'd failed to measure up.

She pushed the self-defeating thought aside and summoned every scrap of courage she could find, forcing herself to look the other woman squarely in the eye as she drew in a long fortifying breath and expelled the next words in one rushed continuous stream.

"My husband left me for another woman and I wanted to know if I have any hope at all of adopting this child on my own."

Priscilla grew quiet as she absorbed the full weight of her words. Then she stood, walked across the room and closed her office door. When she returned to her desk, she folded her hands and gazed at Cressida with a mixture of sympathy and regret.

"I'm very sorry to hear that. I wish I could tell you it's the first time I've gotten that story but in all honesty, it's not." Priscilla steepled her fingers and then tapped them. "Infertility puts an enormous strain on a marriage; on people. You never know how an individual or couple will manage it. It's impossible to predict but the statistics are pretty harsh." Priscilla sighed. "Divorce rates for couples who face infertility are nearly three times the national average. Many times, even solid marriages don't survive."

Cressida leaned forward, gripping her purse so tightly her fingers hurt. "But is it possible? I mean, *for me* is it possible?"

"Well, let's see." Priscilla picked up a pen and flipped open the manila file folder in front of her. She flipped through the documents, studying them in detail. "We don't have much time as the birth mother is in her fifth month."

Priscilla clicked the ballpoint pen in and out several times and then looked up. "Do you have a job?"

Cressida answered reflexively, without taking the time to think through how it might be interpreted. "No. I volunteer."

She sucked in a sharp breath. *Ooo…not good.*

Anxious to put a more positive spin on the truth, she added, "But I'm looking. I'm sure I'll find something soon."

Cressida rushed the words, hiding her uncertainty behind a smile that she hoped looked confident.

Priscilla frowned and made a note in the file.

Cressida squinted and leaned forward slightly, straining to see what she'd written but it proved impossible to read upside down.

"Are you keeping the house?" Priscilla asked.

Cressida shook her head. "We're preparing it to sell." *Crap. That didn't sound good either.*

Priscilla's frown deepened and her pen flew across the page as she scrawled another lengthy note.

Cressida leaned forward and tried to focus on the words she'd written but could only decipher a question mark after a lengthy sentence. And that pretty accurately summed up her entire life right now. A bunch of gobbledygook followed by a giant question mark.

Priscilla looked up. "Do you know where you're going to live?"

"Uh...." Cressida swallowed hard. *Think fast!* "I'm apartment shopping this weekend." Cressida smiled uncertainly. "I'm holding out for something near Trinity Catholic Elementary."

Dummy! Why had she even said that? A private education had been Cal's thing. She wasn't even Catholic. If she kept saying things that weren't true, she'd never be able to keep all the lies straight.

The woman made another note and then looked up, her brow creased.

"Has alimony been discussed? Or whether or not your husband would be willing to assist with the adoption expenses or medical insurance?"

"No," Cressida whispered, barely able to speak around the enormous lump in her throat. This little spur-of-the-moment visit couldn't possibly have gone worse. What in the world had she been hoping to accomplish by coming here?

She set the pen on the desk and shut the file and Cressida tensed, bracing for the worst.

Priscilla leaned back in her chair and steepled her fingers once again. "I think this meeting is a bit premature. You don't have a job, a place to live or any clue as to how you're going to pay for the adoption, let alone how you'll care for the child after she comes home."

Cressida blinked back the rush of tears, certain the woman had already categorized her as unfit for parenthood.

If she'd been thinking clearly, she would've had her ducks in a row before coming here. She would've anticipated these questions and been armed with great answers. Or better yet, she wouldn't have come until *after* she'd spoken with the adoption attorney Gray had promised to refer. She felt like a fool and all she could think about was getting the hell out of there.

"I understand." Cressida stood, preparing to bolt for the door. "Thank you for seeing me."

Priscilla eyed her with brand of steely toughness that would give even Nana a run for her money.

"We're not finished." Priscilla's manner was crisp and businesslike as she gestured to the chair. "Please."

Cressida sat, eyeing the other woman warily. When Nana used that tone, it typically meant she was two seconds from getting an earful.

Priscilla removed her glasses and pinched the bridge of her nose. "I'm not going to lie," she sighed. "It's a little late in the game to be changing paperwork. But before we give in and accept defeat, go home and get answers to the questions I posed today. Come back here with a job, a place to live and a plan for how to care for the child. Then we'll see what we can do to get your file updated." She smiled and her eyes softened. "And do it quickly. At this point in the process, every minute counts."

Relief seeped into every cell in Cressida's body. "Do you think there's still hope?"

The other woman's eyes softened. "There's always hope. You might not get this child but there's a child out there meant for you, whether you're married or not. So let's just stay focused on that and we'll see how things unfold when it comes to this particular little girl."

Priscilla moved to the other side of her desk, perching on the edge as she smiled down at Cressida.

"Have faith. Everything will work out for the best. It always does."

"Thank you so much," Cressida said, weak with relief. Her knees wobbled as she left the office but with each step, her outlook brightened as hope gradually filled her deflated spirit.

She hadn't allowed herself to really believe she might still get a shot at a family despite the demise of her marriage. Not really. Oh sure, she knew single career women who adopted but they had vast resources from which to pull. Her situation couldn't be more different. She lacked a career, an income, a place to live, a husband and the list went on and on. Still, the mere thought that she might have a chance to realize her lifelong dream of being a mother caused the corners of her lips to turn up.

Cal wasn't in charge. He didn't get to call the shots anymore. Now, *she* was in charge and she alone would determine her path. More than a decade had passed since she'd been able to say that and man did the prospect feel good.

As Cressida punched the elevator button, a fountain of happiness bubbled up inside, the sheer force of the unfamiliar emotion fighting for release.

The elevator arrived and Cressida tapped her foot impatiently, hardly able to contain herself as she waited for the people inside to exit. And the second the elevator doors closed, she let loose a whoop of pure unbridled joy that came from the farthest reaches of her soul; a cry she felt sure could be heard from the rafters to the basement. But she couldn't care less.

Cressida danced around in circles in full sight of the security camera, gleefully pumping her fists in the air. She even threw in one of Roxie's trademark hip shimmies for good measure.

When the doors opened, it was all she could do not to skip through the sun-dappled lobby. She restrained herself but didn't even attempt to wipe the ear to ear grin from her face.

Look out world, Cressida Reynolds Wentworth was back. Nothing could stop her now.

Chapter Twelve

Cressida entered the dark auditorium and slipped into a seat in the middle section near the front.

Roxie strutted across the stage sporting a black tank top and leggings under a cheetah print spandex mini skirt. As she belted out Shania Twain's *Man! I Feel Like a Woman!* a team of young male dancers spun around her in synchronized gyrations.

Cressida propped her feet on the chair in front of her, crossing her legs at the ankle as she gazed up in open admiration. In rare moments like this, she got to view Roxie not as her free spirited, cringe-worthy mother but through the lens of her legion of diehard fans—the ever-youthful, always colorful, mega-talented star of one of Vegas' most successful and enduring acts.

Roxie had always dreamed of being a star; of having her own show. And she hadn't relented from that quest until she'd achieved the dream.

Given how completely Cressida's own dreams had slipped from her grasp, she admired her mother's steadfast determination and single-minded focus all the more. By contrast, she'd never discovered a driving career passion. Not really. Like her mother, Cressida loved singing but feared the stage too much to pursue that passion. She liked teaching and had studied hard to get her degree but after graduation, she'd never set foot inside a classroom. Instead, she'd met Cal and had been swept into his ultra-glamorous South Beach world where she'd spent ten years doggedly trying to measure up to the level of perfection the other doctor's wives seemed to achieve with so little effort.

For the first time in her life, Cressida wished she was more like her mother. Strong. Determined. Confident. Fearless. Of course, she wasn't her mother and she needed to work with the strengths she'd been born with, though she had yet to discover them.

Still, despite all her challenges things seemed to be looking up. She finally believed that her future didn't have to be determined by her past. Her failures and disappointments didn't have to limit what her life could become. Today was a new day. This moment was ground zero for her new life. A life free from her old fears and hang-ups. A life free from her super critical husband and even more critical inner voice. A life in which she learned to be as crazy about Cressida as she'd always been about Cal.

She just needed to stay focused on possibilities and silencing the voice of her inner critic seemed a great place to start. Only she could control that.

As the song concluded, the dancers hoisted Roxie high above their heads in a dramatic finish.

Cressida leaped to her feet, cheering enthusiastically. Then she put two fingers in her mouth and let loose a long, shrill whistle.

As the dancers lowered Roxie to the stage, she held a hand to her brow and shouted, "Cut the lights!"

The spotlights shut off and Roxie squinted, peering toward the seats. "Cressie, is that you?"

Cressida stepped into the aisle and skipped her way to the stage. "That was fantastic!" She trotted up the stairs and threw her arms around her mother. "Amazing!"

"There's nothing like a little Shania." Roxie turned to her crew and clapped her hands to get their attention. "Okay guys. That's enough for today. Thank you everyone! Great job!"

The producer stepped forward and bellowed. "Nine o'clock call time tomorrow!"

As the cast and crew dispersed, Roxie threw a towel around her shoulders and looped her arm through Cressida's as they headed backstage. "Come with me while I change."

Roxie led the way down the stairs and through a poorly-lit hallway, lined with dusty props and half-assembled backdrops.

Cressida pointed to a martini glass that stood more than five feet tall. "Is that the one that's giving you trouble?"

Roxie nodded. "It's supposed to go on that steel platform back there." She jabbed a thumb over her shoulder. "I sit inside the glass and the platform whisks me to the stage."

Costa appeared beside them. "And then five huge spotlights zero in on Rox as a dozen super buff dancers pluck her out of the glass and carry her above their heads to center stage. Very cocktail Cleopatra." He sighed. "Fabulous."

"Fabulous, but not working," Roxie said. "Right now the steel lift only works about thirty percent of the time and if we can't get it operating consistently—and I mean every single time—we're removing the whole bit." She eyed Costa sternly as if to say she'd accept no arguments. "It could ruin the entire show if the bit doesn't work the moment it's supposed to."

Costa sniffed. "You mean it'll *make* the whole show."

"Only if it works." Roxie rolled her eyes and in a stage whisper, said, "He came up with the idea so he's having a hard time letting it go." She opened the door to her dressing room and peered inside. "Oh good, it's ready."

Roxie opened the door wider and held it as Cressida and Costa walked inside and then closed it behind her.

"Of course it's ready," Costa said, clearly miffed. "I prepared everything myself."

The soft glow of candlelight emanated from a small coffee table in the center of the room. Three oversized zebra print pillows were positioned on the floor around it.

Cressida's lips twitched. "Are we having a séance?"

She'd assumed her mother's cure for stage fright would involve scream therapy, performance coaching or forcing her to sing in front of a live audience, which she had no intention of doing. She hadn't even considered the possibility that her method might consist of something less orthodox.

She shook her head. She should've known better.

Roxie giggled. "No, silly." She gestured to the pillows. "Plop your little tushy down and make yourself comfortable."

Cressida obliged as Roxie glanced at Costa.

"Did you bring the music?" she asked.

Costa reached over and pressed the button on the iPod docking station and instantly, the soothing sound of waves lapping at the shore filled the room.

Then he strolled over to the table and flopped down on a pillow across from Cressida, folding his legs yoga style.

Cressida pursed her lips and tried to guess at the approach Roxie might be planning to employ.

Meditation maybe?

Probably not a bad idea. It certainly couldn't hurt, though she'd tried meditating before without much success. All the humming and chanting had given her a headache and hadn't calmed her in the least. But maybe, like her experience with *The Secret*, the second time would be the charm.

"I thought we'd demonstrate for you first," Roxie said. She glanced over at Costa. "Ready?"

Costa nodded, his expression serious.

In unison the pair began a bizarre system of synchronized tapping motions on various parts of their bodies—from the side of their right hand to various points on their face to the top of their head—while solemnly chanting, "Even though I feel panicked and afraid, I totally and completely love and accept myself."

They repeated the tapping and chanting cycle five times and in Cressida's view, looked absolutely ridiculous.

She pressed her lips together and sucked them in as she tried to stifle the waves of laughter building inside.

When they'd finished, Roxie glanced over at Cressida, who

raised a skeptical brow and said, "You're kidding, right?"

Roxie and Cressida burst out laughing and Costa flopped onto his back, overcome by a wave of giggles.

Once she caught her breath, Cressida said, "Seriously. Stop joking around. I need help here…"

Roxie shook her head and took a few deep breaths, clearly trying to get a grip on herself. "If you could see the look on your face…" Roxie sniffed and wiped her eyes as she tried to stop laughing. "It's priceless."

Costa sat up and dusted himself off as Roxie sighed.

"I get it though. We look like we've lost our minds. I thought the same thing when I first learned how to tap," Roxie said. "But I swear, it works."

"For everything." Costa nodded. "Tapping cured my lower back pain."

"And I lost five pounds a month ago. Just like magic," Roxie said. "Nana swears by it. Claims it lowered her blood pressure."

Cressida's brows shot up. "Nana does this…what is it called? Tapping?"

She struggled to imagine her sensible, practical grandmother going through those ridiculous gyrations. It seemed like one of those farfetched things that Roxie would've shared with Nana. Not the other way around.

"Swears by it," Roxie said. "In fact, she taught me. She learned the technique at her red hat ladies group. It's called Emotional Freedom Technique, EFT or just tapping for short."

"I don't get it," Cressida said. "What could tapping and chanting possibly have to do with my stage fright?"

"Everything," Roxie said. "The whole premise is based on blocked emotional energy. EFT is an eastern medicine thing that's all about the meridian points in the body. By tapping on specific points while repeating a phrase related to what's bothering you, the blocked negative energy is released and the problem just dissolves."

Costa snapped his fingers. "Like that."

"It's always worked for me," Roxie said. "So typically about ten minutes before I go onstage, I tap on my nervous energy or fears around the performance and a few moments later, I'm queen of the universe."

Cressida regarded them both for a long moment and then shrugged. "Okay. I'm game."

She certainly didn't have anything to lose.

Roxie grinned. "That's my girl." She held up a hand. "I'll walk you through the tapping sequence step-by-step. Once you have the moves down, we'll add the chant." She lifted a brow. "Ready?"

With effort, Cressida pushed away the voice of her inner critic which was trying to tell her the idea was idiotic and instead, focused on following her mother's movements.

She tapped four times each on her right outer hand, her eyebrows, beside her eyes, under her eyes, below her nose, beneath her lip, at her collar bone, under her right armpit and on the top of her head.

"Perfect." Roxie nodded her approval. "Now repeat after me. Even though I have this stage fright."

"Even though I have this stage fright," Cressida said.

"I totally and completely love and accept myself," Roxie said.

Cressida dutifully repeated, "I totally and completely love and accept myself."

"Now let's put it all together."

The trio tapped and chanted for a good five minutes.

When they finished, Cressida glanced from Roxie to Costa. It felt a little anticlimactic, though she wasn't sure what she'd expected. Maybe a bolt of lightning shooting through the roof or an angel descending from on high and proclaiming her healed.

"So...that's it? Am I cured?" She certainly didn't feel any different.

Roxie shrugged. "I don't know if cured is really the right term. I think of tapping as maintenance to clear out all the negative juju we accumulate each day," she said. "It's like brushing your teeth or using a good moisturizer. I even tapped on the flight here last week."

Cressida's mouth dropped open as she tried to imagine what the other passengers must've been thinking.

"You actually tap in front of people?"

Roxie waved a dismissive hand. "All the time."

Costa scoffed. "Oh please. You tapped on the plane so the man next to you would think you were crazy and stop hitting on you."

"True." Roxie scrunched up her face. "He wasn't my type."

Cressida shook her head. "Too old?"

Roxie tittered. "Totally."

"Total geezer." Costa turned up his nose. "And he was wearing a Hawaiian shirt and *black* socks."

"Be nice. You know we don't judge." Roxie stood and dusted herself off.

"Speak for yourself," Costa muttered. He leaned toward Cressida. "I'm a stylist. When it comes to Hawaiian shirts and black socks with shorts, we judge."

Roxie reprimanded him with a look.

Costa clamped his lips shut but the jut of his jaw hinted at a defiance that couldn't be contained.

"Anyway, just keep tapping. It works. You'll see." Roxie grasped Cressida's hand and pulled her to her feet. "We'll practice at home and maybe in a few days, we'll test the results onstage. You know…give the cast a little treat by performing our *Hot Child in the City* duet."

She waggled her brows.

Cressida shook her head so violently her hair tossed back and forth.

"No no no! We're only doing this so I'm not nervous giving speeches. I want all the kinks smoothed out by the time the White Ball rolls around. My singing days are over."

Roxie winked. "We'll see about that."

A knock sounded at the door and Costa trotted over to open it.

Felix, one of Roxie's favorite producers, poked his bleached blonde head inside.

"A Micah Farentino is here for you." He lifted an expressive brow. "And might I add that he's quite the strapping young buck."

"Tell him I'll be up in five minutes." Roxie winked. "And keep the dancers away from him."

"You got it." He grinned mischievously. "I'll see to it personally." His eyes twinkled as he shut the door.

"You better get up there before Felix decides to put the moves on your beau," Costa said. "You know how he likes to flirt."

Roxie put the finishing touches on her makeup.

"Do I look worried?" she asked, tossing a black cashmere pashmina around her shoulders with flourish. "I'll see you guys in a few hours. We're just grabbing a quick bite."

Costa pursed his lips. "Mm hmm."

Like Costa, Cressida wasn't buying her mother's story. "I didn't know you were still seeing Micah."

Roxie's eyes met hers in the mirror. "There's a lot of things you don't know, Cressie."

Or want to know, most likely.

"You'll be home by ten, right?" Cressida eyed her mother sternly. "No more spending the night."

"You know, you really are a downer." Roxie rolled her eyes and then heaved a dramatic sigh as she caught Cressida's warning look. "Fine. I'll behave."

"That would be a first," Cressida said.

Truthfully, the idea of Roxie dating Micah didn't bother her nearly as much as it had a week ago. Their vast age difference still made them seem an odd pairing—at least to Cressida—but given her own track record, she wasn't really in a position to judge. But she didn't want her mother to think she had a green light to do whatever she wanted so it was in her best interests to try to establish some limits.

"Behaving is *so* BORING," Roxie called over a shoulder as she breezed out the door.

Costa's snicker intermingled with the tinkle of her mother's laughter as it echoed down the hallway.

Chapter Thirteen

Cressida blew out the candles as she stole a sideways glance at Costa, busily tidying the mess Roxie had made of her dressing room.

"I've been thinking," Cressida said, hesitating for a brief moment as she tried to figure out if she'd regret what she was about to do. Then she forged ahead. "I'd like to take you up on your offer to help spruce up my wardrobe."

Costa brightened, poking his head around the clothing rack. "Perfect timing! Just this morning, I went through your closet and trashed a whole slew of outfits that didn't pass the divorcee test."

"What?!" She folded her arms and glared at him. "Costa, you can't just throw away my clothes without asking."

He pursed his lips and examined his fingernails.

"You're welcome," he sniffed. "I'll have you know my clients pay fifteen hundred dollars for the full Costa Closet Cleanout. You got my premium service at no charge."

She glowered at him and bit back the harsh retort that sprang to her lips. His little cleanout job had undoubtedly cost her far more than the fifteen hundred he charged for the service but she needed his help right now, so pissing him off would be a bad idea.

Cressida gazed up at the ceiling as she did a quick mental calculation. The White Ball was less than a week away and she needed to find a formal gown for that. Plus she could use something new for her mother's opening night the week after. And goodness only knows what he'd thrown out. She was almost afraid to find out.

"How about Sunday afternoon?"

He studied her as he considered her suggestion. "Okay. I can squeeze it in. I'll have to skip Roxie's midday rehearsal but it's safe to say that you need me more than she does."

Her lips twisted. "Gee thanks."

Costa flounced up behind her and placed his hands on her shoulders. "Sit."

She complied and he spun her chair around so she faced the mirror. He grabbed a handful of hair and contorted his face as if he'd just smelled something foul.

"Are we planning to do something with this mop, too?"

She scowled. "What's wrong with my hair?"

From her perspective, she was having a pretty good hair day. Especially since the humidity level had hovered somewhere around a thousand percent for the past thirty days. Summer in South Florida was a lot like living inside a sauna. The tropical rainforest climate was the sworn enemy of any self-respecting curly-haired girl interested in looking at least somewhat fashionable. But thanks to her new flat iron, her uncontrollable mane looked almost smooth today and just the slightest bit puffy. Pretty good, all things considered.

Costa stood back, hands on hips and assessed her hair situation with cold clinical precision.

His lips curled. "Nothing's wrong with your 'do provided you're headed down to the senior center for a Saturday afternoon shindig."

"What?" Cressida bristled as she ran her fingers through her hair. "Smooth is in."

"Maybe eight years ago."

Costa dug his hands deep in her mane, scrunched and then ruffled. Her locks dutifully puffed into a fluffy mass of red waves.

"Big hair is back, girl. The days of smooth and conservative are over. Thank God!" He rolled his eyes in dramatic fashion. "Of course, conservative was never en vogue in Costa Country. Between the wardrobe and the 'do, you look like a repressed schoolmarm."

She reared her head back, stung by his harsh observation. "What do you really think?"

He shook his head sadly. "You have all these glorious, God-given flame red waves and what do you do? You flat iron them into submission." He held a hand over his heart. "It's tragic."

"But the humidity…"

"Ooooo…the humidity only makes those waves bigger and badder," he declared. "If I could bottle the South Florida humidity, I'd make a fortune on QVC." He scrunched two handfuls of hair again and it puffed even bigger. "There's a caged vixen inside just dying to get out. We're going to set her free."

"How can you be so sure?"

Playing the sexy kitten had always been her mother's thing. Cressida considered herself more shrinking violet.

"It's genetically preordained." Costa shrugged. "Like I said yesterday. It's time to unleash the redheaded fabulous. The school marm vibe isn't working for you."

"Okay, so noon Sunday. Right? We'll start down in Miami, then make our way back to Las Olas and end at Shay's boutique."

"Fabulous," he said. "I have to put away the costumes. See you back at the casa."

After he left, Cressida stood in front of Roxie's full-length mirror and studied her reflection, trying to see herself through Costa's eyes.

She frowned.

Wow. She did look matronly. How come she hadn't noticed before?

Cressida bent over at the waist, buried her fingers deep in her mane, mussed and then flung herself upright, letting her hair settle around her shoulders, full and sexy and loose. Then she jutted out a hip, lowered her chin and pushed out her lower lip.

"Well helloooo," she cooed, batting her lashes and trying to capture Roxie's best come-hither look.

Cressida burst out laughing and shook her head ruefully as she smoothed her hair back into place. Embarking on a self-improvement kick made good sense but that didn't mean she should model herself after Roxie, who she'd always considered a bit on the ridiculous side. And while she appreciated Costa's offer to help spice up her wardrobe, she needed to take his fashion advice with a grain of salt. Otherwise, she'd end up looking like she'd just stepped out of a Frederick's of Hollywood catalog.

She threw her purse over a shoulder, flicked off the lights and shut the door.

As she trotted up the stairs, she tapped her meridian points and chanted, "Even though my life has gone to hell in a hand basket, I totally and completely love and accept myself."

Maybe if she tapped often enough, she'd actually start believing it.

❧

"Let me get this straight." Shay sipped her martini and slid onto the barstool next to Costa. The glint in her eye left no doubt as to the level of her disapproval. "You asked Doner the Stoner to escort you to the ball?"

Cressida lifted her chin, irritated to be put on the defensive. "I did," she said, her tone haughty. "And his name is *Nate* Doner."

"Who's Doner the Stoner?" Roxie asked as she stirred her martini.

"*Nate.*" Cressida cast a warning glance at Roxie. "But he likes to be called Doner. He's my next door neighbor." She swirled her drink. "You've met him twice before but he wouldn't have made it into your little black book because he's gotta be at least forty-five."

Costa's eyes lit up. "He sounds fun. Let's invite him over."

"Let's not," Shay drawled, taking another drink.

Shay wasn't a Nate Doner fan but Cressida had a soft spot for him. With Nate, what you saw tended to be what you got and in her social circle of plastic people, she found his authenticity refreshing no matter how controversial his personal habits might be.

"Nate's a good guy," she shot back at Shay. Then she turned to Roxie. "He sold his technology company a few years ago and moved here from Silicon Valley. Now he owns a medical marijuana business in a few states and he's just waiting for it to be legalized here so he can open a Florida branch."

She had no idea why she felt compelled to justify her platonic date's qualifications as escort but it seemed important to defend his honor.

"Please." Shay scoffed. "He's a pothead who deals on the side."

Cressida cast a level look intended to chastise. "He just rented a retail storefront down on Fourth Street." She glanced at Roxie. "He thought the legislation would pass last November."

"So? What does that prove? That his pot stash is about to be tax deductible because he'll have a business license and his consumption will no longer be illegal because he carries a card that documents his 'official back problem'?" Shay's air quotes punctuated a tone that oozed sarcasm. "Great, Cinderella. Maybe that'll keep you from getting charged with possession and thrown in the pokey when you're pulled over on your way to the ball."

Costa spit out a mouthful of martini, consumed by a fit of giggles while Roxie curled her lips inward and looked to be fighting hard not to follow suit.

"Listen." Cressida shot a dark glare at Roxie and Costa before shifting her gaze back to Shay. "I know he's not your favorite but I didn't ask him to marry me. I asked him to escort me to the ball. As a *friend*."

Cressida rolled her eyes and continued. "Geez…at least I put myself out there by inviting him and considering that just a few weeks ago I thought I'd be attending the ball with my husband, I think I deserve some credit for resilience."

Roxie still looked slightly amused as she said, "He doesn't sound like your type, dear. I mean, granted, just about anyone would be better than that uptight prig you married, but a pot dealer"—Roxie caught Cressida's warning glare and quickly self-corrected—"sorry, medical marijuana salesman, doesn't really sound like someone you'd go for."

"No, he sounds like someone *you'd* go for." Costa snickered and elbowed Roxie in the side.

Roxie lifted her chin. "I'm anti-drug. You know that."

Costa's grin fell so fast, he looked deflated. "I know. I'm just kidding."

Cressida raised her hands and her words sliced through the air, cutting off the easy banter. "Enough! I asked Nate, he said yes and we're going. And you two"—she pointed at Shay and Costa—"are going to help me pick out the perfect dress tomorrow, right?"

They nodded in unison.

She shook her head and sipped her martini as she eyed Shay in disapproval. "If I'd know this would turn into criticize Cressida cocktail hour, I might've rethought the decision to host this little gathering."

Roxie wrapped an arm around her shoulders and squeezed. "I'm proud of you, dear. I'm glad to see some of your old spunk returning. I knew it would. You come from a long line of feisty."

"Whatever." Shay gazed out the window and pointed at Ben, who was leaning against a tree and chatting with the foreman. "I think you should've asked tall, dark and Texas out there."

"I heard *that*," Costa said. "He is soooo…" He clamped his lips shut as he caught Cressida's dark glower.

"I'm not asking the architect my *ex* hired and who no one in the Guild has ever seen before, to take me to the ball," Cressida said. "That would spur endless gossip which is about the last thing I need right now. At least most of the women in the group are familiar with Nate."

While true, she also knew most didn't approve of him. He might be richer than ten of them put together—a trait which usually translated into social currency with her crowd—but he marched to his own drummer and didn't give a hoot what anyone thought of him, so the latter negated the former. And yes, Doner did enjoy the odd toke or two but she liked him. Plus she'd begged him to behave and he'd promised to abstain for the evening. She'd be safe with Nate, he looked great in a tux and with Nate as her escort, she wasn't likely to end up the target of unwanted gossip. And given how far off the beaten path her carefully managed conservative little life had strayed, she figured that was as much as she could reasonably ask for right now.

Cressida glanced out the window. The same could not be said for the gorgeous architect and while she'd briefly fantasized about seeing him in a tuxedo, she'd quickly dismissed the notion of Ben as an escort. Besides, he probably wouldn't have agreed to go anyway. After all, if word got back to Cal that she'd brought Ben as her date—as it most certainly would—his precious on time bonus might be jeopardized and there's no way he'd ever let that happen.

She turned back to the trio. "So when Nate picks me up next week you're going to be nice to him, right? No mentioning of pot or medical marijuana or anything else."

The three musketeers nodded in unison.

Cressida didn't trust them any farther than she could throw them but didn't have much choice. She'd have to hope for the best.

More than anything, she just wanted to get through the White Ball with minimal drama, enjoying the fruits of her labor and seeing hundreds of thousands of dollars raised for her pet charity. All things considered, she didn't think that was asking too much.

❧❦

Cressida studied her reflection, hardly able to believe the glamorous woman staring back was her.

Costa peered over her shoulder and looked about to burst with pride. He made a little circle motion with his index finger. "Spin."

She obliged, causing the silk bias-cut skirt to fan out. "What do you think?"

"A schoolmarm no more," he breathed, placing a hand over his heart. "You look like a Grecian goddess." He tilted his head and sighed. "I swear. That creamy exposed one-shoulder look is enough to make a gay man straight."

Costa reached for a small, turquoise blue padded leather jewelry box and snapped the lid open.

"Here, let me just…" He clipped on a pair of shoulder-grazing gold and diamond-encrusted chandelier-style earrings. Then he brushed her hair away from her ears to make the jewelry more visible.

He stood back and kissed his fingers. "Perfectamundo."

She smiled and reached up to touch the earrings.

His smile morphed into a steely glare. "Remember, those little darlings are on loan. Lose them and we'll both do hard labor the rest of our lives."

The doorbell rang.

"That'll be Nate." Cressida turned to check her reflection once more. She'd experienced butterflies and mild panic attacks all week at the thought of facing those women again. But now that the moment of truth had arrived, panic pulled at her from all directions.

The mere prospect of seeing those women again terrified her. She hadn't spoken to any of the ladies since she'd bolted from the last meeting. Though Lucinda and a few others had called, she'd avoided them. But tonight, she'd have to deal with all of it—her humiliation from the last meeting, her lifelong public speaking fear and the harsh reality of what it meant to become a South Florida divorcee; an outcast.

While she'd fantasized about doing so, she couldn't very well skip the ball given her role as co-chair. Besides, the causes that mattered to her needed the funding they would get from the silent auction, which was the piece she was responsible for.

Her stomach twisted into a knot. "Costa, can you run downstairs and grab me a glass of wine. I need something to calm my nerves."

He squeezed her arm. "Sure thing, doll face."

Apparently sensing her need for solitude, he crept silently across the room and closed the door softly behind him.

Cressida sank slowly onto the edge of the bed and carefully smoothed her white silk gown so it wouldn't wrinkle. Her eyes drifted shut as she pressed a hand to her nervous stomach in an effort to calm the butterflies.

Thank God Nate had agreed to escort her. She'd never have been able to muster the courage to face those catty women on her own. While she felt certain Roxie's approach to calming nerves and gaining confidence was a crock, she'd diligently tapped and chanted all week, hoping the Emotional Freedom Technique would give her the strength she needed to make it through this evening.

She'd written and practiced her speech until she knew it stone cold and just in case she blanked, she'd tucked a handwritten copy into her strapless bra. She might not feel emotionally ready or even particularly brave, but she was definitely prepared.

If Trudy Farentino decided to do the right thing and give her public credit for all the hard work she'd poured into the event in the past six months, she'd stride up to the stage—head held high—and deliver the best speech anyone in the Guild had ever witnessed.

While Cressida sincerely doubted Trudy would recognize 'the right thing' if it pranced up and bit her surgically-enhanced butt, at least she'd done her part and prepared for whatever the evening might throw at her.

Cressida opened her eyes and gazed into the mirror. She stood, turning this way and that, studying her reflection from every angle. Costa really had outdone himself.

Tonight, instead of its usual slightly frizzy mess, her hair cascaded in thick glossy loose waves that reached below her shoulders. Her skin glowed thanks to Costa's adept touch with body bronzer and makeup and her dress looked fit for a princess. To enhance the dramatic flair he loved so much, Costa had added an Egyptian-inspired gold hair ornament. It consisted of two delicate gold chains encrusted with tiny Swarovski crystals which dipped onto her forehead, accented in the center by a teardrop-shaped multifaceted sparkler. She had to admit, while it was not her usual style, the accessory gave the outfit an undeniable wow factor. Very Kardashianesque.

A soft knock sounded at the door.

Costa slipped inside and handed her a crystal flute. In the other hand, he carried the bottle. "Champagne, my queen."

Cressida accepted the flute gratefully and took a long sip.

"Now, let's get those shoes on." He set the champagne bottle on a bedside table and picked up a gold and crystal Jimmy Choo sandal.

Cressida balanced on one foot, using Costa's back for support as he slipped the sandal on her right foot.

Shay burst through the door, her wild-eyed frantic energy sending Cressida's fragile nerves through the roof.

"Houston, we have a prob—" Shay stopped abruptly the moment she spotted Cressida. A hand flew to her throat and her head tilted to the side. "Oh Cress," she breathed, her eyes misty. "You look beautiful."

"Costa did good." Cressida sipped her champagne and turned slowly so Shay could get a good look.

"Bravo." Shay clapped and Costa bowed with a flourish.

"Now, what's all this about a problem?" Cressida asked.

Shay cleared her throat. "Uh...well...um." She shifted her weight from one foot to the other and wrung her hands, a tortured expression on her face.

Roxie breezed through the door, looking as if she hadn't a care in the world as she casually announced, "Your date is three sheets to the wind."

Chapter Fourteen

Cressida spun around and cried, "Whaaaaat?!"

Roxie shrugged.

The knot in her stomach grew tighter. "No…" she whispered. "But he promised…"

"Told ya," Shay grumbled. "You shouldn't have trusted that pothead."

Hurt turned to fury in a blinding white flash.

"Damn him! Now what am I going to do?" Cressida tossed the champagne back and drained the flute dry. "I can't show up without a date."

She thrust the empty glass at Costa who filled it to the brim. Then he chugged a very healthy amount directly from the bottle himself.

Rosie turned to Costa, hands on hips. "Go downstairs and make sure that stoner is still on the couch. If he wakes up, sit on him. I don't trust that he'll behave himself."

Cressida's eyes narrowed. "What do you mean *if he wakes up*?"

"He tried to put the moves on me so I decked him." Roxie looked smug as she added, "He passed out and I dragged him to the sofa. From the looks of that eye, he'll have quite the shiner tomorrow morning."

"Serves him right." Costa snickered. He swigged more champagne and then handed the bottle to Roxie, eyes gleaming with excitement at this sudden turn of events as he raced from the room.

Cressida plopped down on the bed, shoulders drooping. "What am I supposed to do now? I mean…I can't go to the ball alone." Her gaze drifted to the clock on the nightstand. "And it's way too late to find another escort."

Shay turned to Roxie. "Let's throw him in the shower. Maybe we can sober him up."

Roxie shook her head. "He's going to have to sleep it off. On top of being high, he seems drunk as well. And like I said, I socked him a good one. His eye is a lovely shade of lavender and swollen to twice its normal size. No amount of makeup is going to hide that."

"Great," Cressida snapped. "I'm so glad you picked this moment to get a flash of modesty."

Typically, Roxie lived for those occasions when men flirted or came on to her. And while Nate was in his mid-forties—nearly two decades older than her mother's typical beau of choice—by anyone's standards he'd be considered a hottie and of course, was a far more age appropriate love interest. So one would think Roxie would laugh off his advances and revel in the attention, but noooo…not tonight. Tonight—the evening Cressida had worked for and agonized over for six long months—Roxie had to go and clobber her date.

Cressida shot her mother the evil eye as she raced to consider the implications. She didn't much care for the choices available to her. She'd have to either slink into the event on her own like a total loser or spend the evening in her darkened bedroom hiding from the world. Fat lot of good all that godforsaken tapping and chanting had done.

"Don't be mad at me, dear," Roxie said. "That medical marijuana peddler isn't fit to be your escort."

Cressida glared at Roxie. "Well he certainly isn't now, thanks to you."

"Don't worry, I have a plan." Roxie checked her watch. "Which should be about ready. Be back in a flash."

As Roxie dashed from the room, Shay rummaged in her purse and pulled out a pill bottle. She opened it and shook out a little blue tablet, then went into the bathroom and came out with a glass of water.

"Here." Shay held out the pill and the glass.

Cressida reached for them, handing Shay her champagne flute. "What's this?"

"Just a little something for your nerves." Catching Cressida's frown, she waved her hand airily. "Xanax. It's nothing, I swear. It'll just chill you ever so slightly."

Cressida usually didn't even take aspirin but if ever a moment called for medical reinforcement, this would be it.

She popped the tiny blue pill into her mouth and chased it down with three gulps of water.

"Just be sure you don't have any more cocktails because—"

Roxie burst in, grabbed Cressida's hand and yanked, cutting off Shay's last words. "Follow me."

Cressida stumbled after Roxie, trying to guess what misguided solution she might've come up with while simultaneously dreading finding out. Most likely, her 'idea' would involve Costa decked out in Nate's tux and posing as her escort to the ball. While not ideal, she supposed that would be better than going alone. Costa could work as long as he behaved himself, which of course, was asking a lot. Then again, without Roxie there to urge him on, he'd probably be fine. Her mother seemed to amplify Costa's mischievous side.

But as she started down the stairs, Cressida spied broad shoulders filling out a smoky grey tux in the sexiest possible way. That wasn't Costa that was...

She sucked in a sharp breath as Ben turned and gazed up at her. His face broke into a long, slow grin, revealing that elusive little dimple in his right cheek.

A swarm of butterflies took flight. And not the nervous, stage fright butterflies that had pestered her all afternoon and which Shay's little blue pill should soon eliminate. These butterflies were of the heart-stopping, pulse-racing variety—the kind that sucked all the oxygen from your lungs and chased all sanity from your mind. The sort that defied all reason and caused a practical, responsible girl to make bad decisions.

Her heart slammed against her ribs.

Oh my.

Cressida's gaze drifted lower, past his broad shoulders. Was that Cal's tuxedo? Though the men were roughly the same height, Cal had never filled that suit out in quite so…interesting…a way.

She shot Shay an over-the-shoulder look rooted in sheer terror.

Shay seemed oblivious to her panic and shot an encouraging thumbs-up, blue eyes gleaming devilishly.

Her knees wobbled. She grabbed the stair rail for support and held her skirt with her other hand as she descended slowly.

When she got to the bottom, she gazed up at Ben and tried to lighten the mood and distract herself by trying a little humor.

"How did you get roped into this?"

"Just lucky I guess." His eyes grew dark and his face more serious as his gaze drifted downward. "You look beautiful."

"Thank you." Her cheeks flamed under his intense scrutiny.

"Carlton the driver is waiting outside," Roxie called.

Ben extended an elbow and Cressida hesitated for the briefest of moments before she tucked her hand through his arm. As her fingers rested on his muscular forearm, she tried to ignore his masculine scent but he was just so…distracting. All she could think about was him.

As they glided through the foyer, Cressida glimpsed Nate sprawled out on the sofa, snoring with gusto.

Ben far surpassed even a sober Nate in the escort department and as they stepped onto the porch, she decided that she didn't give a damn what anyone in the Guild might think. While her escort would surely spur endless gossip and speculation, a sizeable majority of the women would secretly be pea green with envy. And despite how distracting she found him, it might be nice to have him there to take the edge of the raw humiliation of this first social outing without Cal.

Cressida glanced over her shoulder.

Roxie waggled her fingers, looking about to burst with pride. "Have fun kids!"

"Remember what I said Cress." Shay cupped a hand to her mouth. "No more cocktails!"

As Cressida turned away, her lips twisted at the sight of the mischievous trio framed in the doorway, each looking alarmingly self-satisfied—so much so that she wondered briefly if the three hadn't orchestrated this whole drunken date episode. She certainly wouldn't put it past them.

Oh well. At this point, it didn't really matter. All that mattered was that she was headed to the ball and she didn't have to show up alone.

Carlton the driver held the door open for Cressida and Ben patiently waited while she'd arranged her skirt before he climbed in behind her.

As Carlton shut the door and slid into the driver's seat, she turned and gazed out the window, vowing to keep her focus firmly on the evening to come instead of on the hottie seated next to her. After all, this was her moment to rise to the occasion. To overcome her fears. To deliver the best and most memorable speech about her pet charity that anyone had ever heard. The time had come to prove that Cressida Wentworth could fearlessly face a crowd. That she had passions and causes she believed in. That she wasn't some meek little mouse content to stand in Cal's shadow.

She smiled as anticipation welled inside.

Heck, maybe she'd get lucky and the society page would run a nice little photo with a caption. It would do her charities a world of good and might even help move the adoption forward. The publicity certainly couldn't hurt.

There was no doubt about it. Things were most definitely looking up.

❧

Ben handed her a glass of champagne.

"Sorry it took so long. I had a hard time finding you." His eyes swept the crowded room. "What are we doing all the way back in this dark corner anyway? I thought you were the co-chair of this little shindig. Don't you have to make a speech or something?"

Cressida accepted the crystal flute and took a sip. "We're hiding," she announced.

"Oh." Ben swigged his scotch and looked confused.

She didn't bother to elaborate as she sipped more champagne and surveyed the sea of elegantly-clad women standing next to spouses and partners who were decked out in exquisitely tailored tuxedos.

The ladies had gravitated to their usual cliques. A few of the women had spotted her and waved, appearing surprisingly friendly given the fool she'd made of herself just a week before.

Maybe tonight wouldn't be so bad. The kinks in her shoulders eased ever so slightly.

"I just wanted to scope things out a little before we mingled. You know, get the lay of the land and all." She felt compelled to explain her behavior so he wouldn't think she was some crazy recluse, skulking around in the shadows. "But I think we're in the clear—"

She stopped short and her eyes bugged out as Cal and Graciella glided into the ballroom looking like the self-appointed king and queen of the middle-aged prom.

Cressida zoned in on Cal. Had he ever made her heart race the way Ben did? Had he ever made her blush under the heat of his gaze? Try as she might, she couldn't recall a single time. She'd wondered how she'd feel when she saw him for the first time after he walked out and was shocked now to learn the answer. Nothing. She felt absolutely nothing. No longing. No pain. It was almost as if Cal was a stranger. And in some ways, he sort of was. The same could not be said for his companion.

She zeroed in on Graciella with narrowed eyes. Her flamboyant cousin wore a form-fitting mermaid gown in a rich shade of crimson which stood out in stark contrast to every other woman in attendance, clad in the requisite white. Gracie's dress plunged nearly to her naval, the edges trimmed with delicate little crystals and offering tantalizing glimpses of surgically-enhanced cleavage to anyone who bothered to look. And several men risked both whiplash and the wrath of their spouses by doing just that.

Instead of embarrassed by her showy glitz, Cal appeared proud as a peacock, clearly finding the envious glances of the other men somewhat boosting to his social standing and no doubt, to his fragile middle-aged ego.

If she'd tried to wear a dress like that, Cal would've thrown a massive fit and refused to let her leave the house until she'd selected something more conservative. Not that she would've tried, but still. Yet another reminder of just how much things had changed. As if she needed a reminder.

Cressida downed the champagne she'd been nursing as couples around them started buzzing. More than a few glanced in her direction and whispered.

She had to get out of here. Fast. Before Cal spotted her.

Her eyes darted about the room until she located a potential hideout. Then she grabbed a handful of Ben's jacket sleeve and half yanked, half shoved him into a small, dark alcove several feet away.

"Quick! Hide!"

Caught off balance, Ben stumbled into their little hideaway and crashed against the wall.

She tripped over his feet and fell against him.

He gazed down at her in confusion. "What the—?"

"Cal's here," she hissed. "With *her*."

She'd never imagined—not even in her wildest dreams—Cal would have the audacity to show up at the ball with Graciella. As the full enormity of the situation sank in, she felt the color drain from her face and wondered briefly if she might throw up.

While she no longer felt anything for her husband, that didn't mean she was ready to deal with him and his trollop in a public forum just a few weeks after their separation.

His eyes darted around the room. "Where?"

"Don't look!" She reached up and turned his head toward her, keenly aware that a good number of people in the room were watching their every move.

Just an hour before, she'd been worried about Ben's presence as her escort, assuming it might spur unwanted gossip. Now that Cal had arrived with Graciella, her concerns instantly shifted from defense to offense as she racked her brain, trying to figure out how to avoid being viewed as the loser, the jilted party.

Without stopping to think, she wove a hand around the back of Ben's neck and lifted her chin, raising her lips as she drew him closer.

Ben seemed to hesitate momentarily as his eyes searched her face. Then he came willingly, taking control as his warm moist lips captured hers. His hands skimmed up her hips and came to rest on the small of her back, pulling her closer as a million new sensations exploded inside.

He teased her lips apart, seeking a deeper connection and she surrendered, melting into him.

Her eyes drifted shut and all thoughts of the crowd, Cal and her cousin slipped from her mind as she lost herself in the moment. She moaned softly as her hands slid up his muscular chest and wound around his neck.

Ben pulled away and tipped her chin up, gazing deeply into her eyes as he traced a tender finger across her cheek.

"Cressida…" He sounded rough and raw but the look in his eyes was pure liquid heat.

Her heart pounded so hard she felt certain he could hear it. Her lips felt swollen, still tingling from his touch and aching for more. So much more.

They stood there for what seemed an eternity, gazing into each other's eyes, until the sounds from the ballroom invaded their cozy little alcove.

Practical, responsible Cressida doused her emotions with a bucketful of cold water as the internal recriminations started.

Bad idea, Cress. VERY bad idea.

She stiffened and took a quick step back as Ben gazed down at her, his brown eyes glittering in the semi-darkness. Her cheeks blazed with heat and she took another step back.

Dear God. What have I done?

That kiss had been intended just for show. For the benefit of the crowd. So she wouldn't seem like the pathetic jilted loser she was. She hadn't expected a simple little kiss to be so…terrifying. Terrifying in the most irresistible way. But that's exactly what it had been. An illicit drug she never should've experienced because now she wanted more. So much more.

Cal hadn't kissed her like that in years. Maybe never.

"I'm sorry," she murmured. "I was just…I wanted to…" Her voice trailed off on a sigh. "I'm sorry."

Ben's smile crinkled the corners of his eyes.

She swallowed and looked away, glancing over at the crowd.

Cal and Graciella stood chatting with Naomi, Trudy and their spouses. He didn't appear to have spotted them. But a huge contingent of the room still watched her every move, which meant they'd seen the kiss.

She turned her back to the crowd. "I didn't mean to do that."

"I'm glad you did but I'm hoping it wasn't just to make your husband jealous."

Her cheeks burned as she gazed down at the floor.

"Oh." His eyes scanned her face. Then he squeezed her elbow. "I guess I understand," he said softly. "Let me get you another drink."

Ben poked his head into the hallway and snatched two glasses off the tray of a passing waiter. "Here you go," he said, handing her one of the tumblers.

She took a healthy gulp and tears instantly sprang to her eyes. "What is this," she croaked, regarding the drink with narrowed eyes.

"Looks like a scotch and soda." He reached for the glass, took a swig and then coughed. Twice. "Or maybe just scotch and scotch."

"Whatever." Cressida grabbed the drink and tossed the rest down in one smooth move. She coughed several times and blinked back more tears. "I just wanted to get through tonight without drama, you know?"

She sank into a nearby chair. Between her date arriving stoned and Cal and Gracie showing up at the ball, she'd begun to think she might be cursed. And to make matters worse, she'd actually kissed Ben—the man she'd been dreaming about, obsessed with, since she'd first laid eyes on him two weeks before. The man who'd been hired by her ex to renovate the house she'd never wanted to sell.

And it hadn't been just a friendly little peck on the cheek or a quick stolen kiss done just for show like she'd intended. No, this had been the mac daddy of kisses. It had shot straight to the top of her memorable kiss chart where she felt sure it would stay until the day she died.

What in the hell had happened to her? Between the divorce, the house sale and the adoption, not to mention the surprise visit from her mother, didn't she already have enough problems without introducing a new one? She must be losing her mind.

Cressida dropped her face into her hands and moaned.

Chapter Fifteen

Ben swigged his drink and tried to patch together the tattered pieces of his pride. In the span of five short minutes he'd gone from king of the world to total loser.

That kiss had fanned hot embers of desire into an inferno that raged inside him, yet she'd felt nothing. She'd simply used him to make her snake-in-the-grass husband jealous. Granted, she'd never so much as hinted she might be as attracted to him as he was to her, but still…

Ben tossed back a healthy dose of scotch. It burned a path down his throat. He threw back another gulp and tried to ignore the clusters of curious onlookers, watching their every move.

He glanced over at Cressida. Her head still rested in her hands and she looked like she might be two seconds from losing it.

Ben moved to the entrance of the alcove to block the view of nosy gossips still trying to get a peek. Cressida definitely didn't need a crowd gawking at her like she was some two-headed Texas Longhorn.

He took another long pull of scotch and pasted on a polite smile. Gradually, the gawkers lost interest and went back to their socializing.

Ben snuck another peek over his shoulder. Cressida no longer had her head in her hands but she definitely looked shell-shocked. She needed another drink.

As a waiter passed, Ben swiped a glass of champagne from the tray and handed it to Cressida.

"Here you go," he said gently.

The corners of her lips turned up but the smile didn't come close to reaching her eyes. Without hesitation she tossed the flute back and gulped until she'd drained the glass dry.

He frowned. "Maybe you should slow down a little."

Her fit from the night she'd gotten served with divorce papers drifted back. She'd clearly been more than a little tipsy that evening and had wasted no time in unleashing a verbal assault on her mother. Given Cal's arrival tonight and her rapid consumption of beverages, he feared he might be about to witness act two of that play.

He chewed the corner of his mouth. Maybe he should confront Cal, man to man. That's what any self-respecting Texas gentleman would do.

Ben pushed off from the wall, relieved to have settled on a course of action. "I'll be right back."

Her head snapped up. "Don't leave me," she implored, gazing up at him with those huge green eyes. The kind of eyes a man could get lost in. "I can't face Cal alone," she pleaded as she grabbed a handful of his tuxedo jacket. "Please…"

It took everything he had to resist the urge to take her into his arms.

Cal Wentworth needed his head examined if he preferred that overblown brunette to Cressida. While the other woman oozed an undeniable sex appeal, she exuded a predatory air that turned Ben off. By contrast, Cressida radiated a soft vulnerability and innocent sex appeal she seemed completely unaware of—an appeal he needed to find a way to ignore before he did something he regretted. Like try to bring his endless Cressida fantasies to life.

Ben stepped back to put some distance between them because he felt dangerously close to caving in to his desires and he couldn't; he wouldn't let himself give in to them. Instead, he channeled his frustration directly at Cal Wentworth. He'd hunt down the scumbag, grab him by the collar and toss him out the door—Texas-style. His father had always told him that you shouldn't worry too much how you treat a man who doesn't know how to treat a lady. And he figured now was as good a time as any to put some action behind those words.

"Just making a quick trip to the men's room," he said, not feeling the least bit guilty about the fib. What Cressida didn't know wouldn't hurt her. "You just take it easy and I'll be right back."

He had no intention of going to the men's room and every intention of giving her pompous, unfeeling ass of a husband a piece of his mind. He'd almost certainly kiss the on-time bonus goodbye but some things were more important than money. Besides, he'd just won another big job so his entire future didn't rest solely on this gig any longer.

"Okay," she said. "I need more champagne."

"Why don't we wait until after dinner?" he suggested.

She definitely seemed tipsy and could use a little time to sober up. Given her state of mind, he knew she wouldn't feel like venturing from the alcove so as long as he was quick about it, everything should be fine.

Ben's thoughts shifted to Cal Wentworth as he strode purposefully into the sea of people milling about the ballroom. He unbuttoned his suit jacket and clenched his fists, mentally preparing for a fight.

He didn't plan to hit the guy but he had every intention of making Cal Wentworth feel as small as possible. A good old-fashioned public shaming in front of his cronies. That should straighten him up and send him slinking back to his fancy car like the low down dirty weasel he was.

Ben paused in the doorway and scanned the ballroom in search of the other man. The packed room made it impossible to spot him.

He pushed his way through the crowd, trying to see towards the front.

The lights flickered three times and then dimmed, drawing attention to the brightly-lit stage.

An attractive, though slightly plastic, bottle blonde stood center stage.

"Good evening," the woman purred. "I'm Trudy Farentino and on behalf of the Ladies Guild of Fort Lauderdale, I'd like to thank you for attending our annual White Ball fundraiser."

The crowd clapped politely.

"Please take this opportunity to find your tables as the silent auction and dinner are about to begin."

As the crowd dispersed and made their way toward their assigned tables, Ben developed second thoughts.

What exactly did he plan to do? Challenge Cal Wentworth to a dual in front of an auditorium full of people? Ask him to step outside for a little rumble?

Ben shook his head.

What had happened to him? He was letting his feelings for Cressida get in the way of good judgment. He didn't have a problem confronting Cal or even resigning from the reno job if need be, but decking a respected doctor in public or even verbally confronting him—while it might make him feel better to defend Cressida's honor—probably wasn't the best idea he'd ever had.

Ben spun on his heel and headed back to the alcove.

He'd just have to convince Cressida to leave. At least she'd had the courage to show up but given her husband's decision to bring his new mistress to the event, nothing good could possibly happen from here.

Ben rounded the corner into their little hiding area and stopped short.

Cressida was gone!

His head snapped around, searching the nearby area but the only sign she'd been there at all were the three—no, make that four—champagne flutes, which sat next to the empty scotch and martini glasses.

He frowned. Hopefully Cressida wasn't responsible for all those empty glasses. He chewed the inside of his mouth and whipped his head around, scanning the room in search of her.

Then a light bulb went off. The ladies room. Women always went to the ladies room in moments of crisis.

Ben strode in the direction of the lobby and once he got there, he glanced around.

There was no sign of her.

He leaned against a nearby wall, staking out the ladies room door and checking his watch every ten seconds as he told himself not to panic.

Cressida was fine. Right? Hopefully. But what if she wasn't? She hadn't seemed fine when he'd taken off on a testosterone-fueled whim, determined to defend her honor. What had he been thinking, leaving her alone like that?

Ben loitered outside for several minutes, feeling like a stalker. He even briefly considered poking his head in the ladies room— eyes shut, of course—and calling her name, but couldn't bring himself to do it as the action would violate every rule that governed his traditional Texas upbringing.

A woman approached.

Ben stepped forward and smiled, doing his best to turn on the charm. "Excuse me. I seem to have misplaced my date."

The woman scanned him head to toe, sizing him up.

"If you see Cressida Wentworth, can you tell her I'm out here waiting for her?"

"Cressida isn't in the ladies room," the woman said. "I just saw her in the ballroom making her way toward the stage. They're getting ready to kick off the silent auction and Cressida's in charge of that."

"Thank you," he said, relief surging through every fiber of his being.

He turned on his heel and headed for the ballroom. If she was sober enough to be onstage, she couldn't possibly be responsible for all those empty booze glasses. Granted, Cressida Wentworth could make her own decisions but as her escort, he felt responsible for her wellbeing.

As Ben entered the ballroom, a commotion drew his attention to the stage and his eyes bugged out as a very disheveled Cressida, gold hair ornament slightly askew and mascara smudged across one cheek, crept stealthily toward the unsuspecting blonde with the microphone. She had a menacing, determined expression on her face and looked about to pounce.

The audience started to buzz.

A few people pointed.

And time slowed down in that way it does when disaster is imminent. You see everything; each tiny movement in horrifying, larger-than-life, slow-motion detail as every cell in your body braces itself for the calamity to come.

He had to get to that stage. *Now!*

ᝈᝈ

Ben sprinted across the room, dodging and weaving through the tables at lightning speed, but he arrived at the base of the stairs just as Cressida reached around the blonde, grabbed hold of the microphone and snatched it out of Trudy's grasp.

He froze, gripped with indecision. Now what? Should he go up there and drag her offstage? Or would that make the situation worse?

Trudy Farentino's head jerked around and her eyes widened in shock.

"No!" Trudy grabbed the microphone and yanked it out of Cressida's hands.

"Give me that!" Cressida screeched.

The microphone tug of war devolved into what could only be described as a kicking, scratching, hair-pulling hissy fit. Every grunt, groan and unladylike curse amplified by the microphone they fought over.

The buzz of the crowd increased.

Several folks near the front pulled out their smartphones and started videotaping.

Society reporters crowded the stage, flash bulbs popping. But surprisingly, no one made a move to stop the action onstage.

Ben started up the steps at least half a dozen times but stopped himself. He kept thinking they'd come to their senses and stop and he figured Cressida would never forgive him if he dragged her offstage like a naughty child caught fighting over a ball at recess.

He glanced around in desperation. Didn't events like this have security personnel? Apparently not.

His gut twisted as he gaped at the action unfolding onstage. He should stop her but he didn't want to make matters worse and risk embarrassing her. Of course, she seemed to be doing a pretty good job of that on her own.

The two women circled each other like UFC fighters sizing up their opponent inside the octagon. Suddenly, Cressida made a surprise move, executing a flying tackle as she wrestled Trudy to the floor.

The crowd gasped.

Several tables openly laughed.

A contingent near the back chanted, "Go Cress! Go Cress!"

Cressida snatched the microphone from the woman's hands and then struggled to her feet. She held it up like a trophy, drawing loud cheers from the cluster of tables in the back that seemed firmly in Cressida's corner.

Then she tottered toward the podium, plunged a hand into the bodice of her gown and dug around in a very unladylike manner, finally pulling out a crumpled piece of paper which she carefully unfolded. Then she squinted and started reading, slurring and barely coherent.

"I want to shank everyone fur coming," Cressida said. "This

pash shicks…uh sixth…monsh have been…uh…gwatifying." She squinted and held the paper closer. "I—"

In an attempt to pick herself up off the stage, Trudy grabbed two handfuls of Cressida's skirt and pulled. The delicate fabric of Cressida's silk gown ripped, the pressure proving too much for her one-shouldered gown to handle and the thin strap popped. The bodice of Cressida's dress flopped down, exposing a generous amount of her strapless bra.

More camera bulbs flashed.

In the ensuing struggle, her Egyptian-inspired hair ornament fell over one eye.

Cressida reached up and shoved the accessory back into place which caused her hair to bulge out on one side.

"No!" the blonde shouted as she struggled to her feet.

Cressida whirled around and they grasped each other's shoulders, slapped and struggled as Trudy made a renewed play for the microphone.

Cressida appeared to get the upper hand again until a willowy brunette joined in from the other side and the three pushed and shoved while the crowd watched in fascinated horror. Just when it appeared the two women double teaming her would be victorious, Cressida balled up her left fist, reared her arm back and socked the brunette in the jaw.

The woman spun around and hit the deck.

More flashbulbs popped.

The blonde grabbed hold of Cressida's speech but proved no match for her strength. Cressida gave a final shove and sent the blonde—and her speech—flying across the stage.

Ben decided he couldn't wait another minute. Being dragged offstage by him would be far better for her reputation than continuing on with this cat fight. Or ill-advised speech.

He ran up the stairs and leaned forward, cupping a hand to his mouth as he called, "Cressida!"

She glanced over, frowned and shook her head. Then she

turned back to the crowd.

"Shorry bout that," Cressida slurred. "I…"

"Cressida Wentworth!" Cal stood at the back of the room, just inside the doors, oozing righteous indignation. "Get down from there! You're making a spectacle of yourself!"

Ben glowered at the weasel and clenched his fists, barely resisting the sudden urge to make good on his earlier plan to invite the cad outside. None of this would be happening if it weren't for him. But he'd deal with Cal Wentworth later. Right now, he had to help Cressida.

Her cackle echoed through the ballroom. "You're the spectable. You!" She jabbed an accusatory finger at her soon-to-be-ex and continued slurring, voice shaking as she mumbled, "Shleeping with my coushin."

Cal glanced around and at least had the grace to look slightly embarrassed as dozens of heads snapped in his direction. Graciella stood taller and lifted her chin, seeming to revel in the attention.

"Cressida!" Ben called more urgently.

She either didn't hear him or ignored him as she turned to the brunette, sitting off to the side and rubbing her jaw.

"And you!" She pointed at Naomi Gilligan. "Pretending you're sho much better than the resht of ush when we all know your husband runs around with trannys whenever you're away on your *shopping trips*." She made air quotes. "Which we all know ish really code for meeting your geriatric lover down in Miami."

The crowd gasped as the brunette gaped at Cressida, eyes rounded in shock and disbelief.

"And you!" Cressida marched over to Trudy Farentino, who cowered, putting her arms up in front of her face. "Pretending you don't notice that your husband has shlept with half the *ladies* here."

At least two dozen women glanced nervously at their escorts and then down at the floor.

Ben spun into action. This had gone too far. Fort Lauderdale society might never be the same.

He strode across the stage and tried to pry the microphone from Cressida's fingers but she held on for dear life.

"Enough," he said firmly, gazing deeply into eyes that appeared to be two round pools of pain and heartbreak.

"But...." She gazed into Ben's eyes.

He cupped a hand over the mic. "Enough," he repeated gently.

She nodded and handed the mic to Ben, who placed it on the podium. Then he wrapped an arm around her waist to steady her as they turned toward the stairs.

"It's okay, Cress," he whispered, pulling her closer than was necessary. "It's going to be okay."

Ben glanced over his shoulder. The blonde had managed to stand and make herself somewhat presentable.

"Sorry about that," Trudy Farentino said, laughing nervously. "Oh my goodness..." She patted her hair back into place. "Oh well. What do you expect from someone who hails from Las Vegas?"

A ripple of polite laughter swept the crowded ballroom.

Cressida stopped in her tracks.

Sensing trouble, Ben tried to tighten his grip but she wriggled out of his grasp, spun around and strode back to the podium.

As soon as Trudy spotted her, she jumped back, eyes wide. She cowered, placing her hands in front of her face, most likely to protect herself from Cressida's deadly left hook.

But Cressida didn't attack, at least not physically. Instead, she leaned toward the microphone and gazed into the other woman's eyes, sounding surprisingly lucid as she said, "Oh and your *son* is sleeping with *my mother*." The last two words echoed across the auditorium.

Trudy gasped and the color drained from her face as her jaw dropped.

The crowd erupted into a cacophony of cat calls.

In the span of a few short minutes, Cressida had unleashed the juiciest gossip to hit South Florida in decades. Maybe ever.

Then she stuck her dainty little chin in the air, looped her arm through Ben's and slurred, "Lesh go."

Ben tried to shield her from the flash bulbs and video cameras on the way out. This would undoubtedly be a night no one in Fort Lauderdale society would forget anytime soon. But he felt certain that, come sunrise; Cressida would wish that she could.

Chapter Sixteen

Cressida drifted in and out of the pleasant haze of half sleep, not ready to awaken but unable to ignore the nibbling sensation at her toes.

She pulled her foot away and turned over, nestling further into the pillows.

Nibbling changed to licking.

She kicked her foot, trying to shake the sensation to no avail. She came further awake, senses zeroing in on the wetness.

Licking.

Toes.

Her eyes popped open. She blinked several times in quick succession and then frowned in confusion at the unfamiliar ceiling fan whirring overhead.

Where the hell was she?

She rose up on her elbows, vision blurred from the dried contact lenses stuck to her eyeballs. Alarm bells sounded as she came fully awake, keenly aware of the slick moisture around her toes. What the hell was licking her feet?!

Cressida sat bolt upright and gaped in horror at the enormous black animal seated at the foot of the bed, head cocked to the side and gazing up at her with a mixture of longing and curiosity.

The dog licked his chops.

She swallowed hard and froze, not daring to move an inch.

Terror squeezed the air from her lungs as her mind raced past disturbing, yet far more trivial matters such as figuring out where the hell she was and instead focused squarely on finding a way to avoid becoming doggie breakfast.

Her desperate gaze darted to the door, the window, the bathroom. She'd never make it. She was trapped.

In a last ditch effort for survival, Cressida squeezed her eyes shut and let loose a shrill, blood-curdling scream worthy of a Hitchcock heroine—a cry which emanated from the depths of her soul.

She'd been terrified of large dogs since the age of seven when Billy Dempster's rescued greyhound bit her pinky finger while gobbling down her math homework along with a large chunk of her favorite Scooby Doo pencil.

The beast sprang to its feet, ears drawn together as it emitted a series of ferocious and thunderous barks. Without warning, all hundred plus pounds of girl-eating German Shepherd launched itself onto the bed, straddling her as if she were some sort of prize.

Cressida covered her face with her arms and shrieked louder, certain she was two seconds from death.

The dog barked louder and then threw its head back and howled, seemingly determined to outdo her.

A long gooey strand of dog saliva dripped onto her face.

Eww!

Cressida cowered further.

Ben burst through the door and thundered, "Max! Down!"

The barking ceased, the instantaneous silence almost deafening as the dog collapsed obediently into a lying position. On top of her.

Cressida's screams died away as the enormous semi-smelly dog made itself at home on her torso. To seal the deal, the beast leaned forward and licked her cheek.

Double eww!

She scrunched her face and barely managed to choke, "Can't. Breathe."

Ben snapped his fingers and pointed at his feet. The dog sprang from the bed and sat at Ben's feet, panting and gazing up at him expectantly.

"I see you've met Max," he said, scratching the animal's extremely large head. He appeared to be fighting back a laugh as he studied what had to be a comically horrified expression on her face. "Let me guess. You're afraid of dogs."

"He licked my toes." Cressida glared at the animal with a mixture of fear and accusation as she wiped the slimy drool from her cheek.

"He loves having guests." He squatted down and scratched Max behind the ears. "He's gentle as can be. Only plays with the Chihuahuas at doggie day care. Isn't that right boy?" He scratched Max's face as the dog panted and gazed up at Ben adoringly. Ben grinned at Cressida. "He was trying to make friends."

Cressida didn't bother to acknowledge the comment as she struggled to sit up, keeping the covers pulled tight. She gazed about the room. "What am I doing here? How come I'm not home…in my own bed?"

Ben sat on the arm of a nearby chair and raised his brows. "You don't remember?"

She glowered and bit back a retort. If she could remember, she wouldn't have asked the question. The truth was she couldn't form a coherent thought when her head felt like a legion of jack hammers were drilling from the inside out.

She rubbed her temples. "Can you bring me one of your t-shirts or something? And maybe an aspirin?"

Or six. Her head felt like it was splitting open—whether from the screaming and commotion or the open bar the night before, she didn't know and didn't much care.

Ben rooted around in a drawer and pulled out a t-shirt and sweat pants. He tossed them on the bed and then disappeared into the hall.

As soon as he'd left, Cressida threw off the covers and pulled on the t-shirt and sweats. Ben's clothing swam on her five foot six inch frame but at least her bra and panties were covered. She didn't remember getting undressed. Or whether Ben had slept beside her. Or, pretty much anything after spotting Cal and Graciella at the ball last night.

She must look hideous. Unlike some women, Cressida didn't roll out of bed looking fabulous. It took real work. Her skin looked dull and pasty without makeup and her hair, well, there was no describing the mess in the morning.

Knowing he'd be back any minute, she frantically fluffed and scrunched her hair as Costa had taught her and then slapped her cheeks to bring out some color. She didn't bother to look in the mirror, confident the sight would only upset her further.

Ben returned, carrying a tray which held aspirin, a bottle of water, a mug of steaming coffee and some dry toast. The morning paper was tucked under his arm.

He placed the tray on the bed. "I thought you might need caffeine and maybe something to nibble on."

She mumbled a thank you as she shook out two aspirin. She popped them in her mouth and chased them down with two gulps of water as she surreptitiously checked him out. Whether he wore a tux or a pair of raggedy ole sweatpants, Ben Carrington was a total dreamboat.

Cressida leaned back against the headboard and blew on her coffee as he made himself comfortable in a nearby chair.

He stretched out his legs and crossed them at the ankle as he placed the newspaper on his lap.

Max settled at Ben's feet with an enormous sigh, chin resting on massive paws as the dog gazed up at her with interest.

"To answer your earlier question, you're here because you asked me not to bring you home."

She cocked her head to the side. "That doesn't make any sense. Why would I do that?"

He smirked. "You really don't remember, do you?"

Her stomach tightened as a sense of foreboding descended. Hazy images drifted back but didn't come into focus.

"No." She frowned and bit her lip, certain she didn't want the detail but equally sure she needed to know. She braced herself for the worst. "What happened?"

Ben gazed at her for a long moment, then shrugged and tossed the newspaper onto her lap.

The daily rag landed face up, revealing an enormous full-color front page photo. Of her.

Cressida's eyes bugged out and she nearly dropped the mug. A good portion of coffee splashed onto her leg.

"Ouch!" She brushed the coffee away and placed the mug on the nightstand as she stared at the dreadful photo in disbelief. She lifted the paper and drew it closer, mouth gaping as she scrutinized every horrifying detail of the image.

Her Egyptian-inspired head ornament dangled precariously off to one side and the ripped bodice of her gown revealed an indecent glimpse of strapless bra as she wrestled Trudy Farentino to the ground.

Dear. God.

Cressida dropped the paper and covered her face with her hands as foggy images from the night before came into sharp focus. Some of them made the unflattering front page photo look positively bland.

She collapsed against the headboard and moaned as if her life was coming to an end. And in pretty much every way that mattered, it had.

It seemed funny now that she'd spent the past few weeks obsessing over the potential impact of Roxie's visit and Cal's affair on her social standing. She needn't have worried. As it happened, she'd managed to do a pretty fine job of ruining her reputation all on her own. And it had only taken one evening. Well, one evening and one horrifying photo.

Cressida turned to Ben, eyes shooting accusation and her tone dripping icicles as she said, "And where were you when all this was taking place? Why didn't you stop me?"

Ben held up two hands. "Hey, you disappeared on me. By the time I found you, it was too late. You were onstage. I didn't want to make the situation worse by dragging you off in front of the crowd. I had to wait for the right time."

"What could be worse than this?!" she cried, waving the newspaper as hysteria took a firm hold. "So clearly you decided the right time to intervene would be *after* the onstage WWF match?!"

"How was I supposed to know what you were planning to do? He sounded more than a little defensive. "I didn't want to embarrass you."

She scoffed. "Oh and a grown woman having a knock down drag out cat fight onstage isn't embarrassing."

His brows shot up. "You're blaming *me* for your behavior?"

Their eyes locked each ready to do battle.

Cressida broke eye contact first, gazing down at the newspaper. She expelled a long sigh and flipped the daily over to hide the horrifying image because she couldn't stand to look at it for another moment.

"No," she said. "You're right. It's my fault." She closed her eyes and groaned. "People must think I've lost my mind." She picked up her coffee and took a sip. "Maybe I have. I *must* have." There could be no other possible explanation.

She'd spent her entire adult life avoiding the limelight, fearful of making a spectacle of herself, but clearly she'd learned nothing. Fast forward twenty-three years and on the big night for which she'd prepared six long months; she'd played a starring role in the melt down to end all melt downs. She'd picked the worst possible and most public moment of her private and repressed little life in which to implode.

"This seems like an appropriate time to give you this." Ben reached into his jeans pocket and extracted her cell phone. He pressed the button on top. "This thing has buzzed nonstop since the crack of dawn. You have"—he squinted at the display—"forty-two missed calls."

She snatched the phone from his hands and scrolled through the call log. It was a mixed bag. Some from Roxie. Some from her home number, most likely also Roxie. Some from Cal. Shay. Lucinda. And a few other Ladies Guild members she classified as borderline friendlies.

"Don't check YouTube," he cautioned. "Last I saw, your video had twenty thousand views."

She closed her eyes and swallowed hard. "Someone uploaded a video onto YouTube?!"

He nodded.

She groaned. "I'll never be able to show my face in public again." She gazed up at Ben, panic building inside. "I can't go home."

She wasn't ready to face the humiliation. Not yet. She needed to go somewhere to regroup. To figure out how to fix the colossal mess she'd made of her life.

"Where can I go? What should I do?" Her eyes pleaded with Ben. "Help me. *Please.*"

⬥

Cressida let her head drop back as the sunlight played over her face and chest. She kicked her feet in the lake and smiled as fine droplets of water flew about, glistening like diamonds in the afternoon sun.

Max emitted a half-interested grunt as water rained down on his furry face.

For some reason, despite the fact that she showed him no attention and went out of her way to avoid him, the enormous German Shepherd never left her side.

She glanced over at the dog and found him staring at her, a longing expression in his eyes.

"You know, I'm beginning to believe you wouldn't hurt a fly." Cressida reached over and tentatively patted his head, still uneasy with her newfound friend. "I spent ten years with a man who didn't pay me this much attention."

Max sighed contentedly and closed his eyes.

"You're good company. I could get used to having you around."

Footsteps sounded on the wood dock.

Max raised his head, instantly at full alert. Seeing Ben, he hopped up and trotted over to greet him.

Cressida raised a brow as she eyed the fishing poles in Ben's hand. "I thought you were laying ceramic tile."

"I finished." Ben smiled. "And I'm starving. Time to catch some dinner. There's great bass fishing around here."

"I'm not much of a fisher…person." Cressida fixated on the poles with a healthy dose of apprehension. The one and only time she'd tried, she'd hooked her college boyfriend in the stomach. "I prefer my fish to come from little square-shaped, plastic wrapped containers from Whole Foods."

"Oh no…there's nothing like fresh fish," Ben said. "Trust me. You'll love it." He squatted and placed the poles in the wood canoe tied to the end of the dock.

He extended a hand to Cressida. She grasped it and he pulled her up.

She slipped her bare feet into the flip flops she'd purchased at Walmart the day before, along with the denim cut-offs and tank top she wore and the paperback self-help tome, *The Power is Within You*, from Louis Hay.

Cressida was halfway through the book and loving it but wasn't opposed to taking a break. So she tossed it onto the wood bench seat and then stepped carefully into the boat, grasping the sides as it swayed violently back and forth.

She shot a nervous glance over her shoulder.

"It's okay," Ben said. "Just move slowly and stay in the middle."

An average swimmer at best, Cressida wasn't too comfortable in water more than four feet deep. She sat quickly and gripped the sides of the canoe for dear life.

Max scrambled in next and settled at her feet.

Ben followed, placing the poles and cooler behind his seat. Then he reached out and untied the boat.

She snuck a peak while his back was turned, admiring the ripple of his tanned, and muscular forearms as he pushed off from the dock. But as soon as he turned and took his seat, she averted her gaze and pretended to be preoccupied with Max.

They drifted several feet as he positioned the wooden oars and then grasped them. She peeked at him below her lashes. His arms flexed, thick ropy muscles on full display as he deftly paddled and steered the boat toward the center of the lake.

The oars sliced the glassy surface, causing ripples that fanned out from the boat as they glided smoothly along.

"It's so beautiful here," Cressida sighed as she gazed at the shoreline. "I haven't seen another soul since we left Walmart yesterday. This place is like your own private little oasis."

"I know what you mean." Ben's brown eyes danced as they swept the shoreline. "I love it here. We bought the lake house right before the divorce. Originally I intended to renovate it so we could enjoy it for weekend getaways. After all, it's just a stone's throw from Disney." He paused and grimaced, then shook his head. "But after the divorce, I didn't have the money to fund the improvements so it just sat here. I started working on it a few months ago and it's almost ready to put on the market." He looked around, regret etched deeply into his features. "I'll miss it though."

She tilted her head and leaned back, making herself comfortable. "Why don't you keep it?"

He shrugged. "The kids are getting older and for whatever reason, it's not as fun to come up here alone. After all, I live alone now except for the few days each week that I have the kids. Doesn't make sense to drive two and a half hours just for more alone time." He reached for the poles and changed the subject, handing her one of the rods. "Ever been bass fishing?"

She held the pole tentatively between her thumb and forefinger, scrunching her nose with distaste. "When you grow up without a father and with a mother like Roxie, there's not a whole lot of bass fishing going on."

"Good point." Ben chuckled as he reared back and cast the line. It shot a good distance from the boat in a long smooth stream, landing gently in the water with a delicate plop. He put the rod in the holder and then glanced over at Cressida. "Want me to show you how? These are the kid's spin casting poles, so they're super easy to operate."

She shook her head and leaned the pole against the edge of the boat. "That's okay. I'll just watch."

Ben studied her intently for several long moments. His eyes seemed to peer right into her soul.

She squirmed under his scrutiny. "What? I like to watch."

Despite his challenging gaze, his voice sounded gentle as he said, "I think you've been sitting on the sidelines long enough. Don't you?"

Chapter Seventeen

Cressida bristled, suddenly feeling defensive until his face broke into that heart-stopping grin. Her wariness dissolved, replaced by a staccato heartbeat and an overwhelming desire to lean over and kiss that little dimple in his cheek.

She swallowed hard and gazed out at the shoreline.

"Life is happening right now, Cressida. Get out there and live it."

Her gaze drifted back to his as if drawn by some magnetic force.

His brows lifted as he held the pole out, his eyes issuing a silent challenge as he shook the pole back and forth teasingly.

"Come on," he coaxed. "If you don't like it, then you can watch."

That adventurous spirit—a flame that had dimmed too long ago to accurately pinpoint—reignited inside.

Cressida grasped the pole with something approaching determination, though she lacked even the slightest bit of enthusiasm for the pastime.

But she recognized Ben's challenge for what it was. She'd spent the better part of her adult life on the sidelines. Watching. Supporting. Waiting. Waiting for what? Now that she thought about it, she didn't have a clue but she knew one thing for certain. The time had come to dive back in. To start living. To be the leading lady in her own life instead of a walk-on cast member with a bit part.

"Okay," she said. "I'll give it a try but I'm warning you, the last time I hooked my fishing partner in the stomach. He didn't speak to me for a week."

Ben made a goofy face and wrapped his arms around his stomach.

"Very funny," she said as she placed her thumb on the button.

She reared her arm back and attempted to throw the line as Ben had done but she didn't have anywhere near his level of success. Her line projected just a few inches from the boat and then dropped straight into the water with a hollow kerplunk.

Her lips turned downward. "I suck."

"Nah…it just takes some practice." Ben leaned over and reached for her pole. "May I?"

"Be my guest." She was all too happy to hand over her rod.

He reeled in the line and went through the casting demonstration twice. Slowly.

"Keep your thumb on the button longer. See?" He demonstrated again. "It's actually pretty easy. A lot easier than the more advanced rods like my dad used to use." He threw the line again and it landed perfectly. "Wait longer before taking your finger off the button. That gives the line time to fully cast. You let go too soon, that's all." He reeled it in again and then handed her the pole. "Now you try."

Their fingers brushed as she took the rod back, causing little currents of energy to sizzle through her body. She studiously avoided his gaze and instead concentrated on mimicking his movements.

Her second attempt went better than the first. Though still not great, she deemed the effort good enough and let the line drift five feet from the boat, eyeing the feathery lure expectantly and sitting at attention, anxious for the action to start.

"Now what?"

Ben leaned back and rested against the side of the boat. "Now we wait." He reached for the cooler, opened it and asked. "I have diet soda? Water?" He pulled out a beer for himself.

"I'll have one of those." She smiled.

He popped the top and handed her the cold can. She could feel his eyes on her as she sipped the cold beverage.

"I don't mean to pry but I couldn't help overhearing your conversation with your friend last week. I forgot all about it until this morning but I was wondering. Are you…?" He gazed at her intently.

"I wondered if you heard that. No. I'm not pregnant," she said, pausing for a moment before she continued. "About three years ago, after our first failed IVF attempt, we decided to pursue adoption. Domestic adoption can take a very long time. As luck would have it, now that we've split, we've been selected by a teenage mother." She rolled her eyes and shook her head. "Murphy's Law, I guess. I got the call two weeks ago, just a few days after Cal left."

"Wow." He leaned forward, elbows on his knees. "So, given everything going on…what are you going to do?"

"I'm going to change the paperwork and pursue the adoption on my own," Cressida said, straightening her back in determination. "I'm just waiting for my divorce attorney to refer me to an adoption attorney." She sipped her beer. "Man, there's something wrong with that sentence, huh? Divorce attorney…adoption attorney." She shook her head ruefully.

He grinned. "It's a little non-traditional. I'll give you that. Most people going through a divorce are getting referrals for a good therapist. An adoption attorney is certainly a unique twist."

"It's definitely a long shot. There's not much time to alter the documents and I don't exactly look like a good candidate on paper, so I might go straight to the reject pile. But I have to try."

"Who says you don't look like a good candidate? I think you'd make a great mother," he said.

"Thanks." She smiled and then shook her head. "For starters, I have no job, no income, no insurance and soon, thanks to you"—

she shot him a teasing look—"I'll have no home. If I want to make this work, I'll have to get my butt in gear. And fast." She shrugged. "But I'll figure it out."

"I have no doubt," he said. "Actually, while I'm sure it's been challenging, the adversity is actually great parental training. While it's the most rewarding thing you'll ever do, parenting is also the most difficult."

Cressida nodded. "I'm ready," she said. "Even doing it on my own doesn't feel that scary any more. It just feels…right."

He grinned.

Her pole bent into a u-shape as something tugged hard on the line.

"Help!" She gripped the rod tightly and yanked.

"You got one!" Ben reached over and grasped her pole for reinforcement and then tugged, hard. "Now, reel it in."

Cressida let Ben hold the pole and pull while she reeled.

"That's it." Ben encouraged her, tugging harder.

The fish broke water, wriggling and thrashing. "You got it!" He leaned over and brought the flopping fish closer.

She scrunched her face and moved away as the fish swung close.

Ben grasped the fish and disengaged the hook, laying him on the floor of the boat where he thrashed and gasped.

"Let's put him back," she said. "He's got more life to live."

Ben's head whipped around. "What? No…this guy is dinner! We just need to catch one of his friends."

Cressida shook her head. "No," she said softly. "Let's set him free so he can get on with his life."

Ben frowned and looked about to protest but as he studied her face his frown morphed into a lop-sided grin. "Let me guess. As soon as we get back to shore, we're headed to Walmart for some of those little plastic square-shaped containers. Am I right?"

She smiled up at him and nodded. "Do you mind?"

He shook his head and leaned over the side, placing the fish back in the water and Cressida's smile broadened as the largemouth bass swam away, free and healthy and alive.

࿇

Cressida strolled into the house just before eight o'clock on Monday morning, strappy sandals and semi-crushed head ornament dangling from a fingertip and her ripped evening gown draped over an arm.

She paused in the kitchen doorway, bracing herself for the inevitable battle to come. The sheer volume of calls and texts over the past two days hinted at her mother's state of mind.

Roxie sat at the island, elbows resting on the granite countertop and reading glasses perched on the tip of her nose as her fingers swiped at the screen of her tablet computer.

Costa peered intently over her shoulder.

Cressida squared her shoulders and strolled into the kitchen, feigning nonchalance.

Roxie's head jerked up and her expression instantly morphed from relief into a hardened mask of disapproval.

Her eyes glistened like fiery emeralds as she set the device on the counter with a decisive clank and shot to her feet, hands on hips and peering over the top of her tortoiseshell readers.

"And just where have *you* been, young lady?"

Cressida took her time in responding, carefully arranging her tattered evening gown over the back of a chair. She set the hair ornament on top of the gown and let her sandals drop to the floor.

"You sound just like Nana did when I was sixteen," she said breezily, strolling over to the cabinets and reaching inside. She pulled out a mug and poured herself some coffee as she fought back the wave of giggles fighting for release.

She peeked over at Roxie who looked about to spontaneously combust. Funny how just a few weeks before, the roles had been reversed as her mother nonchalantly strolled in after her evening of seduction with Micah.

The irony wasn't lost on Cressida. Roxie had never embraced the traditional motherhood role but judging from the fire shooting out of her eyes, she'd learned a lot from Nana over the years. Well, this weekend Cressida had learned a few things as well and chief among them was the surprising revelation that she very much enjoyed assuming the carefree, do as you please role for a change. It was easier than being the responsible one and a whole lot more fun.

She splashed cream into her coffee and stirred, not bothering to turn around as she said, "If you must know, I spent the weekend with Ben."

The silence grew thick and heavy as Roxie's simmering angst became a tangible thing.

Cressida could literally feel her mother's laser hot glare boring holes into the back of her head and she couldn't help but feel amused.

She turned and met Roxie's gaze, lifting a defiant brow. "I see you finally took my advice and started wearing readers. Good for you." She blew on her coffee and took a sip. "Your eyes will thank you for it."

Roxie folded her arms across her chest. "Don't try to change the subject, young lady."

She reached behind her, snatched the newspaper from the counter and flung it down in front of Cressida with a flourish. She tapped the front page photo with a frenzy that made clear her frantic state of mind.

"First you make a complete spectacle of yourself in front of your friends and neighbors." Roxie paused for dramatic effect. "This wouldn't bother me in the least but it's completely out of character for you."

Costa nodded, his lips compressed as he mirrored Roxie's disapproval.

"Then you just up and disappear." Roxie spread her arms wide.

"You just vanish! Without so much as punching in a text message."

"Naughty naughty girl." Costa shook his head, making a tsk tsk sound as he eyed her with a reproachful glare. He thrust his hand toward her and waggled his fingers. "Earrings please. Those little luvs were on loan. I expect a couple of Guido's to show up at any moment, threatening to break a kneecap."

"Check the little side pocket in my clutch." Cressida blew on her coffee, refusing to jump at the bait. She shifted her gaze to Roxie. "I decided to follow your lead. You know, the ole do-whatever-makes-you-happy-and-screw-what-anyone-else-thinks routine."

"You didn't think I'd be *worried?*" Roxie's voice cracked on the last word. "The press camped out on the front lawn for *two days.* Two days!!" Roxie paced the floor. "Every time the phone rang, I feared it would be the cops telling me they'd found you at the bottom of a swamp, swimming with the fishes." She paused and waved her arms wildly, clearly working herself into a frenzy. "The mob is big down here, you know. Piss off their wives and they'll take you out!"

"Don't be ridiculous." Cressida blew on her coffee. "This isn't an episode of the Sopranos and we're not in Vegas. The husbands in question are plastic surgeons in practice with Cal."

"Precisely. And Lord only knows the seedy connections those snobby hacks might've cultivated," Roxie said. "I'm beginning to wonder about Ben, too."

Cressida rolled her eyes. "I thought Ben could do no wrong. What could he possibly have done to irritate you?"

"He didn't call, for starters. I left at least three dozen messages." Roxie shook her head, lips pressed into a thin, hard line. "I'm very disappointed in him."

"Ben is not in charge of me. Don't hold him responsible for my choices."

"Well it's a good thing, considering he let you make an absolute fool of yourself. I mean, where was *he* while all this was going on?" She picked up the paper and waved it.

"I don't know." Cressida had wondered that herself. "He said he was waiting for the right time to intervene."

Roxie pursed her lips as she gazed at Cressida.

Despite her endless lectures over the years around not being so uptight and going with the flow, Roxie clearly didn't favor this new and improved Cressida. Well, too bad. She was rather enjoying her new role.

"Shay is beside herself," Roxie continued. "And to cap it all off, your loser of an ex-husband actually had the nerve to stop by." Roxie's face split into a wicked grin. "Of course, he wasn't expecting to see *me*."

Costa snickered. "Rox chased him down the driveway whacking him with your Swiffer." He pulled his mobile phone from his pocket. "I got a few pictures. Wanna see?" He thrust the smart phone at Cressida.

"I'll pass," Cressida sniffed as she blew on her coffee.

Roxie snatched the phone and started flipping through. "Not bad," she said. "These babies are going up on Instagram."

She shoved Costa's phone into her pocket and looked about to speak when Shay burst through the back door.

"Cressida. Ann. *Wentworth!*" Shay's bellow could've blasted holes in the hurricane proof windows. "What the *hell* has gotten into you?"

Cressida groaned. "Not you too. How did you even know I was home? Did you have the house staked out?"

"I texted her." Costa picked up the iPad and refreshed the screen. "Hey, check it out. Your fight video is up to two hundred and fifty thousand likes! And someone just uploaded a second version set to Pat Benatar's *Hit Me With Your Best Shot*."

"Ooo, let me see!" Roxie took the device.

Cressida glowered at them and snatched the tablet from Roxie's grasp.

"Hey! Give me that. I want to comment." Costa tugged the device out of her hand and started punching keys.

Shay stormed across the room. "You drank didn't you?" She stood in front of Cressida, arms crossed and tapping a foot. "Didn't you?! Did you not hear my warning?"

"I heard you," Costa said, not bothering to look up from his video viewing.

"Me too," said Roxie.

Cressida shrugged. "You would've drank too had the roles been reversed."

"Alcohol and Xanax do not mix," Shay announced.

"The Xanax!" Cressida smacked her palm on her forehead. "Of course! "That explains everything."

She'd totally forgotten about taking the little pill and had begun to think she'd experienced a mild nervous breakdown.

"I told you twice not to drink," Shay insisted. "*Twice.*"

"So shoot me," Cressida said. "Try having Jerry show up at a society event with his Brazilian mistress two seconds after you find out he's having an affair." Cressida arched a brow. "As I recall, you spent a week locked away in a dark bedroom when you learned of his secret marriage and by then, you'd already been separated a year. Try confronting the new couple in public in front of all your frenemies. Then we'll talk about the wisdom of abstaining from alcohol."

Shay eyes grew as round as silver dollars. "Cal and Gracie showed up at the ball?"

"Right before I did the onstage takedown on Trudy," Cressida said. "And called out Naomi Gilligan's husband for his cross dressing fetish which happened just before I revealed that Trudy's husband had slept with half the ladies in attendance. Oh, and I capped off the evening by announcing that Roxie is sleeping with Trudy's son. Not that I remember any of that." Cressida grimaced. "Ben told me."

"Oh my Lord." Shay reached for the paper and sank into a

nearby chair as she scoured the article for juicy details.

"Sounds like you made quite an impact, dear," Roxie said, looking about to burst with pride. "The apple doesn't fall too far from the Reynolds' tree."

"No doubt," said Costa. "I'd say the tapping definitely cured your stage fright."

"Tapping didn't do diddly poo," Cressida said. "Shay drugged me."

"Hey, don't blame me—" Shay protested.

The phone rang.

Roxie glanced at the Caller ID and groaned. "It's that Priscilla Davies person again. Will she ever give it a rest?"

Cressida's stomach lurched and she felt the color drain from her face.

Priscilla Davies. Holy crap.

She hadn't even stopped to consider whether the adoption agency had seen her press coverage. She knew all too well the diligent care state agencies took in performing background checks on prospective parents. And Cressida was all for it. Obviously you had to protect the children. But despite her spotless criminal background and blemish free credit, it seemed unlikely a judge would be willing to grant custody of a baby to a single, unemployed woman who'd just engaged in an onstage public wrestling match with two of the pillars of Fort Lauderdale society.

Cressida dropped into a nearby chair as cold tentacles of fear slithered around her, squeezing the air from her lungs. She barely managed to choke out, "What do you mean…*again*?"

The ringing continued. Roxie reached for the phone.

"Don't answer it!" Cressida dove for the phone, swatting Roxie's hand away from the receiver as she repeated in a voice at least three decibels higher. "What do you mean…AGAIN?!"

"That woman is a pushy petunia," Roxie said. "She's called so many times in the past two days I'm convinced she's a stalker. And when I asked what the call was in regards to, she claimed it to be a *confidential matter,*" Roxie said using air quotes. "Since she got so testy with me, I informed her in just as snooty a tone that if you deemed the matter important, you'd call her back. And I asked her not to phone again." Roxie glanced at Costa and scrunched up her nose. "I hate pushy people."

"The worst," Costa said.

Cressida moaned and sank into a nearby chair.

Roxie frowned. "What's wrong, dear? Your face looks as white as Nana's legs." Roxie's brows knit together. "Who is this Priscilla person?" She glanced over at Costa and Shay. "Is she someone important?"

"You might say that." Cressida closed her eyes and pinched the bridge of her nose as she tried to compose herself. Her temples pounded. "She's the director of Children's Hope adoption agency."

Shay beamed and announced, "Cressida's adopting a little girl!"

"Might be," Cressida said. "*Might be* adopting a little girl." Though the likelihood seemed incredibly farfetched at this point. At best, it had been a long shot. Given her stage performance last Friday night, the notion had just veered decidedly toward the impossible.

Roxie's expression morphed from surprise to concern to unadulterated glee.

"How wonderful!" She thrust her arms outward and turned to Costa with a huge grin. "You're going to be an uncle!"

"Glamma!" Costa grabbed Roxie's hands as they gleefully hopped up and down.

"Not so fast." Cressida stood. "Nothing is guaranteed. Nothing at all. Especially after this mess." She smacked the paper on the countertop and glared at Shay. "If you hadn't drugged me, none of this would've happened."

Shay sniffed. "If I hadn't *offered* you that little blue pill, you'd still be hiding in your bedroom too afraid to face any of those horrible women. Or even worse, you would've found a way to drag

Doner to the ball with you which could've turned out even worse than your onstage wrestling match." She eyed Cressida sternly. "I gave you something to take the edge off and I warned you not to drink." She glanced over at Roxie. "By the way, has anyone seen Doner?"

"Not since we dumped him on his living room sofa Friday night," Costa said.

"Well, the important thing is that you seem to have conquered your stage fright," Roxie said.

"No that's *not* the important thing," Cressida said. "The important thing is making this adoption work. If I don't get my butt in gear and get a job, a place to live and some medical insurance—and toot sweet, by the way—then I have no hope of qualifying for this child. She's due in just four months." Cressida shook her head. "Of course that's almost secondary now because if Priscilla Davies and her background checking firm learn of my public meltdown—which I have no doubt they will since it's splashed all over the front page—then I'm toast."

Chapter Eighteen

"Have you started looking for a job?" Shay asked.

"With your degree, finding a job will be a cake walk." Roxie waved a hand dismissively. "Just decide what you want to do and take your pick."

"It's not a cake walk when you haven't done anything but volunteer for the past ten years," Cressida said. "I've never even used my teaching degree. And have you watched the news recently? The unemployment rate is still sky high. Extremely qualified people aren't finding jobs these days and even I couldn't reasonably categorize myself as extremely qualified."

Her shoulders slumped as the reality of her situation sank in.

"*Everyone* is not my Cressie," Roxie said, cupping Cressida's chin as her glittering eyes issued a challenge. "You can do anything you put your pretty little mind to."

She appreciated her mother's confidence but Roxie knew nothing of practical matters like job searching.

"This week my entire focus has to be on the work thing. I don't really even care what I do—at least not right now. I'll take whatever scrummy little job I can land so I at least have an income to declare on the adoption paperwork. I'll figure out the rest down the road."

"I can give you some hours at the boutique," Shay said. "It wouldn't be enough to live on but it's something."

"My daughter is not taking a scrummy little job, as you call it." Roxie pursed her lips and tapped her reading glasses on the counter as the wheels started turning. After a long pause, she said, "My production company could use some help with media relations."

A spark of excitement lit inside but Cressida tried to keep her eagerness in check. She cocked her head to the side. "But I don't know anything about getting media coverage."

Roxie's lips twitched. "All evidence to the contrary." She picked up the newspaper and waved it. "I mean, lookie here! You managed to get yourself on the front page and you weren't even trying."

Costa snickered and Shay looked to be fighting back a shout of laughter.

Cressida glared at them. "Hilarious."

"Oh, qualified shmalified," Roxie said, waving a dismissive hand. "Costa's been filling in but he really doesn't have the time. I just need someone to keep my social media sites updated, schedule interviews and respond to reporters with the occasional 'no comment'.

"Unless of course it's something juicy and in that case, I always confirm it, whether true or not," Costa said.

Cressida shook her head slowly as she considered the practical realities of taking on such a position. She wasn't sure she could tolerate her mother's outrageousness on a daily basis, let alone deal with her ever present sidekick. It was hard enough coping with them in two week increments. To be personally in charge of managing Roxie's over-the-top show-biz image, well, the whole idea seemed...ridiculous.

"I don't know," Cressida said, brows knit together. "I'm not sure I'd know how to do it." And she wasn't entirely sure she wanted to.

"For heaven's sake," Roxie said, her tone veering toward exasperation. "It's not rocket science and I'm not a politician or a corporate executive. I'm an entertainer with a big show and a pretty good fan base. And from my perspective, almost any coverage is good coverage, so how hard could the job possibly be?"

A tentative smile touched Cressida's lips. "I guess I could do it."

If she could work for Roxie, even if only for a little while, it would certainly get her past the biggest hurdle in the adoption process. At least she could support herself and a child. And that would definitely outweigh whatever ridiculousness she might be forced to put up with in the process.

Roxie wrapped her arms around Cressida. "I know you could. We'll need to figure out medical coverage but we'll get online this afternoon."

"And I can help you look for a place this weekend," Shay said. "We'll just have to decide if you want to stay around here or head up to Boca to be near me. It might be a good idea to move north. You know…so you take advantage of the divorce safety zone."

"What's that?" Cressida asked.

"In a divorce, you carve out geographic turf just like you divide up your friends and assets," Shay said. "It's one of those unwritten rules. Cal has claimed Miami by default but he might consider Fort Lauderdale neutral territory since you lived here together. You need your own area—somewhere you can dine out or date without worrying about running into your ex and his live-in bimbette every two seconds."

She hadn't even considered moving out of Fort Lauderdale. This divorce thing seemed to get more complicated by the day. Still, having her job problem resolved—even if only temporarily—was a huge relief. She'd envisioned herself scrounging around to school district after school district, begging for teaching assistant jobs that might never materialize. Or having to piece together an income through a few part-time positions. She hadn't dared even hope that she might find something more interesting. Granted, the media relations gig made her reliant upon Roxie but it wouldn't be permanent. It would just be a bridge until she could find something better down the road.

Despite the tough morning, things were most definitely looking up.

Her cell phone rang.

She punched the speaker button. "Hello?"

"Cress…Ida Wentworth?" An unfamiliar man wrestled with her name.

"Cressida." She issued her automatic correction. "Like the car."

Roxie reared her head back in surprise and shot a confused sideways glance at Costa, who shrugged and shook his head.

"Walter Brimley here," the man said. "Gray Portell asked me to reach out. I understand you need to alter some adoption paperwork. I haven't yet connected with the people at Children's Hope but Gray led me to believe that time is of the essence. How soon can you meet?"

Cressida flipped her appointment book open. "Tomorrow at noon?"

"Noon is fine," he said. "I'm in the same tower as Gray but on the tenth floor."

Cressida scribbled down his address, thanked him and hung up. As she set the phone on the table, she noticed Roxie regarding her with a confused expression.

Her brow crinkled. "What?"

Roxie looked baffled. "Why would you compare your lovely regal name to an obsolete economy car?"

"You ought to know." Cressida shrugged. "You're the one who named me after your old Toyota."

Roxie's jaw dropped. "I most certainly did not!" She shook her head. "You actually believed I named you after my rusted old rattletrap? Which by the way, was a Corolla."

"Oh…well…yes," Cressida said as her brows knit together. "Didn't you?"

Roxie placed a hand over her heart as her eyes misted. "Never," she breathed. "Didn't you take English Literature in high school?"

Cressida shook her head. "American."

"You're named after the lead character in the Shakespearean novel *Troilus and Cressida.*"

"Oh." Cressida frowned. "But I thought…" Her voice trailed off.

"Cressida was a Trojan princess and Troilus, a prince. It's one of Shakespeare's lesser-known works." Roxie sighed. "I wanted to *die* the first time I read that story. It's about the intensity of first love, though like most first loves, the story had a heartbreaking ending. Cressida is strong and beautiful and fierce. I must've read that story a thousand times."

Cressida's eyes welled. "I never knew that."

Roxie tenderly cupped Cressida's cheeks. "From the second I laid eyes on you, I knew you had the soul of a Trojan warrior princess."

Cressida tried to ignore the sting of tears that clouded her vision at this unexpected revelation. To ease the emotion, she made a joke. "I have to admit, that's a better explanation than the one I've been using all my life."

"I'd say so." Roxie leaned forward and kissed her forehead. "A Trojan warrior princess." She tapped Cressida's temple. "Let that notion soak in and forget all that nonsense that loser of an ex-husband has been feeding you all these years."

"Delete. Delete. Delete. Ignore everything he's ever said to you. That's what I do with all my exes," Costa proclaimed, glancing at his watch. "Rox, we need to get going or we'll be late for rehearsal."

As Roxie and Costa headed out of the kitchen, Ben walked in the back door.

Her heart did a little somersault at the sight of him and she smiled shyly as he approached.

Roxie and Costa stopped and stared.

"Hiya Ben." Roxie's eyes twinkled. "Thank you for taking care of our little Cressie this weekend." She shot Cressida a lascivious wink and breezed out the door.

Costa sent two thumbs up as he disappeared behind Roxie.

"I have to go too." Shay skipped out after Roxie and Costa.

"Boy, I really know how to clear a room." Ben smiled down at her, his gaze warm. "So how mad was she?"

"Mad as a wet cat." She laughed. "But she got over it. She couldn't very well stay angry since she's pretty much the poster child for irresponsibility." She tilted her head to the side as she gazed up at him. "I thought you had an appointment down in Miami."

His face split into a lop-sided ear to ear grin. "I needed another kiss." He drew her close.

She nestled into his arms. "Me too," she whispered.

His lips captured hers, lingering with a soul-crushing sweetness. "And I sort of felt like we had some unfinished business…"

Cressida's heart fluttered as white hot desire flamed. She pulled away and gazed up at him.

They'd danced around their attraction all weekend but despite the magnetic pull, she'd resisted the very real temptation to give in to her desire. Not because of any misguided loyalty to Cal. She knew for sure now that whatever they'd shared together had died long ago. No. She'd resisted because she was scared, plain and simple. Afraid of her attraction. Afraid to let him in. Afraid that this time, the hurt might be too devastating.

But for whatever reason, as she gazed up at him, her fears melted away and all that mattered was this moment. Not her past, not what might happen in their future, not what anyone might think. All that mattered was the two of them.

She tilted her head to the side, "How long until your appointment?"

"What appointment?" Ben's voice sounded gruff and his heavy-lidded gaze was dark and sexy.

The corners of her lips turned up as she laced her fingers with his and led the way to her bedroom.

Cressida stood backstage as Roxie, donning a pink satin evening gown and dripping Wilma Flintstone-size diamonds, performed Madonna's Material Girl, vamping it to the hilt with a white fox stole as six shirtless hotties in tuxedo pants and bowties carried her in Cleopatra-like fashion across the stage.

With just two days until opening night, Roxie and crew had entered full dress rehearsal mode and Cressida loved every crazy, semi out of control moment of it.

Costa was right. Roxie really had outdone herself. Somehow, she'd managed to up-the-ante on an already blockbuster and consistently sold out musical variety show, a nearly impossible feat in an industry as fickle as the music business where a show could be considered tired before it even opened.

Roxie thrust her fox stole skyward as the number ended.

A dusting of applause erupted from the crew as Cressida pranced out to greet her mother.

"That was fantastic." She fist bumped her mother. "Even better than yesterday."

Roxie winked. "We're getting there." She turned to the Felix the producer. "Let's call it an early night. Everyone's exhausted and I need 'em rested and rarein' to go in forty-eight."

Felix clapped his hands and bellowed. "Okay folks, that's a wrap! Ten o'clock call time tomorrow."

As the crew dispersed, Roxie grasped Cressida's hand and headed backstage. "Keep me company while I change." She threw an impish grin over a shoulder as she led the way down the back hall. "Then I have a little surprise for you."

"So what's the final verdict?" As they passed, Cressida pointed at the oversized martini glass positioned on the steel platform. "In or out?"

"Unfortunately it's out." Roxie heaved a dramatic sigh. "We tried it today and the darned thing wouldn't budge so I had to pull it. Costa may never recover. He's devastated but hey, that's showbiz."

She opened her dressing room door and flicked on the lights as she flung the fox stole over the back of a chair. Then kicked off her dancing shoes and slipped behind her wardrobe curtain.

Cressida dropped onto the leopard print chaise, legs stretched out in front of her.

"Why are you getting all dolled up?" Cressida asked. "I thought we'd just grab a bite to eat at home. Ben finished the kitchen today so we can actually enjoy a dust-free dinner in the new dining room. They just started the work in the master suite so I'll be sleeping with you for the next two weeks."

Roxie poked her head out from behind the screen. "You don't snore, do you?"

Cressida waved a hand and didn't bother to acknowledge the comment.

"I'm dead serious," Roxie said. "You should hear Costa. He makes more noise than a dying locomotive. When we stay in a hotel, I ask for a different floor."

Cressida rolled her eyes. "It can't be that bad."

Roxie strutted out from behind the curtain and struck a pose. "How do I look?" She twirled around in her black skinny jeans, a flowy leopard print tunic and stiletto booties.

It was the first time Cressida could recall seeing her mother in something that wasn't form-fitting or revealing what she considered an indecent display of cleavage.

"You look cute," Cressida tilted her head as she swept Roxie head to toe. "And kind of conservative. What's up?"

"I have a date." Roxie grinned as she sat down at her makeup table. "I didn't want to look too...well, you know."

Cressida lifted a brow.

She *did* know but couldn't help feeling surprised that Roxie did. Her mother had never given a thought to what others might think of her sex kitten style of dress before.

Her lips twisted. "With Micah, I presume."

"No." Roxie leaned forward and applied a fresh coat of lipstick. "Micah's back in New Haven." She met Cressida's gaze in the mirror and winked. "For some crazy reason, his plans suddenly changed right after the ball and he had to return to school. Imagine that." She giggled and shook her head. "I swear, Cressie. You call me dramatic but your performance the other night put me to shame. You'll be the talk of the town for years to come."

Cressida examined her manicure. Her Xanax and champagne-induced episode still touched a raw nerve.

"I had a good teacher," she sniffed. "Anyway, I'm not surprised about Micah. I'm sure Trudy hasn't recovered from the revelation that her precious and perfect son was sleeping with a woman old enough to be his mother." Cressida grimaced. "Are you mad that I spoiled your fun?"

Roxie regarded her in the mirror for a long moment and then turned to face her. "I know you don't believe me, but I didn't sleep with Micah." She stood and straightened her tunic, then breezed to the door. "Our relationship, if you want to call it that, wasn't even romantic."

She opened her dressing room door and waited while Cressida got up off the chaise.

Cressida scoffed. "You're right. I don't believe you."

Roxie flicked off the lights after Cressida walked by. "Have you always been this judgmental?"

Cressida shrugged. "Call it what you will. I speak from experience."

She'd learned never to underestimate the escapades in which Roxie could become entangled and she'd long ago accepted that her mother had a thing for much younger men. It didn't really even bother her anymore as she'd come to realize in the past few weeks that her issues with her mother's lifestyle had mostly been related to Cal's feelings on the matter.

"Oh, for heaven's sake." Roxie frowned. "I promised to keep Micah's secret but at this point I guess it doesn't matter." She sighed. "If you must know, Micah plans to quit law school. He's formed a Nirvana tribute band and they've landed a few local gigs in New Haven. He wants to pursue a singing career. I gave him some tips on how to break into the biz." Roxie lifted a brow. "There. Are you satisfied?"

"That's it?" Cressida searched Roxie's face for some sign of deception. "Seriously?"

"Seriously. That's all there was to it."

"Wow." Cressida couldn't manage to utter anything more coherent as her mind raced to process this unexpected little tidbit.

Roxie smirked. "You sound disappointed. I can't believe you really thought I'd sleep with a twenty-seven-year-old."

Cressida's cheeks flamed. Put that way, she felt a little ashamed. She'd never considered herself judgmental; more a pragmatic observer of life but where Roxie was concerned, it appeared that she might've leapt to plenty of wild conclusions.

Instead of admitting as much, Cressida changed the subject. "Well, I'm guessing his desire to become the second coming of Kurt Cobain won't sit well with Trudy since she's already announced to all of Fort Lauderdale society that Micah will take the helm of the Farentino law dynasty in a few years."

Roxie cackled. "Well, she better strap herself in because she's about to experience the mother of all career battles. When Micah comes home at Christmas, he's dropping the bomb. Or so he says." Roxie trotted up the stairs and headed towards the stage. "And I say good for him. We all get to live the life we choose and we shouldn't settle for anything less than exactly what we want, no matter who decides to sit in judgment."

Cressida frowned. What else might she be wrong about where her mother was concerned? Had Roxie's relationships with Corey and all those other young men actually been friendships or mentorships instead of steamy May December romances? The possibility had never occurred to her before.

Instead of relieved, she felt out of sorts. "So who's your date?"

Costa bounced up. "Thor!" He leaned closer and elbowed Cressida's side. "And I'm *so* jealous."

Cressida chewed the inside of her lip and searched her memory. Then a light bulb came on. "You don't mean…"

"The hottie with the sledgehammer?" Costa asked. "Oh yeah, baby."

"You matchmaker, you!" Roxie giggled and smacked Costa playfully on the arm. "By the way, his name isn't Thor, its Sheldon."

"Sheldon?" Cressida said. "That just sounds…wrong."

Roxie crinkled her nose. "I know, right? It doesn't fit with his God-like good looks. Too conservative. I asked if I could call him Shelly. He was not amused." She shrugged. "Anyhoo, I'm meeting him up on Las Olas in an hour so we'll have to hurry and do your surprise now."

Cressida whispered to Costa, "Good surprise or bad surprise?"

"Definitely good surprise." He squeezed her elbow. "And be nice. Rox worked really hard on this."

Chapter Nineteen

As they approached the backstage curtain, Roxie turned. "Wait here," she commanded. "I'll be right back." She pranced toward the curtain, calling over her shoulder. "And don't peek!"

Costa air kissed Cressida's cheek. "See you at home, Cress."

Roxie poked her head back through the curtain. "Ready?"

"I guess so," Cressida said. She couldn't help but feel uneasy. You could never predict what Roxie might have up her sleeve.

Roxie dramatically thrust the curtains aside and glided over to Cressida, grasping both hands. "Now, close your eyes."

Cressida did as instructed as Roxie led her slowly to the stage, or tried to anyway. She peeked out from underneath her lashes but try as she might, Cressida couldn't see a thing.

"You're peeking!" Roxie smacked the back of her hand. "Don't peek!"

Cressida yanked her hand away. "No smacking. And I'm not peeking." She shuffled after Roxie, trying to adjust to her mother's steps.

"Okay…stop." Roxie grasped Cressida's shoulders. "Now, keep your eyes closed."

"What are you up to?" Cressida stood awkwardly, listening intently and trying to discern from the sounds what might be in store.

"You'll see."

A chair scraped across the wooden stage. The spotlights above warmed the top of her head despite the chilly auditorium.

"Okay. Open!" Roxie cried.

Cressida blinked twice, trying to adjust to the bright glare of the spotlights.

Roxie sat on a bar stool at center stage, a guitar strapped around her neck. A microphone and stand stood next to her, illuminated by three overhead spotlights. The rest of the auditorium was an empty black cavern. She could barely make out the rows of seats.

Cressida's eyes narrowed. "What is this?"

"We're going to sing," Roxie announced, eyes twinkling. "Just the two of us." She strummed her guitar. "Just like old times."

Cressida shook her head, slowly at first and then more fervently. "No...I can't do it." She swallowed. "No!!!"

For the last two decades, the only singing she'd done had been while alone in the car or in the shower, so her voice was woefully out of shape. Even if she could get past her fear of singing in public, she couldn't endure any more of Roxie's chiding about how she'd squandered her God-given gifts. She'd heard it too many times.

Roxie sighed as she slipped the guitar from around her neck and slid off the barstool. She placed the instrument on the seat and then locked eyes with Cressida. She gripped her shoulders, the look in her eye changing to one of fierce determination.

"Cressie, it's time." She squeezed her shoulders harder. "You can do it. I *know* you can. But you need to prove that to yourself."

She tapped Cressida's temple with her index finger. "You need to believe you can do it in here." She placed Cressida's hand over her heart. "And in here."

Cressida's gaze swept the deserted auditorium. She'd asked for Roxie's help and desperately wanted to move past this paralyzing fear. She truly did. But it was one thing to try tapping or reading books on positive thinking or even mucking her way through a short speech in front of a group of women she didn't even care about. It was quite another to actually attempt to sing onstage with her legendary mother watching her every move.

Cressida took several steps back and every instinct screamed for her to run. And she almost did.

Then she glanced over at Roxie, busily adjusting the guitar strap on her shoulder and caught the whisper of disappointment flash across her mother's face before it was quickly disguised behind an encouraging smile.

But she saw it. She'd seen in her mother's eyes the same disappointment she felt inside. And that reality stopped her cold.

When would she stop running from her fears? What would it take to start believing in herself again?

Cressida stood a little straighter as a strength, a determination she hadn't felt in longer than she cared to remember, rekindled inside. Roxie was right. The time had come to confront her fear. To prove to herself that she could defeat the chains of self-doubt holding her back.

"Okay," Cressida said her voice quiet and tentative. She threw her shoulders back and cleared her throat, trying to feign a confidence she didn't actually feel. But she sounded much more determined as she repeated, "Okay. Let's do it."

She wasn't sure if she'd even be able to choke out the words but she had to try. Ben was right. Life was happening now. She needed to get out there and live it.

"That's my girl." Roxie's lips spread in an impossibly broad ear to ear grin, her eyes suspiciously bright as she lifted a brow. "Ready?"

Cressida nodded and tried to ignore her clenched stomach muscles and her parched throat.

Her mother tapped her hand on her guitar as she counted off. Then she strummed the opening strains of the guitar lead in to 'What's Up', one of Cressida's favorite ballads from the 4 Non Blondes.

"Don't think. Just feel it," Roxie said. "Let the music take over."

Cressida stepped up to the microphone, knees wobbling as she approached the opening cue. Instead of empty seats, she conjured up images of a frowning, jeering crowd.

She closed her eyes to block out the mental images, opened her mouth, hesitated too long and missed the cue.

Roxie stopped strumming.

"That's okay." Roxie counted off. "Let's try it again." She started playing. "You can do it, Cressie."

Cressida counted off the beats and as the opening cue approached, she grasped the microphone with one hand and tapped her leg with the other.

She sounded shaky and tentative, just going through the motions as she sang the first several notes. She tripped up, hesitating slightly as her voice bounced back at her from the acoustic walls. It sounded so bad she almost stopped.

She grimaced and glanced over at Roxie who nodded encouragingly, so she kept going. Her voice sounded stronger with each few notes and as she headed into the second verse, she relaxed into the plaintive, soulful melody and actually started to enjoy it.

She glanced sideways at Roxie, eyes bright with tears and at the chorus, her mother joined in sweet harmony, their voices perfectly blended in a soulful rock style.

Cressida got into it, losing herself in the performance in a way she hadn't imagined ever doing again.

She lifted the microphone from the stand and swayed back and forth as she belted out the words, feeling the music more with each note.

Roxie grinned as they headed into the second chorus. But when she opened her mouth to start the last verse, a hint of movement in the shadows threw her concentration off.

Her voice trailed off as she squinted, straining to see if the movement was real or imagined.

There it was again. A flash of red.

They weren't alone. Someone was out there!

Her vocal chords froze as realization dawned.

Cressida's hand shook as she slammed the mic back into the stand. She spun around on her heel and glared at Roxie as she jabbed a finger at the dark cavernous auditorium and demanded, "Who's out there?"

Roxie stopped strumming and met Cressida's gaze briefly and in that moment, Cressida knew she wasn't going to like the answer.

"Lights!" Roxie bellowed.

The lights flipped on, illuminating the entire auditorium and revealing three rows of dancers, producers and backstage hands at the back of the auditorium, eyes glued to the stage.

Cressida gasped and jumped back as she eyed the group in horror.

Costa held his smartphone up as he taped the entire thing. He waved and shot her the thumbs up as the rest of the cast broke into applause and cat calls.

Cressida's stomach did a sickening double back flip as she gaped at the strangers invading what she had assumed to be a private moment with her mother. Instead it had been a public spectacle and a complete and total violation of trust.

"How *could* you?" she asked, her voice sounding as ragged and raw as she felt. Roxie had taken her greatest fear and tricked her into confronting it in front of dozens of strangers long before she felt ready. She'd never imagined her mother would do such a thing.

Roxie's eyes grew round as she stepped forward, wringing her hands.

"Cressie...I just wanted to find a way for you to prove to yourself that you could do it. That you have nothing to fear." She moved closer, eyes pleading for understanding. "I knew you wouldn't sing onstage if I told you the cast was out there and if it was just us, I didn't think that would be enough to help you truly overcome your doubts."

Cressida wasn't hearing any of her mother's excuses.

"How could you?!" Cressida spun on her heel and bolted

through the velvet curtain that led backstage.

"Cressie!"

Roxie sprinted after her but she proved too fast for her mother as she raced down the back stairs, through the steel stage door and out into the parking lot, stopping only when the stitch in her side became too painful. She bent over, hands on her knees, greedily sucking air into her heaving lungs as hot tears of embarrassment and outrage streamed down her cheeks.

She should've known better than to ask for Roxie's help with anything. Roxie didn't know the meaning of empathy or understanding. It was her way or the highway and next time, Cressida vowed to take the highway.

❦

"Roxie means well. I know you can see that."

Ben poured a generous amount of red wine into the second glass as she leaned forward and scratched behind Max's ear. The dog grunted and gazed up at her adoringly as Ben picked up the wine glasses and headed to the sofa.

"You asked for her help and she's trying to give it to you."

"Oh, so you're on her side. I see." Cressida's lips twisted. "Typical."

"Typical?" Ben handed her the wine glass containing the double portion. "That sounds like an accusation."

"Not at all. It's the truth." She shook her head. "Inside of thirty seconds, Roxie can have any man she chooses wrapped around her little finger. She just bats those come hither lashes, strikes a pose, purrs, *'Well helloooo'* and it's all over." She rolled her eyes and sipped some Malbec. "I hoped you'd be more resistant to her charms but I guess that would be asking too much."

Ben scoffed and settled onto the sofa next to her. "Please. Give me some credit." He shrugged. "I mean…sure, I think Roxie's an absolute hoot and I'd love to introduce her to Uncle Rex but I'm definitely not taking her side. I just call 'em like I see 'em, that's all."

She shifted around so she faced him. "Oh? And exactly how do you see 'em?" She poked him playfully in the side, mimicking his Texas twang. "I'm just *dyin'* to hear."

He drew her hand to his lips and planted a kiss that curled her toes. And just like that, her irritation with Roxie vanished.

"The way I see 'em"—he drawled and winked as he drew her close—"is that crazy mother of yours loves you to bits. Anyone can see that. But with families, actions and intentions sometimes go sideways. All it takes is a little misinterpretation mixed with a little bad judgment"—he shrugged—"and then you've got a big ole Texas-sized mess on your hands."

"A big ole Texas-sized mess." Cressida's lips twisted. "That pretty much sums it up. But I don't think it's due to misinterpretation on my part. Roxie waaay overstepped her bounds."

"She got it wrong, that's all." He placed his wine on the coffee table and turned to face her. "Look at the intention, not the outcome. I'll bet you occasionally get things wrong with her, too."

Cressida swished her wine around in the glass and contemplated his words. Then she smiled ruefully.

"Funny you should say that. I just learned today that I was completely wrong about a situation that happened a few days after she arrived. I thought she was seeing this really young guy"—she glanced up at Ben sheepishly, not quite able to bring herself to reference the most embarrassing episode of her life—"well you know, the one from the—."

"You mean the son of the woman you beat the crap out of onstage before announcing to the entire community that he was sleeping with your mother?" Ben teased. "Is that the one?"

She punched him playfully in the arm and reprimanded him with a look. He rubbed his arm teasingly, feigning injury.

"Anyway, I just found out today that she *wasn't* sleeping with him. As it turns out, Roxie was giving him advice on how to make it in the music business." She crinkled her nose. "I feel awful that I jumped to conclusions."

He gazed down at her. "And you didn't intend to, right?"

"No and I get the point you're trying to make, but I still think what she did is different." She sipped more wine. "She knew better. She knew how terrifying the issue is for me. But of course, I should've known better than to ask for her help with such a sensitive subject. I mean, it's just like Roxie to do the unexpected. To push too hard. To think that her enthusiasm and good intentions will gloss over her bad decisions."

"All I'm saying is that you should focus on the fact that she really does mean well. I'm convinced of it." Ben gazed down at her. "And just remember, you asked for her help. She just tried to give it to you the best she knows how."

"I guess so," Cressida grumbled, amazed that after just thirty minutes with Ben, her outlook had totally changed.

He smiled. "Give your mom a break."

She chewed the inside of her lip. "I guess…" Her voice trailed off as the doorbell rang.

Max barked and hopped up, trotting over to the door behind Ben, tail wagging in anticipation.

Ben pulled the door open and his face split into an ear to ear grin.

"Hey!" He glanced at his watch. "You're early." He waved at the car backing down the driveway. "Wave bye to your mom."

The kids waved and then raced inside. Max stood at attention, tail flipping madly as the kids patted his head. Then the trio took off, heading for the back door. But as soon as the kids spotted Cressida, they screeched to a halt.

Ben sidled up between them, placed his arms around their shoulders and pulled them closer as he said, "Guys, I want you to meet Cressida." He smiled. "Cressida, this is Kaylen and Kyle."

Cressida placed her wine glass on the table.

"Hello." She smiled and stood, rubbing her palms down her jeans. "It's very nice to meet you."

"Hello." Kaylen, tall and gangly with long brown hair and a smile to match her dad's, grinned shyly.

"Are you dad's girlfriend?" Kyle blurted out, his hair a russet brown and a liberal sprinkling of freckles dusted his cheeks.

"Kyle. Don't be rude, buddy." Ben said as Kaylen smacked her brother on the arm. "Cressida's my friend."

Cressida blushed and her gaze locked with Ben's. "I don't want to intrude. I have to get home anyway."

She reached for her purse.

"Nonsense. We're headed to the Shake Shack up in Boca." Ben laughed at the kid's shout of approval and his eyes issued a playful challenge as he said, "Come with us."

Cressida glanced uncertainly at the kids and then back at Ben. "Well, I don't know…"

"Please?" Kaylen stepped forward and grabbed her hand.

"Yeah!" Kyle said. "Their chocolate shakes are the best."

Ben winked. "It appears you're outnumbered. Three to one. You have to say yes."

"You know…" Cressida's face relaxed into a smile as she squeezed Kaylen's hand. "I could really use a chocolate shake right about now."

The kids dumped their backpacks onto the sofa and trotted out to Ben's truck, followed by Max.

Ben slipped his arm around Cressida's waist and pulled her tight as they strolled down the sidewalk.

"Thank you," she whispered around the lump in her throat.

He bent and whispered in her ear. "For what?"

She smiled up at him and shook her head as she slipped her arm around his waist, not sure how to articulate what she was feeling. "Just…thank you."

❧

"You can't hold a grudge forever, Cressie." Roxie poured two mugs of piping hot coffee and handed one to Cressida.

"Forever? It just happened yesterday," Cressida grumbled as she dumped a generous splash of cream into her mug and stirred.

Yesterday afternoon, she'd been ready to throttle her mother for trying to trick her into performing in front of an audience of strangers but after spending the evening with Ben and his kids, she couldn't muster a shred of energy for negativity. She'd gone to bed floating on a cloud of pure bliss and had awakened in the same mood. She wasn't about to let anything spoil it.

Granted, the dinner hadn't technically been anything special. Just hamburgers and milkshakes at a roadside picnic table, but she couldn't recall a more enjoyable evening. The kids had drawn her into the teasing banter and she'd loved every greasy French fry, calorie-laden second of it.

"You asked for my help," Roxie said, still clearly on the defensive. "Maybe I took things a little too far but honestly, I just wanted to push you out of your comfort zone a little."

Cressida sipped her coffee, rather enjoying watching her mother squirm. "Or a lot maybe?"

"Maybe." Roxie raised a brow. "Forgiven?"

Cressida pursed her lips and feigned irritation. "We'll see."

In truth, she was over it but it couldn't hurt to let Roxie sweat a little. Her mother had definitely stepped over the line and knew it. Might be good to let her think she was in a little hot water. Maybe she'd take more care before stepping over the line next time, though Cressida doubted it. Her mother seemed bound and determined to get her back onstage, even if she had to resort to treachery and deceit in order to make that happen.

Chapter Twenty

Costa boogied in, fingers snapping and hips swinging. He stopped short and spun around on his heel in his favorite Billie Jean dance style.

"Girrrl...you rocked that tune last night."

Roxie beamed with pride. "She's a chip off the old block, that's for sure." Her smile faded as she muttered, "Well, strike the *old* part." She pulled off her reading glasses and laid them on the table as she patted her hair.

"Another few weeks of tapping and I do believe you'll have that stage fright totally licked." He plopped down on the stool next to Roxie. "If I could belt one out like that you wouldn't be able to deragggggg me off that stage," he drawled. "I'd enter every talent contest I could find and I wouldn't stop until I won The Voice."

His eyes twinkled as he elbowed Roxie in the side. "Then you could flirt all you want with that dreamy Blake Shelton."

"I'll flirt with him anyway at the next Grammys and I don't give a hoot what Miranda says." Roxie snickered. "He's a little devil, that one."

Costa ran a calculated gaze over Cressida's outfit.

"Very nice." He fingered a lapel on her black silk suit. "And quite a step up from your usual vibe. I'd say our little shopping trip did the trick." He pursed his lips and gazed at her hemline. "We need to hike up that skirt a few inches. You know...show off those gams."

Cressida sipped her coffee and said primly, "My hemline is just fine, thank you very much."

"Sadly, it's not." Costa shook his head. "You must learn to trust me on these matters. Three inches would make a world of difference."

Cressida rolled her eyes. "I may be a divorcee but I'm not going to hike my skirts up past my hoocheekoo just to get a little attention."

"Your loss." He shrugged arms wide. "I can only do so much if you refuse to work with me."

"You two are so silly." Roxie giggled. "Is that my cheetah print top?" Her eyes swept Cressida head to toe as she nodded her approval.

"No." Cressida glanced down. "There's no cleavage."

Roxie pursed her lips. "Good point."

"I finally persuaded our little Cressie to add a few pieces of animal print to her closet." He grinned. "Just a hint of cheetah peeping out. Nice, huh?"

"Very," Roxie said. "Why so dressed up?"

"I have an appointment with Priscilla Davies," Cressida said. And because she didn't want to risk opening the floodgates to Roxie's endless questions, she changed the subject. "How was your date with Thor?" She shook her head. "Sorry. I mean, Sheldon."

Roxie heaved a dramatic sigh. "Unfortunately, he's a bit of a dud."

"He didn't look like a dud," Cressida said. "He's a dead ringer for Chris Hemsworth."

"Well, let's just say the name Sheldon suits him. Thor just doesn't fit. He's not..." She scrunched her nose. "Well, swaggering enough, I suppose." She waved a hand dismissively. "Oh sure, he's easy on the eyes but he's not much for chatting. It was like talking to this chair." She tapped on the legs of her barstool. "After an hour I gave up and called in the troops."

Costa picked up the iPad and started surfing the internet. "We pulled the zero dark thirty on him."

Cressida turned to Roxie and lifted a brow, almost afraid to ask.

"That's where I text ZDT and Costa and a couple of my producers swoop in like Navy SEALs on a rescue mission." Her eyes danced. "They invent some wild excuse about an emergency on set and then I can leave without feeling the teeniest bit guilty."

"It's my favorite," Costa said, eyes gleaming with excitement. "I love it when Rox has a bad date."

"Gee thanks." Roxie shot him the evil eye.

"So you just ditch the guy in the restaurant." Cressida eyed Roxie with disapproval. "Seriously? Don't you even feel the teeniest bit guilty about that? I mean that's just—"

Her cell phone rang.

She glanced at the display.

"Just a sec." She swiped her screen to answer. "Hello?"

"Gray Portell here." Her attorney paused and cleared his throat. "I'm afraid I have some bad news."

Cressida's shoulders tensed as she tightened her grip on the phone, dreading his next words.

"I received a call from the CADs this morning. Apparently, your husband plans to fight any attempt to collect alimony based on the premise that you cheated first." Gray's voice sounded sharp and somewhat accusatory as he added, "You do recall me cautioning you to be discreet?"

"Uh…" Her mind raced, scrambling for an excuse.

"Apparently, they can prove you're having an affair with your architect." He paused several beats. "Is that true?"

Her cheeks flamed, his tone making her feel as if she should be tattooed with a scarlet A.

"Well…yes…I mean…I guess so," she said. "I don't know that I'd call it an affair, really. But I am seeing my architect or Cal's architect or…whatever."

Cressida waved her hand and told herself to stop rambling. She squared her shoulders and lifted her chin. Who was he to question how she lived her life? The first embers of irritation stirred and from the sound of Gray's response, she wasn't the only one annoyed.

"I don't like surprises, Cressida. I thought I made myself clear on that point." He emitted a long, exasperated sigh. "This means I'll have to double back now so I can determine a response."

Irritation turned to outrage in a blinding white flash.

"What does it matter who I'm seeing? I mean...my *husband* is *living* with *my cousin*!" She leapt to her feet. "Cal can't withhold alimony on that basis!"

"He can try and apparently, he plans to which is why I emphasized the importance of flying under the radar."

Cressida chewed her lip and tried to calm down. Cal must've decided to leverage the fact that she'd attended the White Ball with Ben. She should've expected this.

As she processed through the implications, her blood ran cold. Between her horrifying front page photo and Cal's wild exaggerations about her love life, he might very well be able to persuade a judge that she was at fault or at the very least, call into question her good judgment. And she couldn't let that happen. She needed a fair settlement in order to provide a stable life for her and her child while she looked for a more permanent career.

"There's actually more," Gray said. "They're claiming we need to update our financials because you've found a job. Is that true?"

"Well, yes...I mean, sort of." She frowned, wondering how Cal could've learned of her new job. "I'm doing media relations for my mother, at least for a while."

"You'll have to complete a new income disclosure form. I'll email it. Please fill it out and send back to me as soon as possible." He paused. "I'll fight for as much as we can get but you should be prepared to receive less alimony than we originally requested since you now have an income." He paused and his voice held more than a hint of reproach as continued. "No more surprises, Cressida. You're making this process harder than it needs to be."

She narrowed her eyes, irritated at his accusatory tone.

"I don't get it," she said. How could Cal know all of this?" But even as she said it, a voice deep inside whispered the answer.

Gray sighed. "Who knows? Private investigator. Someone from your side feeding them information. Lucky guess. It could be any or all of the above."

It hadn't been a lucky guess. It couldn't be. Cal knew too much. He knew of the adoption. He knew about Ben. He knew of the job with her mother. Only four people knew all of those facts and she'd known and trusted three of them for most of her life. Just one possibility remained.

Her stomach twisted into a knot.

At the very beginning, Gray had warned the divorce might get ugly. He'd cautioned her to stay on guard. He'd told her to watch for new people hanging around who appeared more interested than they should be. But she'd dismissed the notion as ridiculous. So she'd left her guard down which had allowed Ben to just swagger into her life, toss a little romance her way and sell her down the river. And she'd completely bought into his whole Texas good guy act. She'd fallen into his bed and even worse, let him all the way into her heart.

"I know it's unsettling to learn someone close is spying on you," Gray said. "Don't worry. My investigator will find out who's behind these leaks. In the meantime, keep your guard up."

"Don't bother," Cressida said through clenched teeth. "I know *exactly* who's feeding him that information and trust me, it won't happen again."

She hung up and stood with the phone clenched in her hand as she processed through the conversation.

"Watch what you say in front of Ben," she said her voice flat and emotionless. "He can't be trusted."

Roxie lowered her iPad and peered over the top, her brow furrowed. "Huh?"

"I trust Ben," Costa said.

"Nothing more," Cressida said. And as Roxie opened her mouth to respond, Cressida's anger erupted. "You're to say *nothing more*. About *me*. In front of *Ben*. *EVER!*"

Roxie blinked as she and Costa stared at Cressida in round-eyed surprise.

"Better yet, I'm going to take care of this issue once and for all." Cressida's hand shook as she snatched her keys off the counter and started for the door.

If Ben thought he could lure her into the sack and then sell her secrets to her cheating ex just to make a buck or two, he had another thing coming. No wonder he'd let her do the knock down drag out cat fight onstage. That humiliating little episode and resulting front page photo had probably earned him a huge bonus as it had only served to make Cal look better in divorce court.

Her hands balled into tight little fists. If he'd been anywhere in the vicinity, she would've given him two black eyes. She'd most certainly had her fill of dishonest, disreputable men.

Operating on pure adrenaline, she stalked to the door, anxious to get the confrontation over with because she suspected that just behind the fury lay a deep cavern of grief. But she wouldn't let herself dwell on her underlying wounds for fear that once she did, she might never escape their dark depths.

Roxie frowned at Costa. "Am I missing something?"

Costa shrugged. "I have zero idea what's going on. I thought we liked Ben."

"We *do* like Ben," Roxie said and then called out after Cressida's retreating back. "Cressie, where are you going?"

Cressida spun around, eyes blazing. "I'm going to fire Cal's architect."

❧

Cressida ran out of emotional steam before she reached the end of the street. As her car rolled up to the stoplight, her blazing hot rage melted into a simpering pool of sorrow as the full impact of Ben's betrayal smacked her in the face.

The sudden rush of tears stung, making it nearly impossible to see.

When the light turned green, she steered her car into an obscure corner of the Fresh Market parking lot. She shifted the gearshift to park and switched off the engine. Then she sat, staring out the windshield as she tried to silence the voice of her inner critic.

How could she have been so wrong about Ben? So clueless as to his intentions? So easy a target for a calculated guy looking to make a buck? Surely she wasn't that big an idiot. Surely she could recognize an opportunist when she saw one.

Her fingers shook as she wiped the moisture from her cheeks and sank deeper into the leather seat, watching a pair of seagulls peck at the stale French fries lying on the pavement.

Gradually, her tears subsided as sorrow turned to quiet resolve.

She'd confront Ben. He couldn't just betray her like this without consequences. He needed to be called out, to learn that this type of behavior was completely unacceptable.

In the past, she'd always let Cal's bad behavior go unaddressed. His oh so subtle jabs about her weight or her less than perfect hair or outfits. His outright attempts to control everything she did— from friendships to volunteering to hobbies. She'd made excuses for him, blamed herself for her own inadequacies and put up with it for more than a decade. Well, she wasn't putting up with that sort of behavior anymore. Not from anyone.

But now wasn't the right time. When she called Ben out, she needed to be calm and completely devoid of emotion. She didn't know what she'd say, what words she'd use, but she definitely didn't intend to show her hand. When she got through with him, he'd realize that he'd messed with the wrong woman.

She glanced at the dashboard clock and felt a jolt. If she didn't step on it, she'd be late for her adoption meeting and she couldn't let that happen. She'd spent the past few weeks getting her house in order, so to speak.

She'd checked all the boxes and answered all Patricia's questions. Granted, her solutions weren't perfect or even particularly long-term, but no one needed to know that except her. The adoption agency just wanted to be sure she could support a child. And now, she could. She'd found a job and a decent apartment that she'd move into after the house sold. While the job with Roxie was only temporary and her feelings about the tiny two bedroom apartment ranked somewhere just north of loathing, both solutions were workable. She was ready.

Cressida sighed as she moved the gearshift into drive and pulled out of the parking lot. As she drove, she pushed all thoughts of Ben into the same remote little corner of her mind where memories of Cal and her father resided—a place she seldom visited and refused to think about.

When she got around to it, when she felt ready, she'd calmly call him out on his behavior and then she'd casually walk away without displaying even the slightest hint of emotion. She'd prove to Ben Carrington that she didn't care about him any more than he cared about her, which of course, was not at all.

⚭

"Thank you for coming." Priscilla Davies gestured to the seating area in the corner of her cramped little office. "We'll be more comfortable over there."

Cressida set her purse on the table and tucked her skirt underneath her as she settled onto the slightly lumpy beige tweed arm chair. She glanced around at the institutional white walls and the cheap second hand furnishings. The office was so blah, it bordered on depressing. Its looks certainly belied the fact that in this office, families were formed and lives changed forever.

She gazed expectantly at Priscilla. Despite learning of Ben's betrayal just an hour before, she found it impossible to tamp down the excitement building inside. She'd waited for this moment for what seemed a lifetime and it had finally arrived.

Priscilla closed the office door and settled into a worn leather wing chair across from Cressida. She placed a manila folder on the coffee table and then crossed her legs.

"Let's hold off a few minutes. Walter should be here by now." Cressida lifted a brow as she glanced at her watch. She'd met with her adoption attorney the day before and he'd assured her he'd be here. "I can't believe he's so late."

Priscilla leaned forward and clasped her hands in her lap. "I asked him not to come."

"I don't understand." Cressida frowned. "I thought we planned to discuss the final updates to my paperwork."

She reached into her purse and pulled out an envelope which she handed to Priscilla. "I found a job and an apartment. The documents are in here, signed and notarized in triplicate."

She smiled. It felt good to finally take control of her life.

Priscilla took the envelope and slipped it inside the folder. Then she gazed at Cressida for a long moment.

Cressida sensed from both the other woman's posture and hesitation that she was about to hear something she didn't want to hear. She instinctively gripped the arms of her chair.

"I'm sorry Cressida. I'm afraid there's no easy way to say this other than to be very direct."

Cressida's stomach did a sickening twist and she suddenly found it hard to catch her breath. It was all she could do not to shout at Priscilla to get the words out; to just say what she was going to say.

Priscilla sighed. "I've just learned this little girl is no longer available for adoption."

All the air rushed from Cressida's lungs as if she'd been punched in the stomach by an invisible force. She collapsed into the back of the chair as she stared at Priscilla in disbelief.

"But I…what?" Her throat constricted and she gripped the chair harder, as if by holding on to it, she'd somehow be able to hold onto her dream. It took a few minutes before she managed to choke out the words screaming inside her head. "But I did everything you asked of me."

"This isn't about what you did or didn't do," Priscilla said quietly. "The birth mother has changed her mind. She's decided to keep her child."

"No!" Cressida moved to the edge of the chair. "But…I mean…*no*!! Can she do that?"

"The birth mother is able to change her mind at any time in the process and unfortunately, this isn't a usual occurrence." Priscilla sighed again. "This is the worst part of my job, believe me. To deliver this kind of news to a hopeful parent like you is just about the worst thing I can imagine. But I appreciate the other side too. Giving up a child to adoption is a very difficult decision. There are no words for how difficult. And sometimes, even when a mother thinks she can do it, when she's thought through all the implications and believes herself prepared for the emotional impact, sometimes…" Priscilla's voice trailed off and she shook her head. "Many times…she just can't go through with it."

Hot tears rolled down Cressida's cheeks, streaming faster and faster as the full impact of her words sank in. Another dead end.

Priscilla leaned forward, plucked two Kleenex from the box and handed the tissues to Cressida. "There will be other children, other opportunities," she said, her voice soft and reassuring.

Cressida's shoulders slumped and her arms wrapped protectively around her waist. Her head bent forward and her shoulders heaved as gut-wrenching sobs wracked her body.

Priscilla moved to the sofa and slipped her arm around Cressida's shoulders. She drew her close. "I know this is a shock, but this child wasn't meant for you," she murmured. "She was meant to stay with her birth mother."

Even in her pain, Cressida recognized the truth in those words.

She nodded and dabbed at her eyes, her throat too swollen to speak. She wanted what was best for the child and if it was best that she stay with her biological mother then Cressida understood that intellectually. But she'd been so certain, so sure the little girl was meant for her that she couldn't wrap her head around the prospect of not bringing her home in four months. It just felt...wrong.

Priscilla pasted on a bright smile, clearly meant to be encouraging. "And now that we have all your documentation, we can go about searching for the next opportunity." Priscilla patted Cressida's arm.

The next opportunity. Cressida swallowed hard. There might never be a next opportunity. Especially now that she was single. The *first* opportunity had been hard to come by. Even married, three years had passed before she'd received a referral for a child. As a divorced woman on a modest income, she might never be selected. Plus in a little more than three years, she'd be forty and that milestone loomed in front of her like some big fat petrifying dead end.

Somehow, somewhere along the way, she'd taken a wrong turn and she'd ended up on the road to nowhere with no idea of how to find the exit ramp. It seemed that no matter how hard she tried to steer her life in a positive direction, in the direction she wanted to go, the Universe had other ideas. So much for tapping, *The Secret* or letting things unfold in the way they're supposed to. Apparently, nothing she did made any difference at all.

Cressida wiped the last of her tears and stood. All she could think about now was escape. She wanted to be alone, to escape from this moment, this pain.

She drew in a long breath. "Thank you." She kept her tone as businesslike and as devoid of emotion as she could manage.

"Shall we get started on the paperwork?" Priscilla followed her to the door. "We should discuss the option of international adoption. That would open a world of possibilities." She smiled.

"It'll mean even more paperwork because each country is different and there's significantly more cost involved, but many times, international is a whole lot faster. I know of many countries that are single women friendly and of course, there is no shortage of children in need."

"I don't know." Cressida pulled her handbag onto her shoulder. "I just don't know." Right now, the whole pursuit of adoption seemed pointless and she wasn't sure she'd survive the emotional rollercoaster a second time. "Maybe I need to just accept that parenthood isn't meant for me."

Chapter Twenty-One

Cressida pushed her cart aimlessly past the seafood counter. Try as she might, she couldn't recall a single item she needed for dinner but she definitely didn't have the energy to drag herself back out to the car to retrieve the list.

She stopped and stared blankly at the enticing display of fresh salmon, shrimp and sea bass. The fish reminded her of Ben and the weekend at the lake. Her fingers tightened on the cart and she resolutely headed for the frozen vegetables.

Her cell phone buzzed.

Cressida stopped and rooted around in her bag, searching desperately for the device. She'd been trying to reach Shay for hours and once her fingers touched the rounded edges of the phone, she pulled it eagerly from her bag. She was hoping to set up drinks or dinner, but no such luck.

She checked the display and frowned.

Ben.

She chewed the inside of her lip and briefly considered not answering but something compelled her to do it. After swiping her finger across the display, she put the phone to her ear.

"Hello?"

"How about grabbing a quick bite to eat?" Ben asked with a smile in his voice. "Or maybe a cocktail...or something."

She steeled herself against his charm. "I can't," she said, congratulating herself on the clipped and cool tone as she concocted a quick excuse on the fly. "I'm actually up in Boca right now, headed to Shay's boutique and"—she rounded the corner and rammed into someone.

"Oh! I'm so sorry, I..." Her voice trailed off as her eyes locked with Ben's.

Her cheeks flamed, embarrassed to have been caught in the middle of a lie but pure defiance caused her to lift her chin as she clicked the END button and slid the device back in her purse.

Ben pulled his phone away from his ear, looking confused.

"Hey you. I saw you pull in the parking lot a few minutes ago. I called your name as you were walking inside, but..." His eyes searched her face, his brow creased. "Boca, huh?"

She sniffed. "Yes...well...I just meant that I'm headed up to Boca as soon as I drop off the groceries." Her eyes dropped to her empty cart. "Well, I mean as soon as I finish shopping."

His face broke into a lazy smile and despite what she'd learned about his treachery in the past few hours, her heart thumped harder which pissed her off to no end.

This man was the lowest of the low. He'd hung around and gathered little tidbits of her life when she was at her most vulnerable and then he'd fed them to her cheating ex just so he could make a quick buck. There was no way she could still feel attracted to him.

"I've been trying to reach you."

Ben moved closer and reached out to caress her cheek but she took a sharp step back to avoid his touch.

His smile faded. "Is everything okay?"

She lifted her chin defiantly. "You tell me. You seem to be the expert on my life at the moment."

He opened his mouth and looked about to speak but closed it again and shoved his hands into his jeans pockets as he searched her face.

"I'm sorry?" There was no mistaking the confusion in his eyes.

"No," she said.

She looked down and away, afraid he might see the truth in her own eyes. That she longed to touch him. That despite everything he'd done to hurt her, she wished things between them were the same, wished he was the person she had thought him to be. But he wasn't and she just needed to accept that cold, hard truth.

She cleared her throat and lifted her chin. "No everything isn't okay."

Ben shifted his weight back and forth. "Cressida, what's wrong?"

She wrapped her arms protectively around her waist and forced herself to meet his gaze. "I know."

"You know." A deep furrow creased his brow. "Know what?"

Her green eyes flashed. "I know you've been providing information to Cal to help with the divorce."

Ben hesitated for a long moment and then burst out laughing. "That's good. You had me going there for a minute." His laughter gradually faded as he studied her. "Wait. You're serious."

"Don't play games with me, Ben." She folded her arms across her chest, angry that he thought he could just feign confusion and she'd let him get by with it. "I know what you did. I'd just like to know how much Cal paid you."

"Paid me!" Anger erupted behind Ben's eyes as he spluttered, "Wha...but this is crazy! Why would I do anything to help that creep?"

"Oh, I don't know...money maybe?" Her eyes narrowed. "By your own admission you desperately needed that damned on time bonus. If Cal thought he could pay me less alimony for the next five or ten years or maybe none at all by gathering dirt and using it against me, I'm sure he'd be willing to make it well worth your while."

He spread his arms wide. "Dirt. What dirt?" He raised his brows and shouted, "You mean that we slept together?"

Her eyes darted about, taking note of the people milling nearby, not even bothering to pretend they weren't paying attention. But she couldn't care less what anyone thought. She was too pissed.

Cressida glared at him, hardly able to believe she'd allowed herself to be duped by him.

"I have to admit, you have the act down. That aw shucks Texas thing really works for you. But then again, I'm sure you already know that."

He gaped at her with disbelief. "You really believe I'd do such a thing? You believe I'd sleep with you, introduce you to my kids and then turn around and feed a bunch of information to your husband just so he could save a buck or two?"

"No. I think you'd do it so *you* could *make* a buck or two."

He shook his head and scratched his jaw. "Nice. And to think…" He shrugged and expelled a slightly exasperated sight. "Never mind."

After a long pause, he continued. "Listen, I'm sorry that slime ball is trying to weasel out of his obligations to you, though I can't say that I'm surprised. God knows you don't deserve it. But I have nothing to do with whatever he's up to and when you're thinking more clearly, you'll realize that."

"You know, you really are something else." Her laugh sounded as harsh and hollow as she felt as the full weight of his deception sank in, and that pain fueled her next words. "I don't blame your wife for running out on you. There's no telling the lies and deceit you displayed in that relationship. I only wonder why it took her twelve years. She must be even more clueless than me."

Cressida grabbed her shopping cart with shaking hands and strode down the aisle towards checkout, fire shooting from her eyes. If he so much as touched her or attempted to say one more word to her, she was going to punch him right in that arrogant jaw.

He didn't.

She abandoned her empty cart near the customer service desk and clutched her purse like a lifeline as she bolted for the exit. Just before the doors slid open, she glimpsed Ben's reflection in the glass. She couldn't see his expression. Just his rigid posture as he watched her go.

Cressida maintained her composure until she reached the safety of her car but the second she closed the door, the recriminations started.

Why was it that no matter what she did, she couldn't escape lying manipulative men? What was wrong with her that men always chose to leave her in one way or another? Her father. Her husband. Ben.

She slumped against the back of the seat and closed her eyes, trying not to dwell on that painful question and instead, let her mind drift back to the grocery store scene. She'd finally mustered the courage to stand up for herself. Finally rallied the nerve to say the truth to the person she needed to say it to in the precise moment she needed to say it. She should be feeling victorious, proud of herself even. But instead, she just felt sick.

Cressida heaved a long, resigned sigh and cranked the ignition. More than anything, she wished she'd never laid eyes on Ben Carrington.

Ben glanced up from his keyboard when the doorbell rang. He briefly considered not bothering to get up but he was expecting a FedEx delivery, so he couldn't ignore it.

He sighed as he pushed away from his desk. As he pulled the door open, his heart leapt into his throat the second he spotted the red hair. Cressida!

He'd picked up the phone at least a dozen times in the past few hours but every time, he stopped himself. He just couldn't figure out what to say to her, how to convince her how wrong she was. And in truth, he felt more and more that she should be the one to apologize. Maybe she'd come to her senses and was here to do just that.

Ben pulled the door open with an almost super hero strength. Every fiber of his being ached to gather her into his arms and hold her close.

"Cr—" He stopped abruptly as she turned and his heart fell through the floor. "Oh. Hi Roxie." He found it impossible to infuse even the slightest bit of enthusiasm into his greeting.

"Gee, it's great to see you too," she teased, but he detected a deep well of sympathy in her gaze. "I've seen people more excited about a root canal."

"Sorry." His lips twisted and he ruffled his hair, shifting his weight from one foot to the other. The fact that his emotions were so raw and apparent when it came to Cressida, rankled him.

Roxie ran an assessing eye over his disheveled appearance. "You look terrible," she declared. "Can I come in?"

"Sure…of course." He stepped back and held the door open as Roxie breezed inside.

Ben gestured to the sofa and Roxie made herself comfortable, settling in and crossing her legs. He could tell by the expression on her face that she knew what had happened between them. Hell, the whole neighborhood knew. They certainly hadn't exercised the slightest bit of restraint when they'd gone at it right in the center aisle of Fresh Market.

"I hope you know I didn't do what Cressida thinks I did," he said. "I'd never hurt her like that. Never."

She held up a hand. "I know that. That's why I'm here." She gazed at him for a long moment. "You know…my daughter is under the delusional impression that she's completely opposite of me. So conservative, so methodical, so in control." She shook her head and laughed. "But truth is, that's a bunch of hooey. She's more like me than she knows or would ever admit. She's impetuous, temperamental…"—she shrugged—"occasionally clueless." She lifted a brow. "Especially when it comes to men."

He nodded as she continued.

"And when that temper of hers flares, as it tends to do at the most inopportune times…" Her eyes drifted to the newspaper featuring Cressida's now famous public smack down with Trudy and she gestured to it. "I mean…obviously." She sighed. "Well, she's likely to say a whole lot of things she doesn't even mean. That certainly doesn't excuse her behavior, but hopefully it explains her actions a bit. You see…Cressida feels betrayed, deeply hurt by Cal and instead of directing that emotion where it belongs—at him—it landed squarely on you."

"I do understand. Firsthand experience. I went through that same rollercoaster myself. The difference was, it was just me. I wasn't…well…I wasn't involved with anyone." He shook his head. "I've wondered if it…we…might be happening too soon for her. I don't want to be just a distraction to her…or a temporary guy."

He flopped down on the couch beside Roxie. "I mean…well, I guess that doesn't even matter anymore, does it? She'll probably never speak to me again."

Roxie grinned. "She will. I'm sure of it."

He felt a surge of hope at her encouraging words. Then remembering his manners, he asked, "Would you like a cup of coffee? A glass of wine?"

She shook her head. "I can't stay. I have to get down to Miami. We open tomorrow night." She opened her purse and pulled out a large ticket. "Which is actually why I'm here. I came to give you this."

Ben took them from her. "A backstage pass?"

Roxie nodded. "It would mean a lot to me…and to her, I'm sure…if you came."

He stared at the concert ticket for a moment and then shook his head. "I can't accept this. I'm sorry."

Roxie frowned. "Why?"

"Cressida made it all too clear what she thinks of me. What she thinks I did." He stood and raked his fingers through his hair. Then he shoved his hands in his jeans pockets. "She thinks I sold secrets about her to Cal. I mean…can you believe it?" He paced the floor. "And all because I told her how this was my first job and that I was struggling a little with money." He stopped in his tracks and eyed her intently. "But I swear Roxie...I would never do anything to hurt her."

"I know that," she said gently. "And when Cressida has some time to think this all through in a rational way..."—she grinned up at him—"instead of in a Reynolds kinda way...well, she'll come to her senses."

"I hope so," he said. "I really do. But I definitely don't think she'll want to see me at your big opening tomorrow night."

"That's the problem. My daughter has no clue what she wants. Granted, she's starting to get glimpses now that her buffoon of a husband is no longer in the picture, but unfortunately with this crazy divorce and her disappointment with the baby and all..."

He broke in. "What disappointment with the baby?"

She heaved a sigh. "Unfortunately, the baby she was hoping for is no longer available for adoption. The birth mother has decided to keep her child. It's wonderful for that little baby girl...but heartbreaking for *my* baby girl." Her eyes welled but she blinked back the tears. "She found out about all of that shortly before her ill-fated run-in with you. So I'm sure you can understand when I say she wasn't exactly thinking clearly."

"I'm sorry to hear that. I know how excited she was about the baby. How long she's waited." He studied Roxie's face and handed the tickets back. "I wouldn't want to do anything more to upset her," he said. "She's been through enough this past month. I've thought about calling her. Or even stopping by, but I felt it was best to stay away—at least for now."

Roxie stood and slung her purse over a cheetah-clad shoulder. "Roxie knows best." She winked at him and patted his arm. "You just show up tomorrow night. Leave the rest to me."

~∞~

Cressida straightened the rhinestone tiara and frowned at Costa in the mirror. "I can't believe I let you talk me into this ridiculous idea."

"Oh, stop bellyaching." Costa jabbed a bobby pin into her hair with more enthusiasm than was required.

"Hey! Easy now…" She smacked his hand away and glared at him as she rubbed two fingers over the sore spot. "I think you just drew blood."

"Sorry," he mumbled, taking more care as he secured the last bobby pin. Then he fluffed her vibrant red waves around her shoulders and stepped back to study her with a critical eye. "In Rox's last segment, she's dressed as good princess, all in white. You'll show up at the after party dressed in the identical getup, but in black." His mischievous eyes danced. "It'll be a hoot."

Cressida raised a skeptical brow and sipped her martini. "I'm bad princess? No one in their right mind would buy that one."

Costa arched a brow. "I recall a certain front page photo that seemed to suggest otherwise."

"Hilarious." She stood and gazed down at her skimpy outfit with a scowl. "My thighs look like ham hocks."

Costa waved a hand dismissively. "Oh, play along and stop grumping."

"Seriously. This costume is not my friend."

Cressida turned sideways, examining her reflection with displeasure. Then she straightened her spine and sucked in her gut. "Maybe I should throw on a little skirt."

She arched a brow, hoping he'd buy her idea. A skirt could work.

"Curvy is in," he pronounced.

Her lips twisted. "There's curvy and then there's *curvy*. I would be the latter. Too many tortilla chips." She ran her palms over her generous hips. "An adult onesie—"

"It's not a onesie," Costa admonished, cutting her off. "It's a sequined Versace bodysuit with a built-in corset. *Very* J. Lo. And fabulous, by the way."

She rolled her eyes.

J. Lo or not, she wasn't sure she could wear this getup to the after party surrounded by hundreds of strangers and who knew how many cameras. She looked absolutely ginormous. And the corset was so rigid and tight, she suspected two ribs might've been permanently dislocated, not to mention that she could hardly breathe and was sporting a pooch so significant she'd sworn off bread for life.

She grasped the bodice of the corset firmly with both hands and yanked it up, heaving in a long, shallow breath.

"A sequined onesie with black fishnet tights and stilettos shouldn't be worn to anything other than a Fredericks of Hollywood photo shoot. And then, only by a twenty something model who hasn't eaten in a month." Cressida drained her glass dry and thrust it toward Costa. "Refill please."

Costa filled her to the brim. "Stop fishing. You look fabulous and you know it. So does Rox. I swear, you two could be twins."

"In her dreams," she muttered.

"You can say that again." Costa grinned but his smile died away as he studied her face. He leaned forward and squeezed her shoulders, his voice sounding gruff as he said, "But seriously, I'm proud of you, Cressie. The way you're holding up." He wrapped his arms around her shoulders and hugged her tight. "I'm sorry Ben turned out to be such a scoundrel. He had us all fooled."

"Thanks." She patted his hand and blinked back the rush of tears. It had been a tough few days but she'd promised herself she wouldn't go there. Not tonight. This was her mother's night and she wouldn't let anything spoil it.

Costa checked his watch. "We better get a move on. We don't want to miss Roxie's last number."

Cressida headed for the door.

"Bring that pitcher with you," she called over her shoulder. "If I have to wear this ridiculous costume, I don't want to risk my buzz wearing off."

"Come back here." He waved her over with an impatient hand. "You're not finished."

Costa reached into his jewel-encrusted leather fanny pack and pulled out a large makeup brush and compact. Then he proceeded to dust a liberal amount of bronzer on her bare shoulders, after which he attacked her with a cloud of sticky hairspray, his arm moving in wild circles around her head.

Cressida waved her hands to dissipate the haze. "Enough." She coughed. "For God's sake."

Costa pursed his lips. "We're quite the little crankypoo tonight, aren't we?"

"Yes and why is that, I wonder? If you'd just let me wear what I wanted to the after party, I'd be in a little better humor right now."

She rolled her eyes, knowing he'd never get it. It was easier to just save her breath and go along with whatever he wanted.

"Whatever. Let's go."

Costa opened the door to Roxie's dressing room and Cressida tottered past, ankles wobbling in the four-inch black stilettos.

"Stop clomping around like a football player," Costa admonished, as he flipped off the lights and followed her down the hall. "Glide like the princess you are tonight. Think regal."

"I'm trying. It's not that easy," she said. "Now I understand why Egyptian queens demanded that they be carried everywhere they went. It would be a lot easier to look regal if you could just sit and pose."

As they approached the malfunctioning martini glass prop, Costa screeched to a halt and spun around. "Wait!" His eyes danced impishly. "I have an idea."

He bent and set the pitcher of martinis on the floor. Then he grasped a waist high step stool and dragged it up to the glass as he shot an impish grin over his shoulder.

"Let's take some photos of you in the martini glass. Roxie will love it. And it'll be fun for Instagram." He waggled his brows. "Cocktail Cressida?"

She grinned, finding his irrepressible spirit contagious as she handed him the martini and climbed onto the step stool.

"Come closer," she said, leaning on his shoulder for support. With effort, she climbed over the side of the glass and reclined back, stretching her legs out as she assumed an exaggerated va va voom posture, one hand on her hip and the other behind her head.

"How do I look?" She batted her false eyelashes in her best Roxie imitation.

"Oooo fabulous!" He fiddled with his smartphone and then took a few shots.

She thrust out a hand and waggled her fingers. "Martini please."

Costa picked up the glass and handed it to her. Then he stepped back and began barking instructions as he snapped away on his phone, fully embracing his role as photographer extraordinaire.

"Throw your head back!"

Cressida flung her locks over the side of the glass and put a hand to her forehead in dramatic diva fashion. He clicked away, turning his phone this way and that.

"Now, sip your drink!" Snap. Snap. "That's right…"

She dutifully held the glass to her lips as he snapped away. He even climbed onto the stool so he could take a few from an overhead vantage point.

"That's it. Now, kick your heels up."

The opening strains of *Hot Child in the City* drifted down from above. Their laughter died away as Cressida leaned over the side of the glass and thrust her martini at Costa.

"Hold this while I get down. I don't want to miss her last number."

Instead of taking her glass, Costa crept over to the wall.

Irritated, she waved the cocktail more emphatically.

"Costa, come *here*! I can't climb out of this godforsaken glass while I'm holding this. I'll break my neck."

He ignored her and instead, reached out and grasped a large steel handle with both hands. Casting a devilish grin over his shoulder, he slammed the handle down.

"Up you go!" he cackled gleefully.

The platform groaned, lurching violently from side to side.

Half of Cressida's martini sloshed out as she careened backwards, whacking her head against the side of the glass, her legs spread in an unladylike fashion, heels pointed at the ceiling.

"Whoa…!"

Costa doubled over with laughter as Cressida struggled to an upright position while the platform continued to sway violently.

She grabbed the rim of the glass and glared down over the top. "Stop it!" she hissed.

Costa made an effort to compose himself. "Okay, okay…fine." He looked disappointed that his fun might be over as he reached for the handle. "I just wish you could've seen your face…." His voice trailed off as he tried in vain to pull the handle up.

It wouldn't budge. The platform groaned and lurched even faster.

Costa frowned and grasped the lever with both hands, straining with all his might but the handle wouldn't budge.

He spun around, eyes bugging out. "Cressie. It's stuck!"

As he stood there scratching his head in confusion, the platform stopped lurching, emitted a deep grinding sound and then did the unthinkable: it lifted off the ground.

Chapter Twenty-Two

"Whaaaaaaat?" Costa gaped up at the swiftly rising platform as Cressida grasped the rim of the glass prop for dear life.

She peered over the side and then up at the swiftly approaching stage and panic set in. "Costa! I'm serious...make it stop!"

Costa flipped the handle up and down in rapid succession. Then he spun around, face white as a sheet and panic shooting out of his eyes. "Cressie, the glass isn't supposed to work. It's broken!" He wrung his hands. "This can't be happening..."

"Don't just stand there," she bellowed. "Do something!!!"

Costa flipped the handle once more and the lever cracked off the wall. His mouth dropped open as he stared at the worthless metal device in his hands. Then his eyes drifted from the handle to the platform and rounded in horror as it kept rising, now at least eight feet off the ground. He threw the inoperable metal contraption to the ground and clapped both hands over his mouth as he gaped up at her.

"Jump!" Costa screamed. "You have to jump *now*...before you get any higher!"

She was nearly nine feet off the ground. She had to hurry!

Cressida threw her martini glass over the side. The glass fell to the concrete below and shattered.

She struggled forward, grasping the bodice of her onesie with both hands and heaving it up as she tried to reposition the corset. Then she drew in a lungful of air and threw her right leg over the side of the glass, straining her leg as she tried to touch her foot to the platform. Her other leg was hooked over the rim of the glass for support. Luckily, the prop seemed to be bolted down so she didn't fear it toppling off the platform.

Her grand plan was to lower herself to the steel platform and then run like a bat out of hell once she was level with the stage.

Unfortunately, when the platform snapped into place, the violent jolt threw Cressida off balance. Her foot slipped from the platform and swung wildly, pulling her underneath the v-shaped glass. Her other leg remained hooked over the rim she was still grasping with both hands which left her dangling upside down like a circus acrobat.

Cressida blinked, slightly disoriented as she stared into the five blindingly bright spotlights overhead that were now zeroed in on her. She tilted her head back and from her upside down vantage point, saw Roxie's head snap around, eyes rounded in shock.

Without missing a beat, her mother nodded discreetly in Cressida's direction and instantly, a half dozen scantily clad dancers sashayed towards her, snapping their fingers and moving to the beat of the music.

Dear God, no!

And because she couldn't do anything else, Cressida scrunched her eyes shut and prayed.

❧

Ben stood backstage and was rather enjoying the show until a platform suddenly appeared out of nowhere with Cressida inexplicably dangling off the side of a martini glass.

Suddenly the orderly producers and backstage hands erupted into action and judging from the colorful language, he guessed Cressida's arrival was not planned.

"Get me another mic!" someone bellowed.

"Dammit Costa! What were you thinking?!" A tall skinny man with bleached blonde hair glowered down at a breathless Costa who stood gaping at Cressida in panic. "Now what are we supposed to do?"

The red-faced man spun around and screamed. "Team two…you're on!" He shoved a mic into one of the dancer's hands and commanded, "Grab her, carry her to center stage and give her the mic. Now!!!"

Costa shrank back into a corner, more contrite than Ben had ever imagined him capable of being. "Sorry Felix."

The six dancers sprang onstage and joined the six already heading towards her as the crowd burst into applause.

The group shimmied and spun, converging on the glass as Cressida was struggling to pull herself upright. They plucked her off the side with ease and then hoisted her high above their heads as they carried her, Cleopatra-style, toward center stage.

The crowd roared their approval and Felix the producer went positively limp with relief.

༄༄

Cressida lifted her head, eyes darting about in panic as she tried to get a sense of their location. Panic twisted her stomach into a knot. They were headed right for center stage.

Oh, dear God.

She let her head drop back and squeezed her eyes shut. Then she did the only thing she could think of that might help. She started tapping. If ever a moment called for EFT, this would be it.

༄༄

"What in the HELL is she doing now?" Felix thundered. "That Madonna Vogue thing is not retro cool…it's just…retro blah."

Costa moved closer to the curtain to get a better look and his face broke into an ear to ear grin. "She's tapping!" He clapped and then grabbed Felix's arm. "She's tapping!"

"Whatever she's doing, it isn't working." He barked into a mic. "Mimic her moves...make it work!"

Instantly, the backup singers and Roxie started tapping too.

Cressida's fingers tapped the side of her right hand, then her brows, the side of her eyes, beneath her eyes, below her nose and mouth and on top of her head but the only phrase she could manage to chant was a hysterical, "Dear God, please help me!"

And she whispered that phrase over and over again until she was unceremoniously plopped onto the stage, right next to Roxie who was just finishing the first verse of *Hot Child in the City* and oddly, her mother and the backup singers were tapping too.

Cressida stopped tapping as a dancer spun by and thrust a microphone into her hand. She swallowed hard and stole a panicked sideways glance at Roxie, who was rocking the dance moves from their award-winning middle school act.

"Follow me," Roxie mouthed with a playful wink.

After a quick glance at the crowd, Cressida closed her eyes and tried to pretend they weren't in front of thousands of people. Despite her pounding heart; she joined her mother in the simple eight-step dance sequence. Her body moved in a wooden, stiff fashion and sweat poured out of her as she followed Roxie's moves.

When she opened her eyes again, the first thing she saw was Shay, front row center, gaping up in wide-eyed shock, her hands clamped over her mouth and face painted with the same horrified expression Costa had displayed just before she'd lost sight of him.

For some mysterious reason, laughter welled inside. Both of her friends looked exactly like she felt. Mortified.

And then for some equally inexplicable reason—or maybe because of the martinis or perhaps it was all that godforsaken tapping—a warm, soothing calm spread through her every fiber of her being, just like Roxie had promised when she'd taught her EFT.

Her heart rate slowed to normal and the panic dissolved. She was here. Now. And she needed to make the best of it.

Cressida clutched the microphone with determination as Roxie started the second verse, strutting towards her. She pointed to Cressida, indicating that she should take the next line.

She drew in a sharp breath and for a brief moment, panic welled again but something stopped her. Instead of the voice of scared thirteen-year-old Cressida berating her, a stronger voice, quiet and confident and unfamiliar urged her on.

You can do it, Cress.

She opened her mouth and belted out the line, sounding shaky and slightly flat at first but gradually, she relaxed into it. Because she couldn't bring herself to look at the audience, she kept her eyes fixed on Roxie who smiled at her encouragingly as the music take over.

Without warning, the male dancers reappeared and hoisted both women high above their heads as they headed into the final chorus.

Cressida peeked over at Roxie who winked and thrust her arms upward. She followed Roxie's movements as the men spun them around twice and then lowered them to the stage where they executed a perfectly synched and absolutely over-the-top hip shimmy that brought the crowd of cheering fans to their feet.

The dancers clustered around and each woman perched on the knee of a performer, thrusting their hands in the air on the final note.

Flash bulbs popped, partially blinding her as the audience shouted and whistled their approval.

Cressida grinned down at Shay who shot her the thumbs up.

The women stood and the dancers moved back as Roxie stepped close. She grasped Cressida's hand, clutching it tight and then thrust it victoriously into the air.

"Give it up for my daughter, Cressida!" she cried to the roar of the audience.

Then she threw her arms wide and wrapped Cressida in a huge bear hug, rocking back and forth as the applause thundered and reverberated across the auditorium.

As the velvet curtains swung closed, Roxie placed her hands on Cressida's shoulders and gazed deeply into her eyes.

"I'm so proud of you, Cressie." She tweaked her chin, eyes glistening with tears. "So. Damned. Proud."

Cressida's lips trembled as Roxie wiped the tears away, turned and pranced back through the curtains to take a final bow.

※

Ben stood off to the side, every part of him aching to move closer, to take her into his arms. But as he watched her and Roxie, he couldn't bring himself to intrude. He sensed this was a moment for them. A big one. Perhaps one that had taken a lifetime based on what he'd witnessed of their interactions to date. And he didn't want to risk doing anything to take away from that moment.

"Way to go, Cress," he whispered, blowing her a kiss. Then he turned and trotted down the stairs and out the backstage door which led to the parking lot.

He knew what he had to do now. And come sunrise, he was going to do it.

※

"The reviews are in," Costa said, swiping at his iPad. "You wanna hear?"

"I'm pretty sure the answer to that question would be no." Cressida blew on her hot brew. She didn't want any reminders of last night's stage performance. She was proud of herself but she wasn't too anxious to hear the official critiques of her rusty singing voice. She just hoped she hadn't hurt her mother's stellar reputation.

"Nonsense. You were fabulous. I was fabulous. The whole show was fabulous!" Roxie pronounced as she leaned forward, elbows on the countertop and gazed at Costa expectantly. "Let's hear it."

Costa stopped poking at the iPad and scanned the screen. As he read, his face split into a broad grin. "You're famous!"

Cressida groaned as he thrust the iPad towards her. She shook her head and waved a hand. "I'll pass."

Roxie snatched the device and glanced up, beaming. "Cressida Wentworth brings down the house," she read. "And that's just the headline!"

Roxie fist bumped Costa and they launched into the synchronized bar stool dance that Cressida had come to know so well.

When they finished their gyrations, Roxie proceeded to read the article aloud, pausing to emphasize words like 'fabulous' and 'gifted' and 'inspired.' And they all laughed as she recounted the critic's take on Cressida's over the top arrival onstage.

Cressida grinned. "Wow. So they really think that whole dangling off the side of the glass thing was planned?"

"They said…" Roxie peered at the article. "The Cirque de Soleil-inspired arrival of her daughter…"

Cressida cackled. "That's certainly what it felt like." She rubbed her sore rib. "I'm actually bruised from the combination of that ridiculous corset and the contortionist moves."

"Well, Felix covered it like the master he is," Roxie declared.

"He wouldn't have had the chance if it wasn't for me," Costa sniffed. "I made it all possible."

Both women leveled a look.

"I wouldn't let Felix overhear you taking credit if I were you. I'm not sure he'll ever get over that. And if you tried it again, you might not survive it," Roxie said.

He jutted his chin out and pouted.

Then Roxie burst out laughing. "Oh Cressie…if you could've seen yourself dangling upside down like that. It was so hilarious."

Despite herself, Cressida chuckled as well. "I didn't need to see it…I lived it. It was my worst nightmare came to life."

"Right," Roxie said. "But you did it! You conquered your fear."

"Because of the tapping," Costa said.

"I have to admit, I really do think the tapping thing works," she said. "For some reason, right in the middle of it, I just felt calm. Just like you said I would. It was crazy."

Shay bounded through the back door clutching two bottles of champagne. "Bust out the OJ. It's mimosa time!"

Costa pranced over to the fridge and pulled out the juice as Shay reached into a cupboard and pulled out four champagne flutes. As Costa poured the orange juice, Roxie popped the cork from a bottle and then topped off each glass in turn.

Shay distributed the four glasses and Costa raised his in toast. "Here's to the redheaded fabulous. Truly unleashed."

As they sipped their drinks, the doorbell rang.

Cressida slid off the barstool and headed to the foyer. She pulled the door open and her smile instantly morphed into a frown as she saw her visitor.

"Cal." Her voice sounded flat and lifeless. "What are you doing here?"

"Hi." Cal's face looked painted into a forced smile as he stood woodenly. He lifted a brow. "Can I come in?"

"Well, I have company…" she began.

"Just for a minute. I need to talk to you," he said. He gulped and stepped forward, his eyes pleading with her. "Please."

Her frown deepened. It was completely unlike Cal to display even the slightest bit of humility towards anyone, most of all her. She was instantly suspicious. But curiosity got the better of her and she stepped back and opened the door wider.

"I guess so. But you should know…my mom is here." She

figured warning him of Roxie's presence and the potential danger that created for him was the humane thing to do.

"I know," he said, glancing over her shoulder. "I see."

Cressida turned to find three heads peeping around the corner, watching their every move. She waved her hand as if to say 'shoo!' The three heads instantly disappeared back into the kitchen.

She turned back to Cal and folded her arms across her chest. "What do you want?"

He gazed at her for a long moment, a look of uncertainty in his eyes.

"I had to see you, to tell you…well…" he stepped closer. "I've missed you, Cress. I've missed us. What we had together."

Her mouth dropped open and for a moment, she was unable to speak. She shook her head. "I'm sorry…*what are you talking about?*"

He glanced over her shoulder and frowned.

Before even turning, she knew what she'd see. "Back in the kitchen!" she barked, glaring over her shoulder.

The trio of heads, clearly intent upon listening to every word, disappeared again.

"Cressida," Cal stepped forward, looking more confident this time. "I was there last night. I saw your performance. You were wonderful."

Cressida blinked. "You were there? Why?"

"Because I miss us. I miss you." He swallowed. "I'm sorry Cress. I don't know what got into me, walking out on you like that."

She frowned, struggling to try to make sense of his sudden change of heart.

"I know about the baby too and I'm sorry. Truly sorry. But we can try again," he said. "Please give me another chance."

She shook her head, trying to clear the cobwebs and said the only thing she could think of, "What about Graciella?"

Cal waved a dismissive hand. "Gracie and I are over. I ended it right after the White Ball. She's all wrong for me, Cress. You're the one for me and I'll spend the rest of my life proving it to you." He took her hand gently in his. "I want a family with you, Cressida. I want you to be the mother of my children. Please give me...*give us* another chance."

Her instincts told her to ignore his pleas; reminded her that she couldn't trust him. He'd walked out on her and plotted to sell the house from underneath her. Hired an attorney, hid money and ran off with her cousin. And now he wanted her back?!

Anger welled inside but it went to war with a more insidious emotion. Uncertainty. And it was a war that anger would find very difficult to win.

She wanted a family. She wanted her life back. Cal was saying all the right words, words she'd longed to hear ever since the day he'd walked out.

"Cress, remember what we had together," he said, his voice gaining confidence as he seemed to sense her wavering.

He stepped back. "I'll give you some time to think it over." He smiled. "We were good together Cress. We can be again. We can have it all. The family. The life. Everything. Just give us a chance."

She followed Cal out to the porch and watched him drive away. It wasn't until he was gone that she noticed the long white box with the big red bow.

She slipped the box under her arm and carried it into the kitchen where she was immediately greeted by three disapproving stares.

No one said a word at first, as she placed the box in front of Roxie. "From one of your many admirers, I suppose."

"I'm not going to say it..." Roxie said, as she lifted the lid.

"Good. Don't." Cressida shot them all a warning glance. "You just don't understand. None of you. And I don't want to hear it."

Shay clamped her lips shut as Costa downed his mimosa and then grumbled something about her being the one who didn't understand.

Roxie pulled the card out of the envelope and her lips turned

241

up. "These aren't for me," she said, pushing the box over to Cressida and handing her the card.

"For me?" Cressida's brows shot clear to her forehead as she reached for the card. 'C—you were wonderful. Ben.'

Her eyes lifted and met Roxie's. "He was there last night? But how…"

Roxie shrugged and sipped her mimosa, her eyes dancing. "I gave him a ticket. He was supposed to come to the after party but I guess he chickened out."

Cressida crossed her arms in front of her chest. "Mother. You had no right to do that. After what he did to me?"

Roxie set down her glass and moved closer, resting her arms on Cressida's shoulders. "You're wrong about Ben."

Shay nodded her head vigorously but Costa looked uncertain.

Roxie gave her a gentle shake. "And if you even think about giving that snake in the grass husband of yours another shot, well, I'll…" Her eyes glistened. "I know how much you want a family and I know how much it hurts when someone you love walks out but when a relationship isn't right, you have to move on. Even if it means letting go of the things you want the most."

Chapter Twenty-Three

Cressida blinked, still trying to process the bombshell Gray Portell had just dropped.

"I'm sorry…what did you say?"

"My private detective has confirmed that your husband has been bugging your car," he said. "And probably your cell phone, too. That is how he learned of your adoption. Your new job. Your new relationship." He shrugged. "Everything."

"Bugged? How…" she croaked, feeling slightly sick, especially since she'd just stopped by to speak with Gray about putting the divorce on hold. She'd been contemplating changing it to a legal separation; just to see how things unfolded with Cal over the next few months. And now this…

"Well, in this day and age, there are a million devices or applications that can listen in. I didn't ask for confirmation on the specific type, but I can do so if you'd like. In some instances, you can pursue legal action."

Was she wrong or did his eyes just glisten at the prospect of a new lawsuit?

She blew out a long, exasperated breath, a tide of anger rising inside. The nerve of Cal knew no end. Just yesterday, he'd stopped by the house, begging her to reconsider when the entire time he'd been listening in on every conversation.

Unable to contain herself any longer, she shot out of the chair. "I'm sorry…I have to go." She headed to the door with Gray following closely behind.

The lawyer's hand brushed against her bottom and that was Cressida's undoing.

She spun around, fire shooting from her eyes as she lifted her stiletto and smashed it down on the top of his foot.

"Oopf!" he yelped.

"Next time, you'll get worse," she declared, thinking he was damned lucky she hadn't aimed for a more sensitive area.

He grinned despite the pain. "I knew you had fire blazing inside…" his voice trailed off. "Make an appointment with my secretary. We'll need to prepare for our court date next month." He winked.

"We'll finish our dealings on the phone." She strode to the elevator and punched the button, turning just in time to catch her lecherous attorney dragging his eyes from her bottom. "I'm afraid you'll have to find someone else to play with." She smiled sweetly as the elevator doors closed.

❧

"So what are you going to do about the adoption thing?" Shay speared a sprig of broccoli and eyed Cressida with curiosity.

"I've decided to give it some time. I'll revisit the idea of adoption or whatever, when things settle down a little bit." She shrugged. "I was devastated at first, but honestly, it might just be for the best. The timing was off."

"That's putting it mildly." Shay put down her fork and reached across the table to squeeze Cressida's hand. "I think it's a good idea to take a little time. Let things shake out. Figure out the employment thing. See how you feel once you're single…" She arched a brow. "You *are* going through with the divorce aren't you? You're not letting El Cheapo talk you into giving his worthless ass a second chance, are you?"

"Absolutely not. In fact…" Cressida reached into her purse and pulled out her cell phone. She punched in the number to Cal's office and when his receptionist answered, said, "Hello. This is Cressida. May I speak with Cal please?"

"Of course, Mrs. Wentworth."

Instead of putting her on hold while she manufactured a lame excuse, this time the woman put Cressida right through to Cal.

"Hi Honey." Cal's voice sounded warm and confident, as if the turmoil of the past month had never even happened. "I'm so glad you called. How about dinner tonight?"

Cressida didn't hesitate in the slightest as she replied. "No, I don't think so Cal. You see, I've had time to think about your offer and I'm ready to give you my answer."

"But wouldn't you rather do that when we're together? You know…make it special?"

Her lips twisted. Cal's denial and delusion knew no bounds.

"We won't be together any longer, Cal. This time apart has given me an opportunity to see a chance for a different life. And I'm grabbing it." She paused, thinking back to that moment in the car when he'd uttered those words to her and she couldn't resist throwing his thoughtless line back in his face. "One day you'll realize this was all for the best."

Cressida didn't bother to wait for his reply. She just disconnected the call and slid the phone calmly back in her purse.

Shay's eyes twinkled as she extended a teasing hand. "Hi Cressida, I'm Shay. Nice to meet you."

Cressida giggled and smacked her hand away.

Shay's expression turned solemn. "No seriously Cress. I'm proud of you." Her eyes grew misty. "Honestly, I know I talk tough, but if given the same chance with Jerry, I'm not sure I would've had the strength to walk away. I can imagine how tempting it would be to shove the voice of reason aside, to ignore the betrayal and the dishonesty and jump at the chance to save the marriage you thought you had but probably never did. It takes real courage to recognize the truth and walk into a future full of unknowns. A future that looks nothing like what you had expected or hoped it would be."

Cressida blinked back tears and swallowed around the lump in her throat.

"Thanks. But honestly, turning Cal down didn't take courage. Staying for all those years despite the way he treated me, putting up with the constant digs and the putdowns, the manipulation and never ending disapproval as I tried to hang on. To do what I thought was right. That's what took courage."

"Here here." Shay raised her glass of Pinot Grigio. "And here's to never being that courageous, ever again."

The women clinked their glasses together.

Cressida waited down the street for a good ten minutes after Ben pulled in his driveway, feeling a little like a stalker. Her eyes kept darting around, hoping he didn't have nosy neighbors who might call the cops.

But what choice did she have? He hadn't come by the house or reached out once since the morning he'd left the roses so she'd staked out his house for the past two days, waiting for the right moment—when both his truck was in the driveway and she had the courage to face him. There'd been plenty of times when she'd either felt brave enough but he hadn't been home or he'd been home but she'd chickened out. But the moment had arrived.

She put the car in drive and rolled down the street, pulling into the driveway behind his truck as her heart thumped madly in her chest and a mixture of panic and dread stirred inside.

Cressida drew in a long nerve-calming breath, mustering every scrap of resolve she could find as she stepped onto the sidewalk. But as she made her way to the front door, the relentless and never-ending 'what ifs' refused to be silenced.

What if he slams the door in your face? What if his feelings have changed?

Cressida pushed away the self-doubt and pressed the doorbell.

She heard Max barking before the door even opened and that made her smile. She even loved his dog. That had to mean something.

As the door opened, she sucked in a sharp breath and her smile became a little wooden as she noted his cool, guarded expression.

"Hello Ben."

"Cressida." His voice sounded flat, unwelcoming.

She steeled herself to continue. "May I come in?"

He hesitated for what seemed an interminable length of time and then finally stepped back to let her enter. "Sure...sure."

She straightened her shoulders and tucked her hair behind an ear as she stepped hesitantly into his foyer, wondering how she'd ever find the courage to say what she'd come to say.

Max trotted up, tail wagging madly as she scratched behind his ears.

Ben led the way into the living room, gesturing to the sofa, but he didn't offer her something to drink and definitely didn't seem too thrilled about her being there for one second longer than she needed to be.

With great resolve, Cressida mentally deleted the self-defeating thoughts and settled on the sofa, steeling herself against what she sensed might come next as Ben dropped into the chair across from her.

Max sat at her feet. At least he was on her side.

They gazed at each other for a long moment and then both started to speak at the same time.

"I wanted—" she began.

"I guess—" he started.

They both stopped and laughed awkwardly.

Ben gestured to her. "You first."

Cressida swallowed hard, searching his face and looking for some softening, some indication that he still felt something for her. But his face was an unreadable mask which seemed a good indication that she wasn't going to like what he had to say. So she stalled for time, not yet ready to share the real reason she'd come.

"I wanted to thank you for the flowers," she said and meant it, though the flowers were most certainly not the reason she'd come.

"Oh." He raked a hand through his hair and she thought she caught the briefest flash of disappointment before he once again assumed his neutral demeanor. "You're welcome."

"Mom said she gave you a ticket. Were you able to come opening night?" She tilted her head. "I didn't see you."

A grin stole across his face, seemingly against his will.

"I did." His grin broadened as his eyes locked with hers. "Wow Cressida. You were amazing. Really. You're so talented."

She blushed with pleasure. "Thank you." She shook her head with a rueful smile. "My performance wasn't exactly planned. I'd say my contribution to the show came courtesy of Costa."

"Yeah." Ben chuckled. "I gathered that from the mayhem that unfolded backstage as soon as you appeared."

She rolled her eyes. "I can only imagine. It felt a little mayhemish onstage as well, let me tell you. Swinging upside down like an idiot while an auditorium full of people gawked at me…well, it wasn't exactly my shining hour."

"Oh, I don't know…" he said, his smile fading and his expression growing serious.

They gazed at each other for a long moment. She could literally see his wheels turning but she couldn't bring herself to say the words she'd come to say.

Finally, Ben raked his hands through his hair and leaned forward, bracing his elbows on his knees.

"Well, I guess it's my turn, huh?" He heaved a sigh, regret etched deeply into his features. "I guess you're about to get everything you ever wanted. I'm happy for you Cressida." His voice sounded flat and hollow. "You deserve it."

She frowned. "Huh?" She hadn't been expecting that.

He continued as if she hadn't spoken, pushing out of the chair and pacing the floor.

"I'm sorry. That didn't sound very sincere," he said, stealing a quick glance her way. He stopped. "Let me try again. I really am happy for you if that's the life you want. *Really*. But I can't say I'm happy that you've decided to stay with that pompous cheating asshole of a husband."

Cressida went almost limp with relief. She hadn't realized she was holding herself so rigid until his words actually sank in. He still cared for her, at least enough that he didn't care for the thought of her reconciling with Cal.

She drew in a long, soul-strengthening breath as hope bloomed. But still, she kept her cool, afraid to really put herself out there.

"Oh. You overheard us when Cal stopped by," she said, stating the obvious.

Ben nodded. "I was on the porch." He clenched his fists and looked about to burst until he said, "Okay, I'm just going to say it."

He knelt down beside her and gazed deeply into her eyes. "You can't stay with him Cressida." His voice took on a pleading note. "You can't. He'll just hurt you again and besides, he doesn't deserve you and he'll never—"

She reached out and cradled his cheek. "I'm not," she whispered.

Ben stopped short.

"What did you say?" He reached for her hands as his eyes searched her face.

Cressida smiled gently. "It's over. We're over. I told Cal two days ago."

Ben groaned. "Two days?" He placed his hand over his heart in an exaggerated gesture. "You waited *two whole days* before you told me?"

"I would've told you sooner but you haven't been at the house. And I figured you wouldn't talk to me if I called, so I started stalking you here. Why haven't you been at the house?"

"I called Cal and quit two days ago. I referred him to one of my friends."

"What? Wait…" Her brows flew to her forehead. "You *quit*? You walked away from all that money? But why?!"

He shrugged. "I wanted to prove to you that I'm not in this for the money. Granted, it would've been nice to get paid for the full job but not if it meant losing you. I wanted to prove to you that you're more important to me."

Her heart melted.

"I'd never do anything to hurt you. You have to believe that. I don't know how Cal knew those things, but…"

She held up a hand. "I do. He had my car and my cell phone bugged. That's how." She gazed at him. "And I'm so embarrassed that I leapt to such a wild conclusion. That I accused you of selling the secrets to Cal. I don't have an excuse…I guess sometimes I'm impulsive and act a little crazy. Just like…"

"Like your mother," he said.

She smiled ruefully. "Yes. Just like my mother." She arched a brow. "Forgive me?"

He took her hand and placed it against his lips. The combination of the gesture and the look in his eyes curled her toes.

"That depends…" he said, his voice sounding gruff and raw.

She tilted her head to the side, her heart thumping madly. "On what?"

"On exactly how you plan to make it up to me."

"Shall I show you?" she asked.

A deliciously wicked grin spread across his face.

"Please…"

❧

Cressida scanned the crowded lawn. It was a packed house now and the party was in full swing. The crowd consisted mostly of Ben's friends and Roxie's cast and crew with just a sprinkling of

Cressida's close pals. But she didn't mind. Her thirty-seventh birthday had already far exceeded her wildest expectations.

She would've been happy with a quiet dinner at home, just the two of them. But Ben had insisted on a good old-fashioned Texas barbeque and she'd happily relented. She'd helped to plan the event and was even playing host, but his Uncle Rex had done the hard part. One of his many restaurants had catered the party. Rex had yet to arrive but his crew had shown up hours earlier to prepare the tents and set up the banquet tables.

Roxie's band was warming up and she was set to perform some of Cressida's favorite numbers. Cressida had even agreed to a few duets.

Ben walked up and slipped an arm around Cressida's waist. As he took in the scene, he said, "Well, what do you think?"

Costa appeared beside them and answered for her. "It's fabulous," he said. "Absolutely fabulous."

"I agree," Roxie said, eyes dancing. "The band is just winding up and the gang can't wait to bust a move. You would think after back to back shows for three weeks straight that they'd be exhausted, but they're looking forward to some hardcore hoedown action."

"That's good, I—" Ben stopped short as a tall and sinfully handsome older version of himself walked up and slapped him on the back.

"Ben!"

Ben spun around and his face broke into an ear to ear grin. "I wondered when you'd get here. I'm so glad you could make it." He turned to Cressida. "Uncle Rex, I'd like you to meet Cressida."

The other man smiled approvingly and nodded. "Ah. So this is Cressida." He shifted his gaze to Ben. "Nicely done."

Cressida glanced at Roxie and winked as she extended a hand towards the man. "You can call me Cressie Ann."

She'd long since made peace with Roxie's pet name for her and figured she might as well throw it out there since she knew Roxie would eventually do so anyway.

"We don't shake hands in this family. We hug." Uncle Rex pulled her into a rib-splitting embrace.

"This is Costa," Ben continued.

The two men shook hands and the second the other man's back was turned, Costa mouthed, 'Wow' to Roxie who did her best to ignore him.

"And this is Roxie."

Uncle Rex locked onto Roxie like a homing beam, his gaze raking over her tight curvy figure, taking in the black skinny jeans and stilettos and the cheetah print halter top.

Rex stepped forward and licked his lips. "Well helloooo," he said, stealing her mother's typical come hither line.

Roxie blushed crimson under his scrutiny but managed a few batted lashes as Rex gallantly extended an elbow.

"Let's go somewhere quiet so we can get better acquainted," he said, not bothering to address the rest of the group.

Cressida's jaw dropped as her mother slipped her hand through the arm of Ben's outrageously rich and charismatic uncle.

She leaned toward Ben. "I thought you said he always had a young girlfriend in tow."

Ben shrugged. "I guess he's in between right now."

Cressida frowned as the two wandered off. "Did I just see my mother blush?"

Ben chuckled. "She did. Big time. Looks to me like she might've just met her match."

"It's about time she picked on someone her own size," Costa sniffed, as he wandered off in the direction of the dancers.

Ben pulled Cressida into his arms. "I should've warned you. We Carrington's have a weakness for hot curvy redheads. Especially when they're wearing cheetah print."

She tipped her head back and gazed up at him. "Is that so? Well then, I'd say it's a good thing I wore your favorite thong."

"Can I have a peek?" he asked teasingly as he trailed kisses down her throat. "No one will notice if we just sneak away."

"Soon," she whispered on a sigh. "Definitely soon."

Coming Soon

Roxie Ever After – (Princesses of Las Olas – #2)

The *Princesses of Las Olas* series continues in this sequel to Crazy About Cressida. In this over the top romantic comedy, the adventures of Cressida, Ben, Roxie, Costa and Shay continue. Stay up to date on all the latest by visiting AbbyMatisse.com. Sign up for my newsletter, enter contests and much more.

Everything She Wants – (Sweet Home Chicago – #.5)

This prequel to *A Deal with the Devil* features Amanda Wilson's best friend, Kate Montgomery. She's a strong-willed and feisty southern belle from an eccentric and upper crust Birmingham family who finds herself having to choose between the rich and rakish investment banker she's always lusted after and the handsome but penniless young attorney she's finding it impossible to resist. In the process, she must decide whether she'll dutifully follow the path expected of her or find the courage to forge her own.

What Happens in Paris – (Sweet Home Chicago – #2)

In this sequel to *A Deal with the Devil,* Jake and Amanda are about to discover that a lot can happen between yes and I do—especially when so much has been left unsaid. Follow their journey as they venture to Paris, plan their wedding and—once their post engagement glow fades—find themselves dealing with the aftermath of a year spent apart, their sudden reunion, the family dramas and person demons that tore them apart in the first place and an unexpected little surprise. In their case, what happens in Paris will most definitely *not* stay in Paris.

About the Author

Abby Matisse is the author of contemporary romantic fiction. She specializes in romantic comedy and romantic suspense. Each story features a strong, feisty heroine with plenty of heart, something important to learn and an interesting cast of unique characters. Her first novel, *A Deal with the Devil*, was published in July 2012.

Before publishing her first novel, Matisse spent more than fifteen years in corporate America, undertaking various roles in brand strategy and marketing for a series of Fortune 500 companies. But much as she enjoyed the creative demands of her profession, something was missing. She'd dreamed of writing since the age of five and in late 2011, decided she'd delayed the dream long enough.

Matisse writes character-driven stories that focus on a variety of women's issues. Since books have always been a haven for Matisse, her hope is that her stories empower women in some way, give them hope during times of trial and leave them with a smile. And on a good day, she'd love to make you laugh.

Originally from St. Louis, Matisse currently lives in the suburbs of Dallas. Long struck with a bit of wanderlust, fueled by a corporate career which transferred her to eight cities in sixteen years, she's hoping to stay put for a while, though she's always venturing off to somewhere either to visit friends and family or to conduct research on her next novel.

Connect with Matisse on Facebook, via Twitter @AbbyMatisse or on Pinterest. And when you have a moment, stop by her website at AbbyMatisse.com and sign up to receive her periodic HappyMail, a newsletter dedicated to happiness, humor and all the latest news from the land of Matisse.